DON'T TRUST MOTHER

CAREY BALDWIN

BOOKS BY CAREY BALDWIN

Her First Mistake

The Marriage Secret

Second Wives

The Widow Bride

THE CASSIDY & SPENSER THRILLERS SERIES

Judgment

Fallen

Notorious

Stolen

Countdown

Prequels

First Do No Evil (Blood Secrets Book 1)

Confession (Blood Secrets Book 2)

DON'T TRUST MOTHER

CAREY BALDWIN

bookouture

Published by Bookouture in 2025

An imprint of Storyfire Ltd.
Carmelite House
50 Victoria Embankment
London EC4Y 0DZ

www.bookouture.com

The authorised representative in the EEA is Hachette Ireland
8 Castlecourt Centre
Dublin 15 D15 XTP3
Ireland
(email: info@hbgi.ie)

ISBN: 978-1-83618-936-7
eBook ISBN: 978-1-83618-935-0

For Suzanne

"The bird a nest, the spider a web, man friendship."

WILLIAM BLAKE

PROLOGUE

A cold autumn day

A mountain forest near Flagstaff, Arizona

You and I face off in a grove of quaking aspen trees. Their lofty white trunks are crowned by a canopy of golden leaves that hang over us like a shivering sun.

The trembling of the foliage is contagious.

I bend at the waist and place my hands on my knees, trying to still them. "Does she know?" I ask.

Autumn leaves blow around us, drifting into thick, multicolored piles, intermingling with pale bark and trampled grasses. Light beams down between the trees, spotlighting you. The breeze wafting over my cheeks carries the crisp, pungent aroma of fall in the mountains.

"She knows nothing," you say.

My pounding heart quiets, but only for an instant. The relief doesn't last. I've spent decades pretending the past never happened. But you won't let me hide any longer.

I understand what must be done, but I'm still resisting. Still playing mind games with myself, looking for an alternate ending. Trying to hold on to what's left of my humanity until the last second.

I hoped this day would never come, but deep down I knew it would. Secrets have a way of floating to the surface, like bloated corpses in a mossy pond. Now, my darkest secret has dragged itself out of the water and climbed up onto the bank.

Not a corpse at all.

My secret still lives, still breathes, still gasps air into its lungs.

Imperils those I love.

I don't want to give in to the monster inside me—but you leave me no choice.

Every muscle in my body tenses in preparation.

I will do whatever it takes to protect my family.

ONE

IVY

Flagstaff, Arizona

"You have to follow the rules. Do what I tell you to do. It's for your own safety," the voice whispered.

"Mom?" Ivy called out.

"Yes, Ivy. You need to listen to me."

"Where are you? I can't see you."

"I'm right here, Ivy."

Ivy heard a click, and then a dull yellow light pierced her eyelids, triggering them open. Her matted hair stuck uncomfortably to the back of her neck. Her silk nightgown was damp, its beautiful hand-finished *frastaglio* embroidery soaked in sweat. She lay shivering atop a cold, metal slab.

She screamed.

Flung out an arm.

When her fist cracked against hard bone, she bolted upright, her knuckles throbbing.

"Whoa! Ivy. Baby. *Wake* up."

She blinked rapidly and noticed red bumps covering her

arms, coalescing before her eyes into itchy welts. "Clayton? Is that you?"

"Who else? Let me help you." Her husband reached out, wrapping her in a throw that stung her skin as if it were made of nettles instead of the finest cashmere.

She yanked it off, kicked it to the floor and pushed him away.

He held up his hands. "Take a breath, baby. You're having a bad dream. Everything's okay—I promise."

"You're lying." Things were definitely not okay. She was chilled to the core, and she couldn't piece together what was going on. "Am I dead? Is this the morgue?"

Then, in the space of a heartbeat, everything seemed different than it had only a moment before.

A rose-colored coverlet her great-grandma had quilted came into focus. The one nostalgic concession Clayton had allowed her, in an otherwise exquisitely decorated room.

"Ivy, calm down. We're home in bed. You're perfectly safe. I never should've let you see your mother like that—at the morgue. I knew it was a mistake. But I didn't think I had the right to stop you. Now, after all this time, with your nightmares still going strong... I wish I'd put my foot down after the accident."

The accident.

Mom was gone—dead almost six months now.

She put her hand on her stomach and forced herself to take a slow, deep breath, followed by another, and then another. Just like her mother taught her to do as a child whenever she'd wake up from one of her night terrors. When, at last, she got her racing heart under control, she turned to Clayton.

He lifted his hand, partially concealing a fist-shaped mark on his cheek.

"Clayton! I'm so sorry."

"It's nothing. Don't worry about it at all."

"But this is the second time I've hit you." Or was it the third? "Maybe we should sleep in separate rooms, just until—"

"Shh. No way." He reached for her, slowly this time, and ever so gently touched the tip of his fingers to her lips. Then trailed them down her bare arms. "You're broken out in hives, again. I put your tranquilizers on your nightstand. And your antihistamines. You should take them."

"This rash will go away on its own. It usually only takes a few minutes."

"But the pills will help you sleep, too. There's no point prolonging the discomfort when the remedy is right beside you."

Except that the last thing she wanted to do was close her eyes again.

"Do you want to talk about it? Your bad dream? Your mom's accident? Anything at all?"

She swallowed three pills, two antihistamines and a tranquilizer, and then gulped the rest of her water before replacing the plastic bottle on her nightstand. "I had a happy dream at first, but then it changed."

He shifted his position to look directly at her, and the smartwatch on his wrist lit up.

3 a.m.

It was selfish of her to keep him awake. She could read until the pills kicked in. Mom's obituary was in her bedside drawer. "Go back to sleep. You've got that big meeting at the office tomorrow."

"How about you let me worry about my meeting? I want to hear all about this dream of yours."

The room was too cold. She pulled the sheets over her bare legs, careful not to let the fabric come in contact with her stinging arms.

No point prolonging the discomfort when the remedy is right beside you.

Clayton was right. Except it wasn't pills she needed.

He was her remedy.

Clayton couldn't bring her mother back, but he did know how to make her feel like the world would be right again, someday. "Okay. Like I said, my dream started out sweet. I was a little girl. So little that my legs wobbled when I ran. I think I might've been a toddler. But anyway, I did run. And I jumped. And rolled around in the grass. The sun was bright in my eyes, and I kept rolling down a hill. Then the man would carry me back up the hill and I'd roll down again. We played that game over and over until I could barely breathe from all the laughing."

"What man? Your father?"

"No." She pulled her knees up to her chest. "I don't think it was Dad. I can't picture the man's face but I remember it was smooth, with no wrinkles."

"Your dad hasn't always had wrinkles." Clayton smiled.

"It's a dream, so wrinkles or no wrinkles doesn't matter, I guess. But this man didn't smell like Dad. And he had a big smile. I remember feeling so happy when he carried me up the hill. Then, poof, Mom was there. She scooped me up and carried me off. The whole time, I was trying to jump out of her arms, and I kept waving madly at the man at the top of the hill." She paused, struggling to recall what happened next. "Suddenly, the scene switched. I was in our kitchen. And I could smell cookies baking. Mom kept wiping tears from her face with her apron. Then she hugged me, and she wouldn't let go. She kept crying and crying and there was nothing I could do to make it better."

"Did she tell you why she was so upset?"

Ivy shook her head. "No. But I sensed that it was my fault. She sent me to my bedroom, and the dream changed again. I wasn't a little girl anymore—I was a grown woman. I heard music tinkling behind my closet door. I went to check, and on the top shelf, my childhood music box was open, and the little ballerina was twirling. I felt Mom's presence. When the dream switched again, I saw Mom lying in the morgue. And then, it was *me* lying on a cold slab, and Mom was talking to me. She was trying to warn me about something. That's when I woke up. Did you turn on the light?"

"Yes. You were crying and thrashing around in your sleep."

"I'm so sorry for all of this. For punching you. For waking you up at night. I wouldn't blame you for sleeping in the other room, or even... even if you needed a break from me for a while."

"Let's get this straight. I'm not going anywhere. I'm going to stay right here by your side. You can count on it." He kissed her softly on the lips and lay down.

"That's good," she sighed. "Because I don't know what I'd do without you."

"Back at you. Can you sleep now?"

"Soon, I think. Will it keep you awake if I use my book light for a few minutes?"

He frowned. "It won't bother me... but Ivy, you're not going to read her obituary again? It's not helping with the nightmares. And frankly, it's bordering on obsessive—morbid even."

She could understand how it might seem that way, but the obituary helped ground her in reality. Helped her realize that the accident really happened. There had been times, lately, even when she was awake, that she had difficulty distinguishing the truth from dreams, memories from imagination. "Go back to sleep. I took my pills, like you wanted. I'll be out cold in no time."

"If you say so. But I'm officially registering my objection to the bedtime obituary ritual."

"Duly noted." She retrieved the obituary and a tiny reading light from her nightstand drawer.

It is with deepest sorrow that her family announces the passing of Patsy Kane.

If past was prologue, she'd be scouring this scrap of newsprint for hours, searching for clues to solve a mystery that didn't exist—answers to questions her heart would not allow itself to ask.

Obituary: Patsy Kane

It is with deepest sorrow that her family announces the passing of Patsy Kane. At the age of fifty-eight, she succumbed to injuries sustained in a motor vehicle accident.

Patsy was beloved in the town of Flagstaff, Arizona, where she resided for most of her life. There, she was best known for promoting what has been dubbed "the Flagstaff wave". Patsy believed that every resident should show their hospitality by greeting each other with an intentional smile or wave. As a young woman, she published an opinion piece in the Gazette on the topics of friendliness and community spirit and the wave idea caught fire. To this day, many locals adhere to the practice. Patsy's wave will be terribly missed, but each time we lift a hand to greet a passerby we will think of her.

Patsy met Richard Kane, the love of her life and husband of thirty-five years, at the Flagstaff rodeo, when he presented her with a two-hundred-dollar cash prize and the barrel racing Fast-Time trophy. For Richard, it was love at first sight. For Patsy it took a while longer. But Richard didn't give up. They soon bonded over their mutual love of horses and the outdoors. Eventually, he persuaded her to make him the luckiest man alive and the rest is Kane family legend.

After several years, Patsy and Richard were blessed with a daughter, Ivy. Patsy often referred to Ivy as her small miracle. She poured her whole heart into motherhood. Trading her woman's club activities for mommy-and-me classes. Becoming a girl-scout troop leader. Even writing a children's book aimed at helping Ivy overcome her shyness at school. Patsy cherished her family, and they cherished her.

Patsy is preceded in death by her parents, Tom and Catherine Jacobs.

She is survived by her husband, Richard Kane of the Flagstaff Kane Ranch; her daughter, Ivy Pinnacle and son-in-law Clayton Pinnacle, also from Flagstaff; as well as friends too numerous to count.

A private memorial service will be held at the Flagstaff Kane Ranch on Saturday, November 10 at 2 p.m. In lieu of flowers, it is Patsy's wish that donations be made to one of the many state-wide agencies that provide support to vulnerable children and families: see list below.

TWO
SANDRA

After six months of folding and unfolding Patsy Kane's obituary, the words on the scrap of newsprint were smudged and faded, but Sandra Steele knew them by heart. She had just come to the list of suggested charities when she heard her manager's heels clicking across tile.

Hastily, she folded the obituary and stuffed it into her apron pocket.

At the Century Country Club of Fort Worth, the waitresses, collectively known as "the girls", wore low-cut black tops, tight black skinny jeans, and a short waist-tied apron with one large pocket in front. At forty-five, Sandra wouldn't have minded being referred to as a "girl" if only her manager hadn't been twenty-years her junior.

Even with her back turned, Sandra could easily identify the sound of Nora's approach. Unlike the waitresses, Nora's uniform consisted of a classic black dress and stilettos that made a distinctive click-click pause, click-click pause sound as Nora navigated the dining room.

"Sandra, why are you standing still?" Her voice was pitched perfectly—high enough to let you know she was annoyed, but not so sharp as to be considered rude, in case she was overheard by a club member. Nora had perfected the art of setting herself above "the girls".

"I'm setting my table." Servers were not allowed to "screw off". If your tables were taken care of and your shift side-work complete—that never happened to Sandra because she was always helping out one of the new hires—then you were supposed to march from the entry to the kitchen and back again until summoned by a member's lifted finger or pointed glance.

Nora fluttered her extreme eyelash extensions and arched one heavily micro-bladed eyebrow. "What did you put in your pocket?"

Sandra noticed a smear of red above Nora's cupid's bow. Too much lip liner, per usual. And she'd dramatically contoured her makeup to reconfigure the natural shape of her face. She'd be beautiful if only she'd tone down the glam. It was a shame she didn't realize how lovely she truly was. "Nothing."

Nora extended her hand, palm up. "I saw you put something in your pocket."

"It's private." She tried to keep her tone civil. Walk that fine line between being assertive and being a smartass—she needed this job.

"I'm not accusing you; you understand?" Up went Nora's eyebrow again. "But as manager, I have to make sure no one steals from the club. It's my duty to inquire about anything suspicious."

Fair point—if you had an all-inclusive definition of "suspicious". "I didn't steal anything. I was reading a newspaper article."

A look of triumph flashed across Nora's face. "I knew you were screwing off. Need I remind you we provide you with two fifteen-minute breaks per shift? You are allowed to engage in personal activities during those times only. Go ahead, then. Let's see this article."

Sandra bit her lower lip and pulled the folded obituary from her apron.

"Give it to me."

This was simply too much. "No."

"If you don't, I'm going to have to file an incident report."

"I need to finish setting up the table. Charis has members waiting for it."

"Then you shouldn't have been screwing off."

"I apologize." Most people don't realize the difference between apologizing and saying *sorry*. An apology acknowledges you've done wrong, but *I'm sorry* means you feel badly about it.

Which she definitely did not.

"Apology accepted. Now then, let me see that paper."

The easy thing to do would be to hand it over. When Nora read it, she'd assume Patsy Kane was a friend of Sandra's who'd died, and then *she* would have to apologize to *Sandra*. Sandra could go back to setting up her table. Later, she could throw away the obituary and never think about Patsy Kane or Richard Kane or Ivy Pinnacle again.

"Hurry, please. I've got to speak to the new girl. She doesn't understand she can't wear button downs, only V-necks." Nora wriggled her fingers. "Give it up already."

She held out the paper, but then something inside her stiffened. Nora had no right to pry into her private matters—this was too intimate, too important, and Sandra had too much self-respect to allow herself to be bullied. She yanked it back. "I can't. It's personal."

"Then give me your apron." Nora once again extended her hand. "You can pick up your last check on Friday."

"What? No, please. I sincerely apologize. I'll get this table ready in a flash, and I'll work an extra shift every week for the rest of the month. I promise, it won't happen again."

"And you'll show me what you're reading."

"I-I don't want to." *Stupid. Stubborn. Sandra.*

Nora reached behind Sandra's back and untied her apron with a flourish. It dropped, dramatically, to the floor. "I won't be made a fool in front of my staff."

"Please, Nora. I need this job. My son, Dalton, got accepted to the University of Texas. Please, please don't do this. You can read the article. It's nothing." She passed her the obituary.

Nora scanned it, then handed it back. "You're right. It *is* nothing. But you should've given it to me as soon as I asked. I'm afraid your apology is too little too late. And besides, you don't fit in here. I'm trying to set a certain standard at the club. You're good at your job. And you're pretty—which is why I've kept you on this long. But I'm afraid you're past your *sell-by* date." Nora ground the discarded apron under her heel. "Clear out your locker, *darling*—you're fired."

Her heart sank. The cash tips from the club's high society patrons were the only thing keeping her afloat. She loved her other job as a teacher's aide at the School for the Blind, but it only paid minimum wage, and at the moment, the school was on summer break.

Then, the black lettering on the faded obituary caught her eye again.

It is with deepest sorrow that her family announces the passing of Patsy Kane.

She steeled her spine.

Since she was between jobs, there was no longer anything stopping her from making a trip to Flagstaff—if only she could find the courage.

THREE

IVY

Flagstaff, Arizona

Ivy woke up without tears on her cheeks. She brushed her teeth and gathered her long brown hair into a ponytail, donned a tailored white blouse with brass buttons, a pencil skirt and dark pumps. Humming beneath her breath, she made it all the way to the kitchen before reality punched her in the chest.

How could she have forgotten her mom's accident? Even for a minute?

Part of her wanted to turn around, go back to her room, and re-read the obituary.

But then she remembered she'd smacked Clayton in the jaw, again, the other night, and how patient he'd been with her. She thought about his plea to stop the *bedtime obituary ritual.* He was right, of course. There was nothing to be gained from that. She wasn't going to find a cipher written in invisible ink to explain why her mother had been taken from her without warning.

It was an accident, plain and simple, and there was nothing to be done.

Her throat closed. Her heart faltered, then picked up a rhythmic beat once more. A familiar, achy, pit in her stomach announced itself, but more demurely than yesterday or the day before. In fact, she was hungry—a big accomplishment.

If she ate without being reminded, Clayton would be pleased.

So would Mom.

Breakfast didn't have to be a master creation whipped up in the fancy chef's kitchen Clayton had insisted on installing, even though neither of them was a gourmet cook. She could start with baby steps—a nibble or two of her favorite strawberry jam from the farmer's market on a toasted bagel would work.

Outside the kitchen window, two blue jays flitted from ponderosa pine to ponderosa pine, playing hopscotch on the branches and having a grand time, perfectly befitting a beautiful, blue-skyed summer day. Feeling better about what today might bring, she spooned jam onto a bagel and polished off half of it.

So, this is what they mean when they say life goes on.

Put one foot in front of the other without crying.

Eat breakfast.

Enjoy the birds.

Cherish the family you still have.

Hard as hell, but not impossible.

She tugged her shoulders back. She owed it to Clayton and to Dad to make an effort. She'd lost her mother, but Dad had lost the love of his life. His wife of thirty-five years, his soulmate, and *he* hadn't crumbled. Dad was old school. The kind of man who defined himself by working hard, providing for, and most of all, *protecting* his family.

At Mom's funeral he'd stood tall, broad-shouldered and brave.

Ivy had wanted to be strong like him, but she hadn't been

able to contain her sobs, falling into his comforting embrace like a child at her mother's graveside.

Now, she squeezed her eyes closed.

Gritted her teeth.

It was easy to imagine what Mom would say: *It's been six months, Ivy. Shake it off. Act like the woman I raised you to be. And stop reading my obituary!*

Later today, she would transfer it from her bedside drawer to a box at the top of the closet. For everyone's sake—Dad's, Clayton's, her *own*—it was time to get on with life. She needed to find a way to cohabitate with grief without letting it steal all of her happiness. There were so many beautiful moments yet to come, days her mother would have loved to have. It was a crime for Ivy to squander them.

Something clattered in the hallway, followed by the sound of footsteps.

"There you are! What's on your agenda for the day?"

Clayton strolled into the kitchen, in full workout gear, sweat beading on his brow. Somehow, he managed to land a kiss on her cheek without ungluing his eyes from his phone. "Morning, my love. No plans at all. I'm up for whatever."

"You've been to the gym and back already, had your coffee? Why didn't you wake me?"

"You were smiling... and I didn't want to interrupt a sweet dream. It didn't seem like the right thing to do."

"Was I actually smiling in my sleep?"

"I just said so. Do you remember the dream?"

She shook her head. Last night, somehow, she'd slept through the night without nightmares—and without pills.

Dare she hope a return to normalcy was in the offing?

After the accident, Clayton and Dad had persuaded her to take time off from her job as an associate professor at Northern Arizona University. The summer semester had just gotten underway, but it wasn't too late to reclaim her spot in next fall's roster. By now, Maggie Maples would've called dibs on Ivy's favorite class—Introduction to Women Writers—but if teaching Composition and Chaucer was the price of a ticket back to her normal world, she'd have to suck it up.

Clinging to her pain was self-centered. Mom used to say the secret to winning at life was to focus on other people. Reach out to them instead of dwelling on your problems. Her mother had a million such tips.

I'm trying, Mom.

"Ivy?"

"Sorry. What did you say?" She met Clayton's clear brown eyes.

In that endearing way of his, he fiddled with the thick dark hair that curled at the nape of his neck. "I said let's do something fun. Find a movie, or go for a hike. We could meet the Donovans for dinner later. Nothing too ambitious, but, you know, the regular stuff we used to do."

Routine. Life getting back to normal.

"Sounds amazing." She took a breath. "Why are you looking at me like that?"

"It's just so good to see you all spiffed up and happy." He opened his arms.

She scooted into them and rested her head on his chest. His shirt was still damp and musty from his workout.

He shoved her away. "You're dressed up, and I need a shower."

"If we're going hiking, I'm the one who needs to change. There's no point in you showering."

"When you're right—" His words were cut off by a soft chime. He touched his mobile, apparently opening their doorbell app. Then he shrugged. "There's a lady on the porch. You know her?"

He held up the phone for her to check out the woman pictured on the camera's live-stream.

Tall and slender, mid-to-late forties. Wavy auburn hair just hitting her shoulders. Toying with a brass button on a white tailored blouse, shifting from one high-heeled foot to the other.

"No idea who she is. But I'll go find out." Ivy pressed the microphone on the phone's app. "Be right there."

"You wait here. I'll get rid of her." Clayton jerked his phone from her hand and hurried away as if this innocent-looking person might have a grenade in her purse.

Protective.

Just like Dad.

Ivy let him go, but, after a moment, curiosity got the better of her and she followed, landing behind him as he opened the front door.

"Sorry, no soliciting," he said, his tone polite but firm, his finger aimed at a placard affixed to a shingle beneath the bell.

"Oh"—the woman's pretty face flushed—"I'm not here to sell you anything. I'm looking for someone." Her gaze traveled around Clayton and settled on Ivy. "Does Ivy Pinnacle live here?"

A weird feeling raised the hairs on her neck. Irrational though it might be, since the woman had obviously spotted her, Ivy stepped back into the shadows. Suddenly, she was the one imagining this stranger had a grenade in her purse.

"I'm looking for Ivy Pinnacle."

Ivy took a breath. There was no reason for the sense of dread creeping over her. The woman looked perfectly nice. Could be a new neighbor...

"Who are you? What is it you want with her?" Clayton asked.

"If Ivy's here"—the woman crossed her arms—"I'd like to discuss that with *her*."

Ivy reached out and touched Clayton's shoulder, dissuading him from closing the door in the woman's face. With her pulse inexplicably revving, she edged in front of him. "I'm Ivy Pinnacle. What can I do for you?"

"I-I..." The button that the mysterious visitor had been playing with came off in her hand. "May I speak with you alone, Ivy?"

"Sorry, but no. I don't mean to be rude. If you're trying to sell us solar panels or pest control or even if you're trying to save our souls, we're not interested," Ivy said.

The woman rubbed the button between her thumb and index finger like it was a magic coin. "Please, Ivy? If you could step outside so we can talk in private?"

"Whatever you have to say, you can say it in front of my husband. I'm afraid you have us at a disadvantage. You seem to know me, or at least my name, but you haven't told us yours."

The button popped out of the woman's grasp.

Ivy's gaze followed it as it rolled off the front porch into the flower bed.

"I don't mean to interfere with your plans, but I-I think you should know..." The woman hesitated.

The brass button blinked up at Ivy from its new position at the base of a purple iris.

She tore her gaze away and shifted it back to the woman's face. Her features came into sharp relief against a blurred background of blue sky and green pines. Ivy's head felt light. "Whatever you have to say, just get on with it. Dodging and ducking doesn't make a good impression."

The visitor lifted her gaze, her huge, copper-colored eyes swimming with moisture. "All right then, no more dodging and ducking. My name is Sandra Steele, Ivy... I'm your mother."

FOUR

IVY

Ivy pressed her hands over her ears to drown out the chattering of the birds—it was unbearably loud, like their conversation was being piped in over a loud speaker. Then, at once, the world went silent. She dropped her hands and stood statue still, staring at this insane stranger's outstretched hand, noticing her pencil skirt and dark pumps—an outfit eerily similar to the one Ivy was wearing.

We have the same tastes in clothes.

So what? That doesn't make her my mother!

Ivy held her breath, clinging to the wild hope that if she didn't move a muscle, if she willed it with all her might, this woman would vanish, and Mom would appear in her place. Not that long ago, things just as crazy had happened. Like Clayton coming home from work early. Telling her that Mom couldn't make it to their special mother–daughter dinner.

Her car went off a cliff.

She's gone, darling.

I'm so, so sorry.

The stranger pulled her hand away and wiped her palms on her skirt. Seconds ticked by. Ivy didn't move. Didn't breathe.

Then, at last, she allowed her eyes to dart between that woman, *Sandra*, and Clayton. Clayton was making big gestures in the air. Sandra was shaking her head.

The world began to spin. Then, Clayton and Sandra took up a position on either side of her, lifted her arms and draped them over their shoulders.

"Let's get her inside." Clayton's voice came through, calm and strong.

Her hearing had returned, so then, surely, she could get her legs to support her. "I can walk."

"We've got you," said Sandra.

Ivy pushed them away and though, at first, her knees wobbled, she made it through the front door and into the living room under her own steam.

Clayton patted her hand, as if she were a child. "Darling, Sandra says she took a DNA test. She says that, before the accident, your mother hired someone to locate her. I know it's a shock, but I think we should hear her out."

Ivy dropped onto the first available chair and pointed at Sandra. "I don't know who you are. But you are *not* my mother."

FIVE

SANDRA

Sandra took a third turn around Ivy's kitchen, mentally cataloguing its contents.

It wasn't what she'd pictured. She'd assumed Ivy lived in a mansion.

Yes, the house was a major step up from the one she shared with her son, Dalton, back in Fort Worth. And, sure, it was nice enough, single-story, probably three to four thousand square feet. A gated community. Barbeque in the backyard with a partial view of Mount Humphreys. But with all that family money, she'd expected much more.

Ten thousand square feet at least, perhaps an indoor pool and movie room, marble as far as the eye could see. She'd even dreamed up a closet for Ivy that resembled the entire women's clothing department at Macy's. This place seemed far too small to accommodate the luxuries she'd imagined.

But the more she looked, the more she saw signs of quiet luxury.

The kitchen, especially, was like something out of a magazine with its giant white quartz island, *two* entire ovens, and one of those fancy, built-in, furniture-style refrigerators.

And check out the designer tea kettle!

Violets stamped onto creamy porcelain, a wooden handle and a little bird stopper that whistled. Apparently, she and Ivy shared a love of flora and fauna and all the pretty things life had to offer. In fact, Sandra had admired a kettle exactly like this one at Sur La Table for $400—way out of her price range.

Not for long, it won't be.

She intended to enjoy living in luxury—after the life she'd spent working two, sometimes three jobs, in order to make rent and pay for Dalton's school.

She sighed. Time to stop daydreaming. Soon enough, there'd be time to revel in all the creature comforts Ivy's family money could buy. But the longer she lingered in the kitchen, the longer that gave Ivy and Clayton to reconsider the wisdom of allowing a perfect stranger to march through the front door, head straight to the kitchen, and whip up refreshments like she owned the place.

Best get back to them before they picked their jaws up off the floor and realized she'd taken charge of their home without so much as a by-your-leave.

"Just making some tea, sweetheart," she called out, loudly enough to be heard in the family room where Ivy remained parked in a chair with Clayton hovering over her. Was the *sweetheart* too much? "You need a moment to catch your breath."

And I need a moment to regroup and consider my next move.

Sandra hadn't expected the butterflies in her belly when she'd seen Ivy in person for the first time. The photographs Sandra had seen didn't do her justice. Ivy had a certain *je ne sais quoi* about her that went beyond those pretty, symmetrical features; that silky, face-framing hair and lovely figure. Her unguarded brown eyes drew you in—*held* you. Made you want to know and be known by her.

Ivy was the kind of person you wanted to tell your secrets to.

Too bad Sandra couldn't trust Ivy with hers.

"Tea time!" Sandra summoned a confident air, set a lacquered tray, laden with steaming cups, various sweeteners, spoons, and napkins onto the coffee table—as if preparing tea in this house was something she'd done many times before.

As Ivy's mother, it ought to have been.

"You really shouldn't have." The look on Clayton's face told the tale—he meant that literally. He thought it presumptuous of her, and it was. But Sandra *must* be bold if she ever hoped to become part of this family.

Pretending not to get his drift, she gushed, "It was no trouble. I feel terrible about giving you and Ivy such a shock."

"What did you expect?" Clayton glowered at her. She'd managed to get her toe in the door, and to persuade them to give her an audience, but the husband clearly wasn't happy about any of this.

"I guess you were too shocked to take it all in when I explained earlier, on the porch," she pointedly addressed Ivy, "but, I thought you knew you were adopted. I thought you knew that, before her tragic death, Patsy hired an investigator to find your birth family. To find *me*."

"We didn't know anything about that." Clayton's voice rose with each sharply enunciated word.

Sandra had tried to be generous, to cut Clayton some slack, given how surprised he must've been when she showed up on the doorstep. But the way he answered for his wife was getting on her last nerve. A woman deserves an equal voice, especially in her own home. "Your mother never mentioned any of this to you, Ivy? I wonder why not."

Ivy, who'd been staring into her tea for what seemed an

eternity, finally looked up. Her disconcerting brown eyes found Sandra's. "Her death was unexpected."

"I'm so sorry. The lawyer told me she'd been in an accident, but I still assumed that your adoption, and the fact that Patsy had found your birth mother, was out in the open."

Ivy's throat worked. "Mom called me the day she died. We were supposed to meet later for dinner. Just the two of us. And she definitely had something on her mind. I remember how worked up she seemed. When I asked what was going on, she said she didn't want to talk about it over the phone. Now, I wonder if she planned to tell me about *you* that night."

"Mm hm." Sandra settled back into an arm chair, stirring sugar into a Wedgewood teacup. She didn't wish to agree or disagree, didn't want to appear to know too much about Patsy's death. Better to let Ivy draw her own conclusions, rather than appear to be pushing an agenda.

Only the poor thing looked awfully lost.

Sandra had a nonsensical urge to take her by the hand, but settled for making a sympathetic noise in her throat. "I'm sure you'll want to speak directly to the person who reviewed all the testing. Your mother provided a DNA sample for you, and I, of course, volunteered mine. Your mother's lawyer, Mr. Troy Laquay, can confirm—"

"I'll check with him." Ivy edged forward in her chair, and a tight line appeared between her eyebrows. Then she turned to Clayton. "This doesn't add up for me. If it's true I'm adopted, and Mom found my biological mother, why didn't *Dad* tell me?"

SIX

SANDRA

"I've made a mess of this." Sandra got to her feet, speaking quietly, moving cautiously, in order not to startle Ivy, who hadn't taken a sip of the delicious lemon-drop tea Sandra had so thoughtfully prepared. This whole time, Ivy had been staring at the pretty little Wedgewood cup as if it contained hemlock.

Sandra tried to make her voice sound meek. "I don't expect to appear after twenty-nine years and be welcomed into the family. I can't expect you to trust me—you don't even know me." Neither Ivy nor Clayton corrected her. They stood, stiff-backed, clearly ready to escort her out. "You have a lovely day planned and I'm intruding."

Again, stony silence.

Even if Ivy didn't believe her, she should treat her potential, possible birth mother better. "This was a horrible mistake. I should've notified Mr. Laquay of my travel plans. He could've acted the intermediary. He could've worked out, with your father, the best way to inform you. In my defense, I was under the distinct impression Patsy had already spoken with you. Mr. Laquay conveyed to me that your mother was keen on getting things out in the open. I only learned of Patsy's death a few days ago, and the moment I did, I felt compelled to... well, I thought I might bring you some comfort. But all I've done is upset you. And—"

"I'll see you out," Clayton cut her off.

She wiped a nonexistent tear from her cheek. "I understand you need time to let this sink in—I'll get out of your hair so you can get on with your day. Meanwhile, I'm staying at the Thrifty Motel on Santa Fe Avenue."

"What room? And we'd like your cell phone number," Clayton said, his tone cool. "In case Ivy has more questions."

"I'll let you know the room number later today—haven't checked in yet. I was so eager to meet Ivy, I came straight from the airport."

"I didn't hear a cab pull up. I didn't see a suitcase." Ivy frowned, as if this had just occurred to her.

"I walked from the bus stop. My suitcase is at the bottom of your drive. I was awfully tired after lugging it all that way."

"I'll give you a lift to the motel, make sure you get checked in. We'll be in touch, later. Where's home, and when do you plan to return?" Clayton asked, all business.

"I bought a one-way ticket. I assumed you'd want to get to know me a little bit." She made her tone jokey, to soften the clear implication that Ivy and Clayton were being less than kind. "But not to worry. This is your life, Ivy. I'm here if you need me. If you don't, then I'll manage just fine until I can save up the money for my return fare. I was born and raised in Texas, but Dalton and I live abroad now. I've come all the way from Paris, France."

Ivy shook her head. "France... and what do you mean *we*? Who is Dalton?"

Sandra had deliberately held back mentioning her son. He was her ace in the hole. Was there an only child anywhere who didn't long for a sibling? "I keep forgetting no one told you about us. I couldn't afford to bring him with me, but Dalton is your younger brother."

SEVEN

IVY

Alone in her bedroom, in lieu of swallowing the cornucopia of pills Clayton left on her nightstand, Ivy pressed a cool cloth to her pounding forehead.

No need to suffer when the remedy is close at hand, he'd repeated his mantra.

But her head was spinning perfectly well on its own, without the help of a single pharmaceutical agent, and she wanted to remain as clear-minded as possible. The voicemail she'd left Dad made it apparent she needed to speak to him A.S.A.P., but he still hadn't returned her call. She could've told him it was an emergency, but she didn't want to worry him.

Last night, after declining Clayton's cocktail of tranquilizers and allergy pills, she'd had her first good night's sleep in ages. She definitely didn't want to take something now, mid-morning, even after all that had transpired.

A long shuddering breath rumbled out of her chest.

Hard to believe that only a couple of hours ago she'd been bird watching from her kitchen window, believing that life was finally getting back to normal. Then Sandra Steele appeared on her doorstep and destroyed Ivy's new-found peace of mind.

Only if you let her.

She squeezed her eyes closed, trying to think.

Could it be true?

And would it be *so* terrible if it were?

She had to admit the idea of a long-lost brother had its appeal.

But another mother?

She shivered and reached for her tranquilizers—but the sound of the bell stopped her. After this morning's events, she hesitated to open the door, or even check her security camera to see who was on the porch.

Instead, she sat still on the edge of her bed, holding her breath, waiting for whomever it was to go away.

The bell chimed again.

Then came a distinctive rapping.

The cool cloth she'd been holding to her forehead fell to the floor.

Had she really heard what she thought she'd heard?

Once more, someone knocked rhythmically, imitating the beat of the old jingle "shave and a haircut, two bits".

Mrs. Winters.

Our secret knock.

In the old days, when Ivy would hide in her room because a bully hurt her feelings, or a young man broke her heart, Mrs. Winters would wait until Mom and Dad were fast asleep. Then she'd come to Ivy in the wee hours with a tray of sweets and warm milk. She'd use their secret knock to let her know it was her. *I'm awake if you want to talk. Your secrets are safe with me.*

If there was one person who could soothe Ivy's troubled heart, it was Becky Winters. Only, at the moment, Ivy was in no mood to be soothed. Eventually, Mrs. Winters would go away, just as she had when teenaged Ivy refused to open the door and confide in her about a young man.

Then Ivy's breath caught in her throat.

Though Mrs. Winters never pressed, sooner or later, Ivy would always break down and tell her everything.

She sprang to her feet.

Mrs. Becky Winters didn't only keep Ivy's secrets—she knew *Mom's* secrets, too.

EIGHT

SANDRA

Where is he taking me?

After Sandra had explained her situation, that she had no personal vehicle and was lugging a suitcase around, Clayton had offered her a ride. But this was definitely not the way to the Thrifty Motel, where she'd asked to be dropped. According to the directions on Sandra's phone, downtown Flagstaff, and the motel, were to the north. Clayton had turned his Porsche SUV south.

"I think this is the wrong way, Clayton."

He shook his head.

"You need to turn around. I pulled up directions and—"

"We're not going to the Thrifty Motel."

When the car took a dip, her stomach did too. Then she lifted her chin. Clayton Pinnacle had another thing coming if he thought he could load her up into his fancy Porsche Cayenne, drive her out of town, and be rid of her that easily.

He turned, caught her eye and smiled. "That place is a dump. Ivy would kill me if I let someone claiming to be family stay there."

At his congenial tone, her chest loosened. He was treating

her a little better than before. Not as well as a birth mother deserved to be treated, but it was progress. "*Claiming* to be family?"

"You have to understand this came as a complete surprise."

"I am sorry about that." How many times was she supposed to apologize? If he had any manners, he'd move on. "Speaking of surprises, do you want to let me in on our destination? I'm not expecting the Four Seasons, of course."

"This is better."

Than the Four Seasons?

He turned onto a private street, making her mouth water in anticipation.

The road was paved but narrow, winding through a thicket of ponderosa pines intermingled with aspens. She rolled down her window and cool mountain air rushed in, carrying with it a crisp, clean scent she'd almost forgotten. This unending blue sky, these towering trees, the mountain air, transported her back to her youth, making her nostalgic.

"This your first time in Flagstaff?" Clayton asked.

"No. Once, my mother and I took a vacation to the Grand Canyon. That same trip, we spent a few days here. We went to Walnut Canyon and Lowell Observatory. I'll never forget looking through the telescope. I've been a big fan of the night sky ever since."

"If it's stars you're seeking, you've come to the right place. Flagstaff is a dark sky city."

"One of the first in the country—they gave a talk about that at the observatory."

He guided the Porsche through ledgestone pillars. "Almost there."

She stuck her hand out the window, enjoying the feel of the wind whooshing across her palm. Straight ahead, surrounded by magnificent pines, with the San Francisco Peaks as a backdrop, a ledgestone structure stretched toward a yellow sun.

"What hotel is this? I didn't believe you when you promised something better than the Four Seasons, but this place is incredible."

He pulled into a circular cobblestone drive and killed the engine.

"This is my father-in-law's home—we call it the lodge. He and Troy Laquay are waiting inside to speak with you."

Yes! How perfect that he'd brought her here.

But... when did Clayton have a chance to let Richard Kane know she was in town?

She stared at him, half-trying to read his mind, half-trying to unnerve him.

He must've been in quite the rush to notify his father-in-law.

Which begged the question: how much, if anything, did Clayton Pinnacle know?

NINE

IVY

After a round of hugs, Ivy and Mrs. Rebecca Winters settled into opposite-facing armchairs in Ivy's living room. Ivy released the red ribbon that bound a box stamped with the Flagstaff Candy Factory logo. Typical of Becky to arrive with a thoughtful gift. "Thanks for the chocolates. Should we wash them down with something? I can make coffee or tea. I'm out of regular milk, but I've got almond. Or we could have a giant glass of merlot."

"Nothing for me. But you have that wine if you want." Becky plunked a chocolate into her mouth and chewed with her usual enthusiasm for all things sugary.

"I was being facetious—it's not even noon." Although, on this particular day, Ivy would've been happy enough to crack open a bottle before lunchtime.

"Well, from what I hear, you're entitled."

Ivy blinked, trying to get her bearings. Mrs. Winters spoke as if she'd been privy to the entire morning's events, but Ivy hadn't yet had a chance to fill her in. Unless... she did tell her and she'd somehow forgotten? Or what if she was speaking her thoughts instead of thinking them—that had happened once before after a few too many pills.

Mrs. Winters folded her hands in her lap, casting her eyes around the room. "Clayton called me."

Of course! She'd seen him on his phone before he left—sometimes Ivy's brain was simply too addled to bear.

For someone in her late sixties, especially someone who'd cleaned and cooked and managed a household staff for decades, Mrs. Winters appeared remarkably youthful. Though her face was lined around the mouth and eyes, her smile was bright. She kept her medium-length brown hair styled in a simple bob. Today, she looked especially lovely in a white blouse, tucked neatly into trim trousers. Mom had never asked Mrs. Winters to wear a uniform, but for some reason she always chose a white blouse with gray trousers. She might've owned jeans, but Ivy couldn't recall ever seeing her wear them.

"Clayton told me a woman, Sandra Steele, showed up at your door, claiming to be your biological mother." Becky picked up the candy box lid and studied the pictorial diagram of which chocolate was which.

Ivy knew better than to rush her. If she stayed silent, eventually the dam would break, and she would tell her everything.

Becky hovered her index finger over a square milk chocolate, then a round one, then a rectangle. "I better not."

"Oh, please. Help yourself."

Becky consulted the diagram again, and eventually selected a piece, a caramel, judging by the time it took her to chew it. Finally, she cleared her throat. "I suppose you want to hear what I know about this situation."

Ivy merely nodded, somehow managing to stop herself from shaking Mrs. Winters by the shoulders.

"The main thing I can tell you is that your mom, Patsy, had the honor of being your mother." Becky tore her eyes from the box of candy and squared her gaze with Ivy's. "That said, I wonder if this woman might be telling the truth. And with Patsy gone, you owe it to yourself to find out. Perhaps she can bring comfort, or a new dimension to your life, help you find another part of yourself—if she is who she says she is, I think you should give her a chance."

Ivy's shoulders stiffened. This was not what she was expecting from her mother's devoted friend and confidante. She couldn't push the words out of her tight throat; instead, they floated around in her brain like captions on a television screen. *Traitor! Traitor! Traitor!*

TEN

SANDRA

Now this is more like it.

Richard Kane's house was exactly as Sandra had pictured it. His home office was massive—about the size of a church sanctuary. It boasted vaulted, beamed ceilings, carved wooden furniture and vibrant Native American rugs. From floor to ceiling, leather-bound tomes lined three of its walls.

On the fourth, a woman's portrait hung above an elaborate marble fireplace.

Patsy Kane.

Perhaps because it was painted in photorealistic style, it felt, for a moment, as if Patsy were in the room, just waiting for Sandra to make a misstep.

She tossed her hair back and made eye contact with Patsy—as well as one can make eye contact with a painting—then turned and unabashedly took in every inch of the two men standing beside Clayton.

One towered over the others. Deadly handsome, for a man in his sixties, with a full head of silver hair, dressed in worn jeans. She cocked her head to get a peek at the back of his dusty suede boots, and sure enough he was wearing spurs.

The other man was billiard-ball bald and stocky, in a blue silk suit, narrow gray tie, and expensive-looking leather loafers.

It wasn't hard to figure out who was Richard Kane, the family patriarch, and who was Troy Laquay, the lawyer.

"I didn't know they were permitted in the house, or I would've worn my spurs." She locked her gaze with Richard Kane's steely blue one, and offered her hand. "You must be Richard, Ivy's adoptive father."

"I'm Ivy's *father*." His deep, gravel voice echoed in the cold, stone-walled study. Other than a slight emphasis on the word "father", he showed no sign of annoyance. "I've been out riding. I apologize for my appearance."

Bull. He didn't give a damn how he looked, but he knew how to make an impact. It wouldn't surprise her if he'd deliberately cowboyed up to intimidate her. He looked like he'd just walked off the set of a television show. One of those family sagas, which had gotten so popular, about rich, ruthless ranchers —Richard Kane exuded wealth and power.

Maybe he was a real cowboy, or maybe it was an act—either way he wasn't going to ruffle her. "Nice to meet you..." She turned and stuck her hand out to the lawyer. "And you as well. I'm Sandra Steele, Ivy's birth mother."

"Clayton, may we have the room?" Troy Laquay's voice fit his style. Weak, soft and bordering on obsequious.

Clayton's sneakers squished over the stone floor, and then the door closed heavily behind him, leaving Sandra alone with the patriarch and the lawyer.

ELEVEN
SANDRA

Indicating a highbacked chair that looked to be straight out of the Spanish Inquisition, Laquay said, "Please make yourself comfortable, dear."

Sandra scanned the room for the advertised comfort. Most of the furnishings were high-end natural wood finishes without a cushion in sight. Only the tufted leather production behind the colossal snakewood desk, where Richard Kane presumably reigned, looked comfy—the most inviting piece in the room and the most menacing in juxtaposition.

"Don't mind if I do." Sandra rounded the desk and claimed his highness's chair.

One side of Richard's mouth *might* have quirked, but she wouldn't lay odds on it.

"I'm afraid there's been a misunderstanding." Laquay grimaced.

Ignoring Laquay—he was a mere lackey, and she couldn't care less what he had to say—she kept her eyes on Richard, stroking her fingers over the supple leather that encompassed her.

Never in her life had she sat in such a chair.

"How much do you want?" Richard ventured at last.

"For what?" She feigned ignorance.

"Let's not play games." Laquay attempted to engage her again.

"But you're paying me to play games."

Laquay produced a handkerchief and wiped his forehead.

"I am an actress." That's how she'd billed herself, anyway, and she did have a part in a school play once. "You hired me to play a role. I'm simply fulfilling my end of the bargain."

"I terminated your employment." Laquay began pacing in front of the desk. "Mrs. Kane passed away, unexpectedly, and your services are no longer required. Six months ago, I sent you her obituary along with a check."

"Yes, but the check was only for half the amount." At this point, she wouldn't even accept the full amount. Not after Laquay reneged on their deal. Not after she'd been fired from her job at the country club. Dalton was going to get the education he deserved, and she was finally going to find out how the other half lived. She was after much more than the original sum now, and why not? Richard Kane could well afford it.

"You cashed the check, and that indicates you accepted it as payment in full," Laquay said, as though she should take his word as law.

"That was only a first installment. We have a contract, and I'm here to hold up my end of the bargain."

"Coming here in person was *never* part of the bargain, and you damn well know it. I hired you to play Ivy's birth mother. Your son was to play a biological half-brother. All of it *online*. You were *never* supposed to meet Ivy in person. You were supposed to say you lived in Paris. You were supposed to provide up to ten hours of online face-to-face chats, ostensibly from France, with the option for more if needed. You were supposed to answer all of Ivy's questions, in whatever manner I directed you. But since Mrs. Kane... since she isn't with us any longer, the gig is cancelled. Apologies for any inconvenience but considering the tragic circumstances, I'm *appalled* you'd show up and make a fuss."

This guy seemed genuinely, morally outraged. Rich, considering the con he and his boss were trying to pull. She wasn't backing down, but the more information she could squeeze out of him, the more leverage she'd have. "I did get your check and your voicemail canceling the contract. But you didn't explain why Mrs. Kane's death meant—"

"Because Ivy doesn't know she's adopted—at least she didn't until you showed up. It's true that Richard and Patsy were planning to tell Ivy, but after the accident, Richard changed his mind. Why are you so determined to cause this family more pain?" Laquay's voice squeaked up an octave.

"Why did you hire me?"

Richard Kane sauntered over and bent down, laying his hands on the arms of her chair, getting so close she could smell the outdoors, the wind, the horses. Apparently, he really had been out riding. "Mrs. Steele, I can see you're a curious woman. And you must've put on quite a performance earlier with Clayton and Ivy. I believe you're a fine actress, dedicated to her craft. But the show's over. It's time to take your final bow. I'll write you a check for the original amount—in full, plus travel expenses. You will go back to wherever it is you came from. You'll send Ivy a note explaining you've been called back to Paris—Troy will dictate; you can write it out in pretty penmanship. We'll handle everything else."

"No, thank you."

"I thought I'd give you a chance to do the right thing, but as I suspected you might, you've refused. You obviously came here intent on stirring up trouble. Well, I'm going to pay you anyway. I'm a man of honor, and I will not have you hurting my daughter. You will go home, wherever that may be, and forget this ever happened." Richard flicked his gaze to Laquay. "Troy, round up Clayton. Send him home to Ivy. Is Mrs. Winters around?"

"Clayton asked her to check on Ivy, but she should be back shortly."

"As soon as she arrives, tell her I need her to arrange a one-way flight to anywhere Mrs. Steele chooses. Book her first class to Paris if she wants."

She climbed out of the world's finest leather chair and glared up at Richard. "You're confused about who's calling the shots. You hired a fake family to trick your daughter. I don't know why you did such a despicable thing, but unless you're prepared for Ivy to find out, I'm not leaving."

"I did not hire you."

Richard spoke so emphatically she almost believed him. "Your lawyer did not do this on his own. You signed my check. And if you didn't authorize the contract, then who did?"

Laquay dotted his handkerchief across his glowing forehead, yet again. "It's none of your concern, but if you must know, the fake family was all Patsy's doing. Richard knew nothing about our arrangement until after Patsy's death. At that point, I was obligated to tell him, and the moment he found out he ordered me to call you off."

"That's enough, Troy." The tremor in Richard's voice was barely detectable, but real. When he turned back to Sandra, his complexion paled—the man was shaken. "I may not have hired you, but this is still my fault. I never should have ordered a search for Ivy's birth parents. But after Ivy married, I thought she should know her medical history before having kids of her own. I'd give anything, now, to have never brought it up. I knew how terrified Patsy was of losing Ivy. When she was a baby, Patsy constantly worried the birth parents would try to reclaim her. And when Ivy became an adult, Patsy feared she would choose her biological family over us if she learned she was adopted."

"Richard instructed me to find the birth parents, and to make sure they were good people, before letting Ivy meet them," Laquay added. "But Patsy begged me not to, and against my better judgment, I acquiesced. She wanted me to hire actors and present them to Ivy and Richard online. That way, she could control the narrative, have them enter and exit Ivy's life quickly. Patsy wasn't only worried the real parents would be scammers or addicts—she was most afraid that Ivy would bond with them, and then she would lose her forever. I tried to reassure her that wouldn't happen, but I think after all her miscarriages—"

"Stop talking." Richard glowered at Laquay.

"That's quite a story," Sandra said, uncertain how much of it was true. Not that it mattered. Because she'd figured out how she and Dalton could get the most benefit from these people. "Take my bag to your best guest room." She waved a hand at Laquay. "And don't forget to leave spending money on the bedside table—however much cash you have on you will do... for now."

"And why would I permit that?" Richard asked.

"You're afraid of what it will do to Ivy if she finds out about Patsy's intended plan. If you weren't, you would've explained it to her the minute you found out I was in town. So, here's what's going to happen. I'm going to stay right here in Flagstaff and get to know my beautiful daughter."

TWELVE

IVY

With the room spinning around her, Ivy gripped the arms of her chair. She inhaled a long breath, and as soon as the vertigo subsided, she intentionally relaxed her posture. If Mrs. Winters sensed her distress, she might try to spare her feelings by leaving out certain details.

"I can see the shock on your face. But I have to call it like I see it," Becky said.

"I'm grateful for your honesty. Please, continue—and don't hold anything back. I promise I can handle the truth, and I value your advice."

Mrs. Winters sat up straighter. "Stop me anytime if the going gets too rough, or if you have a question."

"I promise I will."

"All right then. Here goes. Thirty-three years ago, I started work as a part-time cook for your family. During that time, your mom cried more than she smiled. Three times, that I know about, she became pregnant but miscarried. The last time, she nearly died, and the doctors warned her it wasn't safe to keep trying. After that, she cried every day. Often, she wouldn't even bother to get dressed or come out of her room."

"But Mom always seemed so strong, so resilient."

"Because *you* turned her into a fighter. Your mother was all lioness after you came along." The housekeeper sniffled.

Ivy took a tissue for herself and passed the box to Mrs. Winters.

"One day, your father came to me. He lifted me off the ground in a bear hug and twirled me around. He'd never done that before, and he hasn't done it since. He told me he'd found a young woman, a teenager, who was looking for a good home for her unborn baby. He offered me a raise to move into the house after the baby was born. That baby was you. From the day they brought you home, you were the light of your mom's life. Mine too, if the truth be told." She blew her nose, noisily.

Ivy put her face in her hands.

Mrs. Winters leaned toward her. "Take a breath, sweetheart. You'll get through this. Here's what else I know. Shortly before Patsy's accident, Mr. Laquay put a private investigator onto finding your birth parents. I don't know how that came about, but the day before she died, Patsy confided in me that Laquay had located your birth mother. And that's why I believe this Sandra Steele person might be for real."

Ivy nodded. "Sandra said she took a DNA test. But even if she did, I'd want her to repeat it. I don't mean to sound paranoid, but Dad does have a small fortune."

"Nothing small about it. And I'm all for you checking things out for yourself. Verify, verify, verify." Becky glanced at her wrist. "Oh dear. I didn't realize it was getting so late. I gave Felicia the afternoon off, so I've got to get back to the ranch to pick up the slack. Are you okay for me to leave you on your own?"

"Not to worry. I'm fine—now that we've had this talk." Those weren't just words. Ivy did feel better. Hearing the truth brought her relief, made her stronger. "One more question before you leave. Mom told you Laquay found my birth mother, but he was looking for both my parents, right?"

"Yes."

"Did she tell you anything about my birth father?"

Mrs. Winters clucked her tongue. "Only that he ran off before you were born. If Mr. Laquay had any luck finding him, Patsy never mentioned it."

THIRTEEN
SANDRA

This place seemed more museum of western art than home, but in the main house, unlike in Richard Kane's study, Sandra detected the subtle insinuation of a woman's influence. Amidst the carved wooden furniture and stone floors, the Ansel Adams photographs and table-top Frederic Remington sculptures, you'd find a small vase of violets here, a handmade quilt tossed there.

And the family photos were *everywhere.*

Apart from the photographs of Richard and Patsy on their wedding day, Sandra couldn't spot a single one that didn't feature Ivy.

Baby Ivy red-faced and wailing.

Sitting.

Crawling.

Smashing birthday cake into her mouth.

Toddler Ivy stepping into Richard's outstretched arms.

Ivy with a bow, nearly as big as her head, in a frilly pink party dress blowing out six candles.

Preteen Ivy in full riding gear on horseback.

Blossoming Ivy posing stiffly at the bottom of a staircase with her adoring prom date.

Ivy was the center of this family.

Her life was so well chronicled, it was no wonder she'd never suspected she was adopted. It was easy to overlook the absence of Patsy's pregnancy photos when the entire home was flooded with Ivy's childhood memories.

Sandra halted, waiting for Laquay, who trailed behind with her lone suitcase. "Are we there yet?"

Hopefully, her room wouldn't be much farther. The walk from the study to the kitchen alone was enough to make her miss her little house in Texas.

"Just another mile or two," he deadpanned. "You said you wanted the nicest guest room."

"I was hoping it would be in the same county as the front door."

Laquay threw up his hands. "Look, Sandra, there is no need for you to stay more than a night. Just until we can arrange a ticket home for you. Or why not choose Paris? Doesn't that sound nice? If that doesn't strike your fancy how about London, Auckland, Tokyo? You can pick your spot. Mr. Kane is a generous man—and imminently reasonable. Anyone else would've thrown you out on your ear—or had you arrested."

"Arrested for what?"

"Fraud."

"You and his poor deceased wife hired me to commit that crime —and he signed a check to compensate me after he found out what Patsy had started. So, no, I don't think you'll be calling the cops."

He massaged his forehead. "I shouldn't have said that. There's no real crime here... yet. Just a man trying to protect his family. But if you continue down this path, the crime becomes real. Blackmail is certainly—"

"Protect his family from what?"

"From you. Or any other unscrupulous person trying to take advantage of Ivy. I'll show you to your room now, it's only a little farther."

Her gaze skipped ahead to an open door up the hall and to her right. Inside, she spied a room that wasn't like the others. She crossed the threshold into a tiny space that held a twin bed and a thin, tall chest. Not a single photo or painting adorned this space. Not a quilt. Not a vase of flowers. Not even a rug.

It looked like a nun's quarters.

Or a place you'd send a child without dinner in order to reflect on their crimes and misdemeanors.

This was definitely a place for penitence.

If Laquay thought he was going to stick her in here, he was sorely mistaken. This was downright appalling. "This isn't—"

"No, no. This is Mrs. Winters' room. She's the house manager."

Her throat tightened. "I'll take it. Please leave my suitcase by the bed."

"Don't be stupid. First of all, this is the smallest bedroom in the house—the only one without a private bath. And second, it's occupied, as I've said, by Mrs. Winters."

"The way they treat their servants says a lot about the Kanes."

"Mrs. Winters is hardly a servant. She helped raise Ivy from the time she was an infant. Mrs. Winters is *family*. This room was specially converted from a laundry room into a bedroom because Mrs. Winters *asked* to be near the nursery. She didn't want a long walk for the late-night feedings. It was strictly for her own convenience."

Didn't add up. Ivy was grown and married and living in her own home, yet Mrs. Winters was still stuck in what had once been a laundry room. These highfalutin people didn't give a fig about the comfort of their staff. And Sandra didn't like it one bit.

"I want *this* room."

"Mrs. Winters is a creature of habit. She doesn't like change. Trust me, she will not budge. This is *her* room."

"Not any more it isn't. Please have one of the other staff members pack up her things so she doesn't have to bother. She doesn't need to be near the nursery these days, so there's no reason not to move her into the room you were going to give me."

"But you asked for the nicest guest room in the house."

"Exactly."

The sound of footfalls in the hallway preceded a long shadow. And then a trim woman in her late sixties appeared in the doorway.

She planted her hands on her hips and looked sharply at Laquay. "What's all this?"

At the sight of her, Sandra's heart skipped a beat, but she managed a quick recovery. "You must be Mrs. Winters. I'm Sandra Steele. Mr. Laquay is moving you to a larger room—I'll be staying here during my visit."

"You'll do no such thing." Mrs. Winters sucked her teeth. "This room isn't fit for a guest."

"True enough. Come to think of it, there's no need for *anyone* to stay in here when there's luxury all around." She smiled at Laquay. "I'm sure you can arrange more generous accommodations for *both* Mrs. Winters and me."

"Becky? What do you say?" Laquay sent Mrs. Winters a seemingly imploring look. "It's time for you to spread out. May I have your things transferred to the Mountain Room? We'll put Mrs. Steele in that lovely room right next door."

"I really don't see the point, but..." Mrs. Winters' hunched shoulders relaxed. "Thanks. I can move my own things though."

The look that passed over Laquay's face suggested to Sandra that he might have a soft spot for Mrs. Winters.

"Good. It's all settled," he said.

"Fine. If you wouldn't mind, please give Mr. Kane and the rest of the staff a heads up that I'll be packing, but I'm still available for anything that might come up—Felicia has the afternoon off," Mrs. Winters said. "Meanwhile, I'll show our guest to her room."

As Laquay hurried away, Sandra took a good hard look at the woman in front of her. The fine wrinkles around her eyes, the lack of makeup, the proud lift of her chin, the determined set of her mouth. But what struck her most was the cast-iron strength of her unflinching gaze.

Once the sound of Laquay's footfalls were no longer audible, Mrs. Winters kicked the door closed behind her and took a step toward Sandra.

Their eyes met and locked.

Sandra pushed her shoulders back, took a breath, and said, as casually as she could manage, "Hello, Mother, you're looking awfully well."

FOURTEEN

SANDRA

Sandra dragged her suitcase across the threshold of her new quarters before diving onto the bed. It felt soft as snow and warm as whiskey. The chandeliered ceiling rose so high above her she was tempted to break into an aria. Lofty French doors led to the balcony, and when she turned her head, postcard-pretty Mount Humphreys appeared behind spotless glass.

This room would definitely do.

Her mother, Becky, trudged behind, remaining near the door with her back against the wall, as if bracing for a quick getaway.

A silence, borne of decades of resentment, stretched between them.

"You should never have come here," Becky muttered through tight lips.

"I've missed you, too," Sandra snapped back. Old habits were like riding a bike—in this case a tandem bike.

Becky studied her hands, clasped tightly in front of her. "Don't misunderstand me, Sandy. I'm glad to see you. I never wanted this... distance between us."

"And yet you're the one who sent me packing."

"That's not the way I remember it. You decided to leave."

"You decided to stay. Tomato. Tomahto."

"I don't want you stirring up trouble—although I guess it's too late to lock the barn, now that you've been to see Ivy. Richard and Patsy have been very good to me. Especially Patsy." Becky's voice wobbled when she spoke Patsy's name. "This family means a lot to me. I don't want to see them get hurt."

So, nothing new here. Her mother still valued the Kane family's welfare over that of her own flesh and blood. When Becky offered Dalton and Sandra a chance to make some fast money off her precious Kanes, Sandra dared hope her priorities had changed. That, for once, she was thinking of her own family.

"I wish I'd never gotten you involved," Becky said.

"Why did you?" That came out more bitterly than she'd intended. "I never once saw this place in the years I lived in Flagstaff. That's how hard you worked at keeping me away from your fancy employers. So, what changed?"

"It was an impulsive decision. One you've made me regret, by coming here. Troy asked me if I knew of anyone who might want to make a quick buck and not ask questions. After some time, I wormed it out of him—he told me there was a plan to present Ivy with a fake birth family—"

"Are you sleeping with that skeevy lawyer?"

"No! We're friends. He sometimes confides in me. I don't think he has anyone else who really listens to him."

"You're a great listener, *Becky*." Again, she wanted to bite her stupid sarcastic tongue. She didn't want to fight with her mother—she was tired of their estrangement. Especially since Becky and Dalton had been getting along so well recently. She was envious of her son's relationship with his grandmother. "Sorry to interrupt. I'm glad you're not sleeping with Laquay— please, go on."

"He wouldn't tell me anything else, except that there was no stopping the plan—he said he'd already tried. My first instinct was to go to Patsy to argue against it, but he warned me that would likely cost both of us our jobs. I believed the Kanes would never do anything to hurt Ivy—and even though it seemed wrong, I figured there must've been a good reason. And, whether you believe it or not, you and Dalton are always in my heart and on my mind. So, I told Troy that a friend of a friend of a friend knew an actor. I thought if this was going to happen anyway, why not give you the benefit of a nice payday?"

Becky paused and shook her head, as if reprimanding herself for her own foolishness. "And I hoped that if I helped you financially, you might... well, I thought it could be a second chance for you and me. May I ask why you took the job?"

After the chilly reception she'd received, it was obvious she and her mother would never get over the past. "For the money, Mother. I wasn't looking for us to reconcile. I'm sorry if that disappoints you. But you can't throw someone else's money at me, after all these years, and expect me to forgive you."

"Forgive me for what? I'd really like to get your take on my failings as a mother."

"For leaving me alone all those years."

"I know I made mistakes, Sandy. But you're grown now. You have your own son. I hoped, by now, you would understand that I had to put bread on the table."

"From the time I was eight years old, you left me to cook my own meals, watch television by myself, scratch out my home-work with no help from you."

"I wasn't out partying. I was earning a living."

"You were cleaning *other people's* houses, cooking dinner for *other people's* families. Making sure *other people's* children were safe and tucked snugly into their beds."

"But why show up out of the blue, Sandy? Are you sure you didn't want to see me even a little bit?"

"I told you. I'm in this for the money. I'm going to milk every dime I can out of Richard Kane."

Becky paled. "He's a powerful man. It's risky to cross him."

"Risky for who? If you're worried about your job, don't be. I'll never tell Kane or Laquay you're my mother." She rose and crossed the room, placed her hands on Becky's shoulders. "I won't do anything to hurt you. Whether I like it or not, you're the only mother I've got."

FIFTEEN

IVY

Ivy suggested to her father that they move things outside onto the Zane Grey balcony of the Weatherford—one of Flagstaff's most historic hotels. It was a beautiful day, and their conversation called for more privacy than even the quiet bar offered.

She grabbed her cosmo, Dad his whiskey, and they settled into a pair of director's chairs facing the street.

He nudged Ivy's athletic shoe with the toe of his boot. "I cleaned up especially for you."

She eyed the dirt layered on his jeans, the twigs clinging to the brim of his Stetson, and the stark contrast of his impeccable white dress shirt.

It was a running joke between Mom and Dad. If her mother asked him to change his clothes before going out, more often than not he'd simply put on a different shirt and call it good. Mom always said she only let him get away with it because he looked too damn handsome for her to argue with.

"Mom would be proud," she teased.

Dad crinkled his eyes, and then swiped at them.

At a moment like this, it would be easy to get lost in her

emotions. Let her father off the hook like everyone always did, which was probably what he was counting on.

But this was far more important than changing into clean clothing—she couldn't just let it go.

"Dad? Are we going to talk about this or not? Because you've put me off a full day, and I would love some answers."

"I'm sorry for putting you off."

"I'm not after an apology. I only want to understand the thinking behind keeping my adoption a secret in the first place."

He sighed. "We were planning to tell you, Ivy, I swear. But then the accident happened, and you were so devastated by Mom's death, I didn't want to upend your world all over again. You needed to grieve the mother you knew, the one who loved you your whole life, before you found out that there was another."

"I'm not asking you why you didn't tell me about Sandra Steele." *Yet.* She swallowed, her mouth suddenly dry. "I want to know why you and Mom didn't tell me I was adopted at all. You must've had a reason. Why keep it a secret?"

SIXTEEN
SANDRA

Sandra should've known to bring an umbrella. After all, she'd endured some of the worst years of her adolescence in this small mountain city with its fickle weather.

Now, the sunny skies, so delightful when she'd left Richard Kane's "*maison*" this morning, had suddenly taken a turn. They looked as if they were about to dump one of their famous Flagstaff monsoons onto her charade.

"*Mai*-zahn?" She attempted to imitate the accented, disembodied voice that was enunciating into her earbuds. "*La grande mai*-zone?"

In school, she hadn't been a terrible student, but no way, no how, was she going to get good at French in a day or two, merely by downloading an app.

Before Patsy died, and he'd tried to back out of their deal, Laquay had created a biography for Sandra. It specified that she and Dalton had been living in Paris for decades. The distance was supposed to limit her encounters with the Kane family to online meetings. The whole Paris fairytale was designed to decrease the chances of their web of lies being sussed out. But now that she was here, that fairytale was no longer protecting her—it was putting her at greater risk.

Other than a few cool curse words, she didn't speak a lick of French. And apart from the Eiffel Tower, she couldn't name a Paris landmark—except of course the river Seine, but that was only because of the televised Olympics.

Anyone who'd actually been to Paris could trip her up with a simple question.

Thank goodness she hadn't spouted the entire biography at Clayton and Ivy's house. She hadn't actually mentioned how long she'd been abroad.

So, screw it.

Now that she'd turned the tables on Laquay and Richard Kane, she didn't have to tell their story. She could invent her own. She'd rewrite Paris. Claim she and Dalton recently moved there for a new start. Sadly, things didn't pan out. That sweetheart of a job she'd been promised fell through. They'd been looking for a way to make it back to their home state of Texas. And, oh, how she'd struggled with the language—why, toddlers in Paris spoke better French than she did.

Et voilà!

Just like that she'd freed herself from the burden of learning a new language. She halted, clicked off the app and stuck her earbuds back in her purse, just as two teenagers plowed into her. They all but knocked her to the ground before racing past without even a *sorry, lady*.

"Excuse me! I'm so sorry!" A woman in distressed jeans and a bejeweled tunic-top hustled toward her. "Girls! Girls! No running! Stop right where you are!"

The young ladies turned around but kept walking—backwards—eyes fixed on the woman. "Can we go in here?" Clearly unrepentant, they gazed longingly at the Main Street Cake Factory.

The woman cupped her hands and shouted over the wind.

"You can each pick out one treat—but only one! I'll be there in a sec!"

Sandra shot her hand into her purse, hoping to grab the earbuds in time to fend off any unwanted conversation. To her way of thinking, this town was far too friendly. All that waving —and being up in your business even when they'd never met you. And then there was the bumping into your neighbor, your postman, your dentist, every-damn-where you went.

But she hadn't lived here since she was a teenager, and it was unlikely anyone would remember a sad little nobody whose invisible mother scrubbed other people's floors.

"Again, I'm so sorry about my girls." The woman sent her a warm smile.

Dammit. Sandra snapped her purse closed and looked up. It was officially too late to mount the earbud defense. "No worries."

"It got windy so fast!"

"Erm. Yeah. Looks like rain. No umbrella, so I'm just going to..." Her words faded as she studied the woman in front of her. There was something familiar about her—not so much the face as the voice.

"My girls aren't deliberately rude, more like oblivious. They didn't see you, that's all. But one hundred percent, they should've stopped to be sure you were okay."

"I'm okay."

"I'll talk to them."

Sandra should have seized the chance to get away. Instead, she froze, like a deer about to become roadkill.

"Are you sure you're not hurt?"

"Oh, no. Sorry. I lost my bearings for a moment. Like I said, no worries." She pulled a souvenir map of downtown Flagstaff from her purse. It'd been so long since she'd lived here, she truly didn't remember the lay of the land. Plus, it made a good prop. "I'm late for an appointment. Could you point me to Café Mocha? I've got an interview there in five minutes."

"What kind of interview?"

Yep. Up in her business like they were best buds. "For a job."

"Oh." The woman's brows drew together. "It's up ahead. I can show you, if you like."

"No thanks. Your girls are waiting for you."

"Straight ahead on the right, then. Just a few doors down. You can't miss it."

"Thanks!" Sandra whirled around with a relieved sigh, only to feel a hand on her shoulder.

The woman again...

Gina! Sandra suddenly recalled her name. *Gina from gym class.*

Her shoulders stiffened.

Gina walked around her in a circle until they were face to face again.

Sandra commanded her breathing to slow.

This is nothing. No big deal.

"I'm sorry. Sorry, to keep apologizing, too. But you look so familiar. My name is Gina Crenshaw. Used to be Gina Jordan. Have we met?"

She certainly wasn't going to admit it. They'd had one class together thirty years ago, and they were not friends. *Hold your head high. Stand your ground.* She could hardly hide behind a potted plant every time she bumped into someone who might recognize her. If she was going to pull this thing off, she had to be daring. "Funny, I was thinking you looked familiar, too. Have you ever been to Texas... or Paris?"

"I'm afraid not."

"Then I guess you just have one of those faces—and me, too. It's nice meeting you, Gina. I'm Sandra Steele, by the way. But now I've really got to run." She strode briskly up the sidewalk, then ducked into Café Mocha. She filled out an application for a server's position and left it with the young woman behind the counter.

She had no intention of taking a job—Richard Kane would be supplying her with all the money she needed for the foreseeable future. But she ought to at least appear to be trying to find work. She'd told Ivy and Clayton she couldn't leave town until she'd saved money for a ticket home. If she was going to stick around and get close to Ivy, she had to sell that lie.

SEVENTEEN

IVY

"Honey, the only thing I can tell you is the truth." Dad looked Ivy fully in the face. His gray-blue eyes were full of love, but she didn't detect regret.

Which was perfectly fine, wasn't it? She only needed him to explain. "The truth is all I'm after."

"I'm sorry, but there was no big reason we didn't tell you. When we brought you home, you were only a few days old, and we were so busy, so in love with you, we didn't have a spare second to worry about when or whether or not to tell you that we'd adopted you. We were figuring out how to make a bottle and how to make sure you were warm without putting blankets in your crib because the pediatrician said that wasn't safe, what to do about that red rash that kept popping up under your chin... we were trying to keep you *alive*. It sounds dramatic, but wait until you have a newborn of your own..." His voice trailed off.

She wished he hadn't brought up the subject of grandchildren. She and Clayton had only been married a year. They hadn't planned on starting a family anytime soon, and now, her chest ached with the knowledge her mom would never get to hold her grandbaby.

But she could cry about that later.

As painful as this conversation was, she wasn't giving up on it. Surely there was more to it. "I get that. But as time went by, you must have talked about it. There has to be some reason. Ignoring the issue was a choice."

"It's not a satisfying answer, but we didn't have a concrete reason. Or at least I didn't. It was a closed adoption at the request of the birth mother. We didn't know her name. I suggested we pick a time to tell you, but your mother couldn't decide on the right age. So, I said, let's just wait until the moment seems right, and we left it at that. Then, after so many years passed, not making a decision defaulted into the decision itself." He paused, his throat working, his voice catching almost imperceptibly. "We never meant to hurt you."

Of course they hadn't. "But you and Mom had Laquay searching. You knew he'd found my birth mother, and my half-brother. Is that right?"

"I guess so. Yes."

His hesitation seemed strange, like he was holding something back. She could see that this whole conversation was hard on him. "I understand why you didn't want to tell me right after the accident. But it's been six months. So, *when* were you going to tell me about Sandra and Dalton?"

He reached for her hand. "The truth, honey, is that I wasn't. After Mom's accident, I changed my mind. Troy told me the woman lived in Paris. She never searched for you. You didn't know she existed. My instincts told me to leave it alone. You're our daughter, and you always will be."

"But you knew Laquay had already contacted her."

"I didn't think she'd show up at your door. It's totally up to you, but, frankly, I don't like the idea of you getting involved with her. She's not going to replace Mom."

"I know that, Dad. But I am curious about things. There's so much that would be good to know. And not only my family medical history."

"What sorts of things?"

"My half-brother, for one. And for another" Ivy paused, knowing this might be difficult for Dad to hear.

"I'd like to know something about my biological father."

EIGHTEEN
SANDRA

By the time she exited Café Mocha, Sandra's case of nerves, from her encounter with her old classmate, had dissipated. If you assert something is true, enough times, people *will* believe you. All she had to do was stick to her story. Stick to her plan. She could ride this ride however long she wanted and then walk away with a load of cash.

Except...

Becky had recommended her to Laquay.

If he or Richard Kane ever found out it was the faithful housekeeper's prodigal daughter screwing them over, Sandra might escape unscathed, but what would happen to her mother?

She'll be fired.

Or worse.

Richard Kane was hell bent on protecting his daughter, that much was clear. If he learned Becky was part of the fake family scheme, he wouldn't just fire her; he'd banish her from Ivy's life —and that would devastate Becky.

I won't do anything to hurt you.

That was the promise she'd made to her mother.

Sandra looked up at the gray sky. It was going to dump on

her at any moment. She was about to summon an uber when someone touched her shoulder, making her jump.

She stifled a curse—that would be Gina again.

But then, she felt a hard pinch on the side of her neck.

Sour breath wafted in her face, and Troy Laquay hissed in her ear, "You're coming with me."

"Get your hands off me," she ground out.

He got an arm around her waist. "I said, you're coming with me."

"No!"

He tightened his arm so that she could barely breathe.

Pushing her from behind, he marched her toward a parked Lincoln Town Car and forced her into the back.

When she grabbed for the door handle, the locks clicked shut.

She could breathe again, but it was too late to scream. The tinted glass would surely keep passersby from seeing or hearing her cries. These windows were likely soundproof.

The vehicle pulled away from the curb, and into traffic, passing other cars on the road at a speed that prohibited her escape, even if she could somehow unlock the doors.

The only way out of this vehicle was to go through Richard Kane.

Just as she should've predicted this afternoon's pending storm, the instant before Laquay shoved her into the Town Car, she should've guessed Richard Kane would be waiting. Now, here she sat, wedged between him and Laquay.

She balled her hand into a fist—preparing to fight for her life if need be.

NINETEEN

IVY

Ivy wondered if she could trust her own eyes. On her way to her car, after lunch with Dad, she'd witnessed something that had set her heart pounding and her mind racing.

Had she imagined Troy Laquay grabbing Sandra and pushing her into the back of Dad's town car?

No. It definitely happened, but perhaps she'd misinterpreted the situation.

Her father's lawyer had always acted the perfect gentleman around Ivy. And she hadn't been herself of late, forgetting lunch dates with Clayton, misplacing her keys—all the more reason to kiss those sleeping pills of hers goodbye.

There had to be a perfectly reasonable explanation for that surreal scene on the street. Attempting to remain calm, she drove to the ranch, hoping Dad could supply the answer. He was out, so Felicia, the assistant housekeeper, took her to the next best source of information.

Mrs. Winters.

In the Mountain Room!

Despite her worries, she couldn't help but marvel at the change of scene for her beloved nanny. "About time you upgraded. I think this bedroom has the best view of Mount Humphreys on the ranch."

"It's grander than I deserve, that's for sure." The upholstered chair she occupied seemed to swallow Becky whole.

"Nonsense. You deserve the world."

Throughout Ivy's life, Mrs. Winters had stayed next door to what had first been Ivy's nursery, and later her childhood lair. Modest as it was, Ivy loved that tiny room—especially the secret door she'd discovered behind the chest of drawers.

Once, when Mom and Mrs. Winters were out shopping, Ivy squeezed her skinny six-year-old body between that chest and the wall, and wound up getting stuck.

She was still stuck, and quite terrified, when Mrs. Winters finally returned.

Mrs. Winters freed her, and then showed her that the door led to a space even smaller than the bedroom. Ivy understood it was probably meant to hold laundry equipment and supplies, but, as a child, it was fun to speculate that it had once housed elves, or boxes upon boxes of peppermints and chocolate-covered pretzels.

The lack of paintings and other decorative objects in Mrs. Winters' room had given wings to Ivy's imagination. She liked to pretend the walls were covered with cryptograms written in invisible ink. No furniture, except for a bed, and that tall chest of drawers meant there was no place to sit. No place to sit meant Ivy had to crawl into bed with Mrs. Winters to talk.

Sooner or later, she'd tell Mrs. Winters every single secret.

Now, the distance between them yawned.

"Are you sure you don't want to chat in the dining area? I could make you lunch," Becky offered.

"No thanks. I ate at the Weatherford—out on the Zane Grey balcony with Dad. And besides, I don't want anyone eavesdropping on our conversation." The quick tears that came to her eyes surprised her. The past twenty-four hours had been a lot. "It's a relief to have someone to talk to."

"Oh, sweetie, what's this all about? Tell me everything."

Ivy dabbed her cheeks with her fingers and then remembered she had a tissue in her pocket. "I saw something upsetting. Something bad. I was hoping Dad could explain it, but since he's not here I'd love to talk things over with you—like old times."

"Did something happen at lunch—does it have to do with your father?"

"I'm not sure." The more she played it back in her head, the more questions she had. "I *think* I saw Troy Laquay grab Sandra on the street. He pushed her into Dad's Lincoln. The windows were so dark, I couldn't tell if Dad was in the car or not. I assumed he was, but then I thought the chauffer might be driving only Troy around."

Red splotches bloomed across Becky's chest, then climbed her neck. "What do you mean he *grabbed* her?"

"Just that. I saw Sandra come out of Café Mocha, and Troy raised his hand high, near her neck. He seemed to be pushing her down the sidewalk, and then he shoved her into the back of the car—like something out of a mob movie. I yelled at him to stop, and I ran toward them, but I was a couple of blocks away. I couldn't get there before they drove off."

Becky's back arched, and her mouth opened in apparent disbelief.

"I thought they might've come back to the ranch. I don't have Sandra's number, but I've been trying to reach Dad and Mr. Laquay. My calls keep going straight to voicemail."

Whenever Ivy got upset about anything, Becky would always bring perspective and calm to the situation. Now, Ivy waited for reassurance. Waited for Becky to say she must be mistaken or exaggerating. To not let her vivid imagination run wild. That Troy Laquay was probably just helping Sandra into the car.

A beat passed. Then two.

Still, Ivy waited.

Becky brought a trembling hand to her mouth, then let it drop, uncharacteristically at a loss for words.

"You don't think Troy would hurt Sandra, do you? If Dad was in the car, he'd never allow that."

"I hope you're right, honey."

What?

That was not the answer she'd anticipated from the voice of reason.

"How was your father at lunch?" Becky spoke slowly, apparently weighing her words. "Did he seem angry about Sandra?"

"Not at all. We had an open conversation. He explained some things about my adoption. Everything was fine when we said goodbye."

Mrs. Winters' hand flew to her heart. "That's a relief."

Again, not the reaction Ivy had anticipated. "Look, I know Dad doesn't confide in you or anyone else."

"He keeps his own counsel."

"But Mom shared so much with you. Is there anything more you can think of that might shed light on my situation with Sandra?"

Mrs. Winters looked about, avoiding Ivy's gaze. "After you married Clayton, your mother told me that she hoped you'd want to start a family. She and your father argued about whether they should finally tell you about the adoption. I'm not sure what the bone of contention between them was. On the day of the accident, Patsy told me Laquay had found your birth mother, but your dad didn't know, and I wasn't to breathe a word."

This was more than Becky had revealed before, but Ivy was

certain she was still holding something back. "Is that all? What-ever you know, Mom would want you to tell me. The night of her accident, she insisted on meeting me for dinner—just the two of us. She said she wanted to discuss something important."

"Why don't I make us some tea while we talk? Or, if you don't mind, I could use a real drink."

Take a breath. "Sure. I'll have one too."

Mrs. Winters was killing her. But there was no rushing this woman. There never had been.

"I don't want to say anything that might betray Patsy's trust, you can understand that, can't you?"

Ivy was having a hard time getting Becky to meet her eyes. "Of course. I get it. I—'

The sound of approaching footsteps stopped her mid-sentence.

A knock followed, then Felicia poked her head in. "Sorry to interrupt, ma'am, but there's a policewoman at the door."

TWENTY

IVY

Ivy had never been paid a call by the police. When Mom died, it had been Clayton who'd broken the news. She realized the case wasn't closed, and heaven knew that played on her mind, but as she needed drug cocktails just to sleep, Clayton had kept the police at bay.

Now, she played with the hem of her blouse, wondering what was so important an officer had come to her father's home. Just a few more seconds and then she promised herself she would meet the eyes of the policewoman seated across from her in the ranch-house living room.

But for now, she kept her mind squarely focused on the mundane. The rumpled appearance of Detective Winthrop's blue suit jacket. Her short, shiny brown curls. The deep tan that crept from her forehead, past her unadorned earlobes, across her jaw, stopping abruptly at her shirt-collar. Judging by the few creases on her forehead, and the faint lines around her mouth, the woman was old enough to have experience, and young enough to still have ambition. Her unpolished nails, chewed to bits, proved she had bad habits, the same as everyone else. *Nothing to be afraid of here.*

Mrs. Winters reached over and gripped Ivy's hand.

Ivy's mouth went dry.

As long as she avoided the detective's gaze, she could still pretend that whatever this woman had to say would not change her world. That she'd come here about a burglary in the neighborhood, or to collect a donation for some community cause the police were sponsoring.

Her jaw ached from clenching her teeth.

What if there'd been another accident?

Since the moment she'd seen Laquay shove Sandra into the back of Dad's town car, Ivy had been trying to reach her father. He'd never picked up. Her calls to Clayton had also gone straight to voicemail. What if something had happened to Dad or Clayton?

Detective Kathleen Winthrop shifted forward. "Sorry to disturb your day."

Ivy lifted her chin and looked directly into a pair of unreadable brown eyes.

"I'll try not to take up too much of your time. In the interest of that, let me come straight to the point."

Ivy's jaw relaxed and she released an audible sigh of relief.

Promising to come straight to the point was not the way one delivered a death notification. That would certainly be preceded by platitudes.

Whatever this was, it wasn't that. And anything else, Ivy could handle. "I'm not in any rush. Please, take your time."

"Great." Kathleen Winthrop nibbled her thumbnail, then seem to realize it and dropped her fist to her side. "I'm trying to close your mother's case, and I have a few loose ends I need to tie up."

"Oh, of course. How can I help?"

"As you know, the medical examiner hasn't yet determined the *manner* of death. Due to the trauma sustained in the car crash, certain physical findings that might've guided us, conclusively, were obscured. And the circumstances surrounding the accident are still being looked at."

"What?" She must've misheard. "But we've already scattered her ashes. I don't understand."

"They gleaned all they could from the body before releasing it to you—to the family. But some results are pending, and we're still analyzing certain facts patterns, trying to put all the puzzle pieces in place."

Hadn't Clayton said closing the case was merely a formality at this point? It'd been weighing on her mind, but he'd been so quick to shut down her concerns. He'd insisted that if there'd been anything out of the ordinary, the police would've told them.

"In a one-car accident, before we close the books, we need to look carefully. I have a few unanswered questions, if you don't mind."

If the manner of death had not yet been determined, then this was a bit more than a formality. Momentarily unable to catch her breath, she nodded her consent.

"Did you speak to your mother the day of her death? Can you describe her state of mind?" the detective asked.

"Yes. We spoke on the phone. We planned to meet later that evening for dinner. Just me and her. The telephone conversation was brief. She seemed like she was either in a hurry or didn't want to talk over the phone. Not sure if that's what you want to know."

"Very helpful. Thank you. So, other than being in a hurry, how was her mood? Did she seem sad or worried? Was she slurring her words?"

"She wasn't drunk if that's what you're implying. My mother wasn't a big drinker."

But something had seemed off.

Just answer the questions. Don't get defensive.

Ivy took a breath. "I'm not sure I'd characterize her mood as sad, but she was a bit agitated—nervous. Like she had something on her mind."

"Mm hmm."

"I might be reading you wrong, but you did bring up the fact that it was a *one-car* accident. If you're wondering whether she might've *intentionally* crashed her car, I can assure you she didn't. My mother would never deliberately hurt herself. She loved her family too much."

"You're not reading me wrong. A nonaccidental manner of death is under consideration. There were no skid marks to indicate she tried to brake."

"Well, that's a mistake. I'm *sure* she tried to stop. Just because you didn't find marks doesn't mean she didn't apply the brakes. The *absence* of marks can't prove something like that."

"That's true. It's not proof, but it is evidence. The absence of marks isn't conclusive—it's *suggestive*."

"And why ask about slurred words? If there was alcohol in her system, you should have found that out from the bloodwork."

"Again, you're right. The toxicology didn't show the presence of alcohol or any other substance. But there was an empty bottle of whiskey in the car, and her clothing reeked of it." The detective arched an eyebrow. "You seem to know more than most people about forensics."

"Only what I've learned from reading true crime. And Mom didn't like whiskey. When she did drink, it was one or two glasses of white wine at the most and that's it."

"The empty whiskey bottle's one of those puzzle pieces I mentioned. How would you describe your relationship with your mother?"

"Perfect. I don't mean we never squabbled, but that was rare. My mother was my best friend. She was the best mother I could ever hope for."

"I'm sorry for your loss. What about her relationship with

your father, was there any trouble there? Affairs on either side? Arguments?"

"No. Absolutely not. They were an ideal couple. Very, very happy together. I can barely recall any disagreements between them. I'm sure they argued—every couple does—but I never saw it."

"Excuse me," Mrs. Winters interrupted. "May I add something?"

"Please." Detective Winthrop shifted her position to better include Mrs. Winters.

"For about a month or so before the accident, I noticed more squabbles."

"What about?"

Mrs. Winters cast her eyes away from Ivy. "You'll have to ask Mr. Kane the details, but they did begin a search for Ivy's birth parents—she's adopted."

"I only just found out," Ivy said.

"Curious timing." Detective Winthrop frowned.

Ivy didn't like where this was heading, or the gnawing feeling in her chest. "Do you mean it seems coincidental with the accident? Do you think Mom was distracted by the adoption issue? That she wasn't paying attention to the road because she was worried about telling me?"

"That could be." Detective Winthrop held up her hand. "I have to wonder why there was an issue in the first place. You're an adult. I would think it would be a no-brainer to tell you the truth about your adoption. I'm just spit-balling here, so try not to take offense. But sometimes families have secrets. Do you think your mother might've had something to hide?"

TWENTY-ONE
SANDRA

Trapped between two muscular, potentially armed men, in the back of a speeding car, Sandra had two choices. She could give in to the panicked voice in her head and do something stupid that might get her killed, or she could harness the energy pumping through her balled-up fists and redirect it to her brain where it would serve her better.

She relaxed her hands into open palms and forced herself to breathe evenly.

She couldn't out-muscle these two, but she could outwit them. They might have physical control of her at the moment, but she was the one who held the cards.

Touching her knee with his fingertips, Richard nonverbally directed her to face him. "Good morning, Mrs. Steele."

"Good morning, Mr. Kane."

"Please, call me Richard."

A painful welp was forming on the back of her neck, where Laquay had pinched her, but she sure as hell wouldn't give either of these men the satisfaction of seeing her cry.

Fixing her gaze on Richard, she said, "If your errand boy lays a finger on me again, I *will* go to the cops."

"I highly doubt that. However, I am sincerely sorry about Troy's manners. I don't condone brutish behavior—especially not when it comes to a woman. It won't happen again." Richard leveled a commanding look at Laquay. "Apologize to Mrs. Steele, Troy."

Laquay hesitated, but then it seemed a quick gut check told him his boss wasn't kidding around. "Sorry."

"And it won't happen ever again." Richard's voice was steely, his eyes daggers.

"I promise," Laquay said evenly.

"Next time I ask you to *escort* a lady to my car, I'd like you to do just that."

Maybe Richard hadn't ordered him to force her after all—he seemed sincerely displeased with Laquay, and he must know that if he'd simply asked nicely, she probably would've gotten in the car voluntarily.

"Where to, sir?" The driver hadn't so much as scanned the rearview mirror this entire time. He obviously knew better than to stick his nose in.

"Sky Harbor," Laquay answered.

No! Not the airport!

Richard Kane didn't get to decide when this game was over —*she* did.

As the privacy window rose, cutting off the back seat from the rest of the universe, her stomach tightened.

Her purse was on her shoulder.

Her phone was inside her purse.

If she raised her voice, she could ask Siri to call 911, and they might not be able to stop her before it was too late.

But hopefully that wouldn't be necessary—it was more of a back-up plan in case she was presently underestimating the evil that men will do.

The *probable* worst-case scenario was that she'd be stuck in their company for the two-plus-hour drive to Phoenix's

International Airport, and then she'd be coerced into getting on a plane to Paris. It would be cheaper to send her home, to Fort Worth, but she suspected they wanted her as far away from Ivy as possible.

Ivy.

Ivy was Richard's Kryptonite.

She sat back, feigning composure. "I'd like to discuss this further. But would it be okay to detour to the house? I need to collect my things."

"Your suitcase is in the trunk. There's no time to waste, so I had Troy pack you up."

"You must be pretty sure I'm going to go along with your plans."

"I worry about the impact your ill-advised intrusion into Ivy's life will have, especially followed by your sudden, but necessary, disappearance. My daughter is still grieving for her mother, so naturally, I'd like to make this as painless for her as possible."

"Naturally."

"None of this should've ever happened. I wish Patsy hadn't come up with this disastrous scheme. I'd like to think the whole charade was more preliminary concept than hardened plan. She loved Ivy so, so much. If she'd lived, I can't believe she would have gone through with it. I'm sure she would've come to her senses and canceled your contract, once she realized the damage it could do to our daughter." Richard's tone softened. "So, I'm asking you to accept my terms, for the sake of all concerned. They're more than generous, I assure you."

She'd let him drone on about Patsy's good intentions and his own magnanimity long enough. "You may be right about your wife, but she did hire me. I'm here, and that can't be undone. Sending me away now won't fix your problem."

"*You* are the problem. I will not allow you to take advantage of Ivy. Her welfare is my number one priority."

Kryptonite.

Richard's devotion to Ivy was exactly what gave her the upper hand. She could make the argument that leaving so suddenly would hurt Ivy even more. Persuade him to let her stick around longer.

But was it in her best interest to do so?

She'd already created enough chaos to bilk him out of a small fortune.

Was it only her ego, the desire to leave on her own terms, that was making her want to hang around?

Why wasn't she salivating in anticipation of hearing his offer?

Why wasn't she thrilled to get out of this on-the-way-to-somewhere-else mountain town with its unpredictable monsoons, brutally cold winters, and zero nightlife?

There's nothing for you here.

"Maybe we can come to terms on a settlement," Sandra said, careful not to sound too eager, and puzzled that, in fact, she was not.

"How does fifty thousand dollars sound?"

"Low."

"One hundred, then. And in return, you'll write a letter to Ivy. Say you made a mistake coming here. You were worried about her, after Patsy died, and you wanted to make sure she was okay. But now that you've seen for yourself what a wonderful husband and father she has, you want to go back to your life in Paris. You do not desire any further contact. You'll say it's important that she respect your wishes on this matter, and that you absolutely do not want her to contact either you or Dalton again."

"She might not honor that."

"I believe she will. Ivy isn't the kind of person to force herself on anyone. The wound has already been inflicted, but it's not too late to cauterize it and stop the bleeding. I'm going to make sure she has all the support she needs to get through this."

Richard knew Ivy a lot better than she did, and what Ivy did or didn't do was *not* Sandra's problem.

But was Sandra really going to get on a plane without saying goodbye to her mother... again?

Why not?

She'd be doing her a favor. Becky wouldn't have to worry about her own part in the scheme becoming known. "I could use a European vacation. One hundred thousand dollars, a ticket to Paris, *and* you transfer *all* your flyer miles into my account so I can see the world."

"That works for me. Laquay, you've got a pen and paper in your briefcase?"

"Of course, sir."

"Then it's settled." Richard held her gaze. "I want to be sure you've asked for all you need, because you're not making this deal with my lawyer this time. You're making it with me, and I will hold you to it. You got that?"

Her hands clenched in her lap. She'd been estranged from her mother for so long, and seeing her again had sparked long-buried emotions. But Sandra didn't come here for a reunion with Becky.

She came here for the money, and this was as good as it was going to get.

The last thing she needed was to flail around with some stupid scheme. Sooner or later Ivy was bound to discover the truth, and then Sandra would have no cards left to play. She could wind up walking away with a lot less than one hundred thousand dollars and a gazillion flyer miles.

"Well?" Richard asked. "Do we have a deal?"

Sandra squeezed her eyes closed and breathed in deeply. Her heart was still racing after being dragged into the car, and she couldn't ignore the feeling that Troy Laquay was a dangerous man. He knew he'd screwed up by hiring her behind Richard's back, and after the dressing down Richard just gave him, she could feel the steam coming off him.

If Laquay thought he could clean up his mess by getting rid of her *permanently*, with or without Richard's knowledge, he might not hesitate. And Richard had agreed to everything she'd asked for. Dalton's college fees would be completely taken care of—with change left over.

It would be crazy to turn him down... wouldn't it?

TWENTY-TWO
SANDRA

The flight from Phoenix to New York City had seemed much longer than five hours. Now, faced with a three-hour layover at JFK, Sandra would love to stuff a jacket under her head, stretch out, and doze blissfully off—like the jerk in the row across from her. But taking up four seats in a crowded airport lounge wasn't her thing. She might not be a model citizen, but she knew how to put herself in someone else's shoes. Luckily, the drinks in first class had taken the sharp edge off her stabbing conscience.

She did *try* to say goodbye to her mother in person.

Not hard, but she had at least asked Richard to stop by the ranch.

Twice.

Or was it only once?

In reality, she held enough leverage over Kane that if she'd insisted on returning to the ranch before leaving, he would've likely arranged it. Whatever. That ship had sailed. Or rather that flight had flown.

So, what's your excuse now?

She had plenty of time to kill before her connection to *Paris, France!* boarded.

And she had her mother to thank for her new-found wealth. Not that $100,000 was a fortune, but it was more money than Sandra had ever had at one time. Enough to pay in-state tuition for Dalton at UT, and enough to put a down payment on a house. A house that would accrue equity. Sandra was about to become a participant in a time-honored American tradition— home ownership. The way a lot of everyday people, like her, attained financial independence.

Something her mother never managed to achieve.

Becky Winters would probably be slaving away in other people's houses for the rest of her days.

I do it for you. She could hear her mother's voice in her mind.

And perhaps that was so.

But all Sandra had ever wanted was for her mother to be present in her life. To be there for her like she was for her employers and her employers' children. The hard cold truth was that Ivy Pinnacle had gotten more love from Becky Winters than Sandra ever had.

You're not being fair to Becky.

Sure she was, but as long as she was hanging out, waiting for her flight, it wouldn't kill her to give her mother a heads up.

She frowned at her phone. Turned it over in her hand. Frowned again.

The screen lit up—it was a sign.

"Hey, I was just about to call you," she said. "You'll never believe where I am—JFK."

"First, please tell me you're okay." Becky's voice sounded strained.

"I'm okay. Why wouldn't I be?"

"Thank heavens." Becky let out a sigh so long and loud, Sandra turned down the volume on her cell.

"Mom." She hadn't called her that in years. "Are *you* okay? What's going on?"

"I'm worried about you is all. Ivy said Troy pushed you into the town car."

"Yeah. He did. Quite the gent, that Troy Laquay. But it worked out. I got a big payday. All I had to do was write a fare-thee-well note and agree to disappear from Ivy's life forever. I'm sorry I didn't get to say goodbye. I guess it wasn't in the stars."

"Wait. What are you doing at JFK?"

"I told you. Richard paid me off. I'm all done playing the bio mom."

"But what about Ivy?"

Everything had to be about Ivy. What else could she expect from Becky? "She'll get over it. It's for the best. The longer I hung around pretending to be her birth mother, the more it was going to sting when I left."

"I-I don't know why you have to go *now*."

"A ruse like this one has an expiration date. Did you think I was going to move Dalton to Flagstaff and keep playing the part forever? That we'd all be one big happy family? If so, you're living in a fantasy world. That would *never* have worked."

Another long sigh, and then, "I'm not under any such delusion. You're the one who showed up at Ivy's door uninvited. But since you did, I hoped you would stay a little longer. And, yes, as a matter of fact, I would love to see more of my grandson."

"Dalton's a grown man, Mother. How much time he spends with you is up to him." Becky playing the victim was too much. "You've never been there for either one of us."

"It was *your* choice to live so far apart. Not mine," Becky said.

True enough. She had put physical distance between her son and her mother—to stop Becky from letting him down. She hadn't wanted her to hurt Dalton like she had Sandra. "Well, he can do what he wants to now."

"Please come back to Flagstaff. Something's happened, and I need to talk to you about it."

"You're talking to me now."

"I wouldn't ask if it weren't important. It's too complicated to get into over the phone."

"If you have something important to say to me, then say it. Waiting for the perfect moment is a recipe for disaster. Just look at what happened to Patsy and Ivy."

"I love you." Her mother whispered the words so softly Sandra could barely hear.

"What?" The phone suddenly felt slick in her hand. She dropped it in her lap. Put it back to her ear. "Mom? Sorry, I-I dropped the phone."

She wanted to say "I love you, too", but she couldn't.

Not just like that.

Not after all these years.

Apparently, calling her "Mom" twice in one conversation wasn't enough for Becky—the other end of the line remained silent.

"Mom? You still there?"

Whose voice was that in the background?

She heard a strange, muffled gasp.

Followed by a distant crash.

"Mom? What's going on?"

No response... and then the call disconnected.

TWENTY-THREE

IVY

Ivy's head hurt. Her stomach hurt. Her *heart* hurt.

Propped up against the bed's headboard, she currently had three pillows behind her back and more under her feet and at her sides. In a fit of solicitousness, Clayton had trapped her in a fortress of down. She kicked a couple of pillows to the floor, as if by accident.

Clayton grabbed her hand. "You okay?"

"No. Dad has got to stop treating me like a child."

He'd called, earlier, to tell her Sandra caught a plane back to Paris. He said he had other news, too, but it would keep until tomorrow.

She'd begged him not to make her wait. But he wouldn't budge. "He acts like I'm too fragile to deal with more than one problem at a time. He thinks I'm made of glass." She was aware of the irony of saying this as she casually slipped another pillow from the pile Clayton had stacked behind her back.

Clayton brought her hand to his lips and kissed it. "He's looking out for you. You've had quite a day."

That was an understatement, what with Sandra's sudden

departure piled on top of everything else. "Did I tell you the detective thinks Mom's crash might not have been an accident?"

It had rattled her, even though she'd had an odd feeling since the accident.

"Three times. I'm sure the detective is only doing her job, considering every possibility. But... even if it was a suicide, that doesn't make it your fault, honey."

My fault?

Why would he put that idea in her head? She looked away from him. "You make it sound like she meant to leave us—Dad and me. Like you think..."

"No, no, no. I only meant to say that *if* your mother was worried about her relationship with you, it wasn't your fault."

"Mom and I didn't have any problems with our relationship. Not ever."

"Yes, but what if finding your birth mother made her feel insecure?"

Clayton was trying to be honest. She knew he meant well, but this line of conversation was only making things worse. She tried to ease her hand from his. "Let's just get some sleep."

"I love you, Ivy." He clung to her hand and squeezed—so hard her bones crunched. Pain arrowed up her arm. "Clayton! You're hurting me!"

He dropped her hand.

She rubbed her sore arm—it felt like he'd literally hit a nerve.

"I'm sorry, sorry, sorry." Clayton leaped out of bed and ran around to her side, bent over her, inspecting the damage.

"Maybe I *am* made of glass."

As he probed her hand, she wiggled her fingers. "Nope. Not broken."

"Should you get an x-ray? Oh, man. I did not mean to hurt you."

"I know you didn't. And I'm perfectly fine. But next time,

keep in mind how big and strong you are." She mustered a smile, but he couldn't seem to.

He vanished into the bathroom, and soon returned with water and a bottle of pills. "Ibuprofen for pain. Your tranquilizers are in your nightstand—they'll help you sleep."

"No thanks. The pain is already gone—really, it is." That was a lie. Her hand and her arm were still throbbing, but she was so tired of waking up in a fog. The pills were more hindrance than help. They did knock her out, but she had such crazy dreams...

"You need rest. Take these." He tapped pills out of bottles and extended his hand, palm up.

It took three gulps of water to get all the tablets down. She didn't want them, but it would make Clayton feel better, and both the detective's questions and that scene on the street between Sandra and Laquay had left her shaken.

Was Laquay the reason Sandra left so suddenly?

Ivy tossed the remaining pillows to the floor and lay flat on her back, staring at the ceiling.

Above her, shadows danced and changed, morphing into strange shapes and silhouettes.

Light became dark, and the dark was timeless.

How long did she lie there? A minute? An hour?

The bed was so big.

And she was so little.

She climbed down, her bare feet hitting the cold floor, her chubby legs tangling in her white nightgown. Then she toddled to the window, crawled up into the chair and stood on her tip toes, peeking out at the man.

Follow your safety rules!

Mommy's voice.

Ivy promised Mommy not to go outside. But he was right there, by her window. And she wanted to play. Wanted the man to pick her up and swing her around and make her giggle.

Too cold!

The night wind whipped straight through her thin nightgown.

She wrapped her arms around herself for warmth.

Ivy! Get back inside!

She was running now, as fast as her little feet could carry her.

Hurry, Ivy!

She fell and scraped her knees.

Got back up.

Then everything shifted. She was back in bed, hiding beneath her warm quilt.

Morning light drifted between the curtains, and she bolted upright. Tossed off the covers.

Her beautiful white nightgown was covered in blood.

"Ivy! Ivy!" Clayton's voice reached her, floating to her amid the sound of her screams.

Her eyes popped open.

"It's only a dream, baby. I'm here. I promise, I won't let anyone hurt you. Not ever." Clayton tightened his arms around her—squeezing her so tightly she couldn't breathe.

TWENTY-FOUR
SANDRA

Something was definitely off about her text exchange with Becky.

Sandra: What happened? Are you okay? Can you pick up my calls, please?

Becky: Sorry, we got disconnected! I tripped over my suitcase.

Battery's low. Can't call. Will text news instead.

I love you. Sorry if I've hurt you. I haven't been a perfect mother, but everything I did was for you. I'm past retirement age, and I want to put myself first for a change. Patsy's gone, and the family doesn't need me like they used to. Don't know where I'll go, but love the idea of not being tied to any plan. That's my news. Take care!

Sandra didn't expect, after all these years, to suddenly develop a rosy relationship with her mother. But she also didn't expect Becky to go dark on her without a solid explanation—and this message didn't fit the bill.

If Becky tripped over a suitcase, that might explain most of what Sandra heard on the other end of the line. But if Becky's big news was that she was leaving town, why had she begged Sandra to return to Flagstaff just before the call disconnected?

And why wasn't she responding to Sandra's calls and texts? Becky had had plenty of time to charge her battery by now.

On the other hand, she and her mother hadn't been on good terms for decades. Maybe she'd decided to cut off communications again.

She begged you to come back to Flagstaff.

Sandra could twist herself into a pretzel to make this make sense, but it wasn't easy.

What if there was more to this whole scheme of Patsy's than Sandra knew?

Becky and Patsy had been very close—what if her mother had gotten herself into something messier than she'd admitted?

And that awful gasp over the phone...

Thanks to Richard, Sandra had plenty of flyer miles—she could visit Paris anytime.

If she chose to, she could book the first flight out of JFK, and call Clayton from the Phoenix airport to take her back to the ranch. Since he'd been acting as a liaison between her and Ivy, she had his number.

She didn't necessarily trust Clayton, but he hadn't done anything to make her *distrust* him either. As far as she knew, Clayton wasn't party to this whole charade. As far as she knew, Clayton believed that Sandra was, in fact, Ivy's birth mother.

She re-read Becky's text, and the knot in her stomach tightened.

What kind of trouble had her mother gotten herself into?

Did Sandra really want to blow up her $100,000 deal with Richard Kane in order to find out? Given her recent encounter with Laquay, she couldn't help wondering how far he might go to get her out of his way.

If she returned to Flagstaff, would she be safe?

When she'd needed her mother most, Becky hadn't been there for her. Now, she had to decide whether or not to put everything on the line, in order to be there for her mother.

TWENTY-FIVE

IVY

When Ivy was ten years old, her best friend moved from Flagstaff to Japan. Then, Dad had tried to soothe her broken heart by picking her up early from school and presenting her with a six-week-old Maltipoo.

Now, he stood before her, in the front room of his ranch house, with an identical look on his face. Only instead of a wiggling ball of fur, he was holding an orange box.

"Is that my consolation prize for my birth mother appearing and disappearing without so much as a good-bye?" she asked, trying to keep her voice from sinking. She'd meant it as a joke, but it came out sounding pathetic.

"No occasion needed to treat my little girl to something special." Dad held out the box.

"Is it a puppy?" she quipped.

"If you want one, I can arrange it. Fifi's been gone for years. It might be time for you to open up your heart again."

Had he taken her remark seriously? The *last* thing she needed was to open her heart up—to either a puppy or a person. "I was kidding, Dad."

"I promise it's safe—not a puppy." He extended his offering again, and this time she accepted.

Lifting a soft, draw-string pouch out of the box, she peered inside. "A purse. I love it!"

"You barely glanced at it."

She wasn't much of a purse person, but she'd never been able to convince either Clayton or Dad, who seemed susceptible to the marketing gurus' insistence that a designer handbag makes the perfect gift for the woman in your life. She removed the purse, to properly inspect it, and spied the receipt.

Oh, no.

Putting a supportive hand underneath, she tried to give it back. "Seriously, Dad? This cost more than my car."

"It cost more than *Clayton's* car. But why can't you just accept my gift and enjoy it?"

"I don't want you to spend that kind of money. This is so, so generous, and I am grateful to have such an amazing father. I know your heart is in the right place. But if you really want to cheer me up, pick me a handful of wildflowers."

He looked away, then back again.

"Oh, my goodness, Dad, please don't cry—I'm such a goose. You must've gone to great lengths to get this for me. It's wonderful. I'll keep it."

"Real men are allowed to tear up around their daughters from time to time. You don't have to keep it—I'm only trying to show you how much I love you."

"You truly don't mind if I give it back?"

"Not at all. Next time I'll bring those wildflowers. I should've known better, honey. You're so much like Mom."

She replaced the purse in its pouch, the pouch in its box, and then set it on the coffee table. "Just the fact you made an effort means a lot."

He scrubbed his hand over his face. "I bring you a Hermès bag, and you tell me it's the thought that counts?"

She smiled. "I guess that does smack of a spoiled brat. But thanks for lifting my spirits. I was pretty low when I woke up this morning. And I'm nervous about this other news you say you have. Is it about Sandra? I can't believe she left like that."

He swept his arm in the direction of the couch. "Let's sit."

Her knees locked. The extravagant gift, the stalling. He must be building up to something awful. "Hurry and tell me. At this point, the anticipation has to be worse than whatever news you have."

"Becky... Mrs. Winters quit. I came home last night and found a letter of resignation on the kitchen island. All of her belongings are gone. She said it was past time for her to retire. To take some time for herself. She didn't leave a forwarding address."

Ivy couldn't possibly have heard him right. "Becky can't be *gone.*"

"I'm afraid she is, honey."

Ivy shook her head. "Well, she must be planning to come back for her pay. That's why she didn't leave a forwarding address. When she does, you can offer her a raise. I'll talk to her. I'm sure she'll listen to reason. I'm sure she'll agree to stay on when she realizes how much we need her." She balled her hands into fists. "We should never have let her stay in that tiny room all these years. We should've bought her a new car instead of loaning her that Jeep from the ranch every time her old clunker broke down."

"I don't think she'll be back, Ivy." Dad put his arm around her and tilted her chin to get her to look at him.

She pushed him away and strode to the window—now it was *her* eyes that filled with tears.

"We've used direct deposit for years, so she doesn't need to collect a check in person. Her salary has always been generous. And don't worry, I plan to add a big bonus to her last payroll.

I'm going to miss her, too. But we can't be selfish. She's opening a new chapter in her life, and we have to be happy for her."

Ivy was more than selfish enough to want Mrs. Winters to stay on. She wrapped her arms around her waist and choked back a sob.

"I'm sure it was a tough decision. Let's give Becky some space and see what happens."

Her heart felt like a stone, rolling around uselessly inside her chest. Why hadn't she told Becky how much she meant to her when she'd had the opportunity? And not only Becky. Ivy hadn't treated Sandra well, either. She'd all but called her a liar, and now the chance to get to know her biological mother had slipped through her fingers. "I suppose I should give Sandra space, too. But I wish I had a do-over. Do you think if I apologize, she'll give me another chance?"

"I don't know, honey." He cleared his throat, then fished around in his vest pocket. "I should've given this to you right away, but I wanted to tell you the news about Becky first."

"What's that? Did she leave me a letter? Why didn't you say so?"

"It's not a letter from..." Dad's words trailed off at the sound of a car coming up the drive.

Ivy pulled back the curtains in time to see Clayton's Porsche coast to a stop.

The passenger door opened, and Ivy's hand flew to her throat—that was Sandra Steele climbing out of the car.

TWENTY-SIX

SANDRA

As she entered the front room, Sandra saw Richard slip an envelope into his vest pocket.

The letter.

The one he'd paid her to write. The one that said she never wanted Ivy to contact her again.

"Sandra! You're back!" Ivy practically leaped at the sight of her.

She caught Richard's eye—clearly, he hadn't yet given Ivy the letter. Would he do so now? Confront Sandra in front of Ivy and let the chips fall?

Ivy's eyes were red, and Sandra suspected those were tear stains on her cheeks.

"Welcome back." Weirdly enough, Richard sounded relieved. He strode to her side and clapped her on the back, before turning to his son-in-law. "Clayton, you should have called us with the good news."

After the money and miles Richard had transferred into her accounts, she didn't believe, for a minute, he was glad to see her —but she had to admit he was a damn good actor.

She cast her gaze around the room and down the corridor,

hoping to catch a glimpse of her mother. Even if Becky was serious about retiring, she would have proffered notice. Sandra had given up on Becky picking up her calls, but she had hoped to find her here on the ranch, safe and sound.

"I thought it would be a wonderful surprise for Ivy." Clayton glanced at Ivy from under arched brows. His look seemed to ask: Did I do the right thing?

Ivy's smile was huge when she answered, "Thanks, honey. I can't believe you took off work to bring Sandra back to us. You've outdone yourself."

Sandra wasn't sure what had brought on Ivy's change of heart. She was looking at her like she was a skittish colt she didn't want to frighten away. "I'm sorry I left without saying goodbye. I should have spoken to you first, Ivy."

"I wish you had, so I could've talked you into staying. I'm sorry for the way I acted before. I handled things badly."

So far so good. Ivy was happy to see her. Richard hadn't kicked her out of the house—yet. But she'd feel a lot better after she met with Becky. She couldn't have left town already. "Where's Mrs. Winters? I've been traveling all day, and I'd love something to eat."

At once, Ivy's smile disappeared. She looked as if she were about to cry again. "Mrs. Winters moved out—retired, I should say. But I'd be happy to make you something. We have plenty of sandwich fixings, or I could—"

"Don't bother. The granola bar in my purse will tide me over until dinner." It was true she hadn't eaten all day, but this killed any appetite she might've had.

Even though her mother had few belongings, it would take at least some advance planning to move out. She'd need to find a place to stay, put up a deposit and such. She itched to pull out her phone and re-read Becky's message, but she didn't dare do that until she was alone. Anyway, she knew it by heart:

I don't know where I'll go, but I love the idea of not being tied down to any plan. That's my news. Take care!

Something was definitely off. Her mother was a planner. She wouldn't shop without a list, or go away for the weekend without a detailed itinerary.

"We're *all* thrilled you're back," Richard said. "I'll have Felicia get your room ready."

She nodded, and the motion sent acid flashing up the back of her throat.

Becky loved being part of this family. She wouldn't have left so suddenly without a damn good reason. What if someone had learned the truth about Becky and Sandra's relationship?

Had she left under threat of harm or... had someone already hurt her?

TWENTY-SEVEN

SANDRA

Despite the perfect day, there was no one else around.

Sandra and Ivy had the woods, the gurgling, high mountain streams, and the glory of nature all to themselves. Moments like these, places like this, made Sandra wish she'd never left Flagstaff.

As a teenager, she'd taken its beauty for granted. But now, she couldn't help thinking how wonderful it might be to wake up, every day, to the pines and the blue, blue sky.

"This hike was a good idea. I don't think I've ever been on this trail before." That was a mistake—her *character story* didn't include having lived in Flagstaff.

"This one's not in the guide books—so most people don't even know it's here."

Luckily, Ivy didn't seem to have taken note of Sandra's slip.

"I truly am sorry for the way I acted that first day you came to the house," Ivy said. "I understand why you'd turn around and leave. What I'm wondering, though, is where you want to go from here. What made you decide to come back?"

Good question.

Given her troubled relationship with Becky, it hadn't made

much sense to return. The old Sandra would have gone on to Paris and simply waited for the day Becky popped up again. Only it would be so much better to bring Dalton along on such a grand vacation—and he'd never forgive her if she left the country without making sure his grandmother was okay. And this new version of herself worried about her mother almost as much as she worried about her son.

New Sandra was busy rewriting history.

Her entire life, she'd believed in the memoir a lonely little girl had created—and there was much truth in that version of events. But she was beginning to realize that child had been wrong about *some* things. There was no denying her mother left her too long and too often, but that wasn't the same as neglect.

Becky Winters had been an absentee parent, but she'd always made sure Sandra was safe and fed.

She closed her eyes and pictured Becky peeling off dollar bills, or searching the bottom of her purse for change to pay the sitter. Opening the fridge to check on whether she needed to add milk or eggs or orange juice to her grocery list.

The way Becky would kick off her shoes and Sandra would make fun of her big feet. Then, she hadn't realized they were swollen because Becky's worn-out shoes didn't provide enough support for her long work days.

Later, Becky would bathe her and wash her hair, and they'd snuggle into the same bed for sleep. Sandra had her own room, but she rarely slept in it, because the only time they could be together was at night. Her mother would say a bedtime prayer, thanking the lord for keeping them safe, and Sandra would fall asleep happy.

When morning came, her mother would be gone.

I know I haven't been the perfect mother, but everything I did was always for you.

Sandra opened her eyes.

Where did you go, Mother?

Ivy was staring at her, expectantly.

"Sorry, what was the question?" She shouldn't let herself get lost in memories. She needed to stay on her toes.

"It doesn't matter. I'm just glad you came back. To tell the truth, I'm feeling a little lost at the moment, with Mrs. Winters leaving."

"I should've asked you how that made you feel. It must be hard for you after everything you've been through."

Ivy pressed her lips together. "Honestly, not great. I'm worried about Becky."

Me too. "Oh?"

"I can hardly believe she'd leave without saying goodbye. She's taken care of me my whole life. And now she just leaves a note and disappears?"

"It seems off to me, too. But she might change her mind, like I did, and come back."

"You think so?"

"I *hope* so." Sandra dared hook her arm through Ivy's.

Ivy didn't push her away, and that was a good thing.

They trudged on, in silence, for a bit, save for the sound of twigs cracking beneath their feet, the blue jays chattering. "What was Mrs. Winters like, when you were growing up?"

Ivy stopped, withdrew her arm and looked at her, puzzled. It was a strange question, she supposed. But she wanted to know if her mother read to Ivy. Prayed with her at night.

"Whenever there was a thunderstorm, Mrs. Winters would let me come into her bed and snuggle with her."

"Why didn't you go to your parents' room?"

"Believe, me. I tried. But Dad would lead me back to my room and tell me big girls sleep in their own beds. So, I'd pretend to go along, and then, as soon as the lights were out, I'd sneak into Becky's room. It's a wonder I didn't get her fired. She was always letting me have my way, even when my parents disapproved. I could see her struggling to send me back, to say 'no', but it was too hard for her. I swear, if I cried a single tear, she'd let me get away with murder."

Becky had never been able to say "no" to Sandra, either. "Maybe that's why she left without saying goodbye. She was afraid you'd ask her to stay and she wouldn't be able to refuse."

Ivy's hand climbed to her throat, and she caught a loose tendril of hair between her fingers. "I bet you're right. That's super insightful for someone who just met her a few days ago."

"I'm only going off of what you told me."

"Still, it's a great insight, and one that makes me feel better. Thank you."

"You said most people don't know about this trail. Do you take it often?" She suddenly realized she should steer the conversation away from Becky lest she slip up and reveal too much.

Please be okay, Becky. Make me look like a schmuck for worrying.

"It's one of my favorite trails. A short drive from town. Not a lot of foot traffic. I like the solitude, and in summer, the wildflowers put on a splendid show." Ivy bent at the waist, as if trying to get a closer look at the petals on a star flower. Then she frowned and pointed. "What is that?"

Sandra followed her gaze to some dark spots in the dirt. "Looks like dried blood. Probably an animal—" The muscles in her throat tightened into a painful spasm, cutting off her words, rendering her unable to speak.

No, no, no!

Ivy straightened slowly. "These droplets are leading off trail, into the woods. Someone might need help. We'd better check it out."

TWENTY-EIGHT
KATHLEEN

At this time, Detective Kathleen Winthrop could not be certain the detached arm she was looking at belonged to a homicide victim.

Most years, you could count the number of murders in Flagstaff on one hand. But in a small city, that put them smack in the middle of the rest of the country for murders *per capita*. She wasn't a cynical cop, hardened by a thousand horrible crimes, but this wasn't her first rodeo, either.

Flagstaff was no more or less crime-ridden than most places —it only *felt* safer.

Which was why most residents didn't give a second thought to walking around at night, or worry if they realized they'd forgotten to lock their doors. They seemed blissfully unaware that theft and assault were among the most common crimes in their city.

Far more common than murder.

"Could've been a bear done it." Officer Wadley had been the first on scene. He poked the bloodied forearm, with the tip of a makeshift walking stick—a branch he'd picked up.

"Don't." She knelt to scrutinize the evidence. The arm was mangled, most likely chewed by an animal, but who knew if that happened before or after it was severed from the rest of the body.

"I didn't touch it." He held up his gloved hands.

"But you disturbed it. The techs need to process it just as you found it."

"Sorry. I don't think I disturbed it in any significant way."

"I'm sure you didn't. But let's do this by the book. No sign of the rest of the body?"

"Haven't done much of a search. I took a quick look around, but I didn't want to leave the scene until you got here."

"And our lucky hikers?"

"The ladies are in the back of my patrol car."

"What'd you get from them?" she asked.

"Not much. Only that they saw a trail of blood and followed it. Found this here, and called nine-one-one. They're shook up. I'd say the right amount of shook. Not too much, and not too little."

One thing she knew was not to judge a book by the cover. She had good instincts when it came to reading people, but she didn't rely heavily on instinct. She put her faith in evidence. "Thanks for that observation. Stay here and wait for the techs. I'm gonna walk."

"Will do."

Kathleen removed her sunglasses and snapped them onto her shirt pocket. She wanted to scan the ground without the lenses in order not to miss any subtle discoloration.

The forest floor was covered in all the usual stuff. Leaves, branches, rocks.

No obvious tracks, either human or animal.

She could wait for the canine officers, but she wanted to make a preliminary check of the area.

That arm looked fresh.

Which meant its owner might still be around, might even still be *alive*.

"Police!" she called out, drawing her weapon, not knowing if criminal, victim or both were out here. Leading with her pistol, she kept her eyes peeled. Tread gingerly. Her senses on high alert for anything that looked, smelled or sounded out of the ordinary.

The usual mix of chattering birds.

Hissing wind.

The musty scents of damp earth and animal droppings.

The feel of hot sun, scorching her cheeks in the thin, high-altitude air.

"Police!" She walked a grid. All the while her mind slotting through open missing-person cases.

In the distance, she heard vehicles and voices.

The team had arrived. She pivoted, intent on returning to Wadley and handing the scene over to the techs and the dogs. The two women who'd found the arm had yet to be interviewed in depth. Chances were, they were simply unlucky enough to stumble across this mess, but it bugged her that one of them, Ivy Pinnacle, was connected to another case.

She was hardly a suspect in her mother's death, which was likely going to be ruled an accident.

Coincidences happen.

The itching in Kathleen's throat was allergies, not intuition... but the lump her foot just hit, the unpleasant tang in her nostrils, was something more.

Much more.

She took a step back.

A deep breath.

Holstered her pistol before squatting.

She didn't brush away the dirt and leaves from the mound

in front of her—didn't need to. She could see, plainly enough, without disturbing the scene, what was in front of her. She sucked in her stomach to quell her nausea, then pulled out her radio.

"Wadley. I found the head."

TWENTY-NINE

IVY

Earlier today, Kathleen Winthrop found Troy Laquay's detached head.

Ivy had sought refuge on the back porch to clear her mind and have a good cry. She'd been sitting on the steps, with the porch light out, ruminating for the better part of an hour. But so far, she hadn't shed a tear. Nor had she been able to banish the image of that mangled arm—Troy Laquay's arm—from her mind's eye. Worse, though she hadn't actually seen it, she kept picturing his severed head.

The screen door creaked open.

"Want some company?" Clayton sat down beside her on the steps, without waiting for a response.

She hadn't wanted him to see her in distress—he worried too much about her as it was, and even though she had yet to break down in tears, the bright wolf moon would reveal the trepidation that had to be written all over her face.

He reached for her hand. "When's your interview with the detective?"

"Nine o'clock tomorrow morning."

"Want me to come with?"

Clayton had missed a number of important work meetings already on her behalf, but pointing that out wouldn't be a winning argument against him tagging along. Like her father, despite his success in business, family was his first priority. "She won't let you sit in, I'm sure."

"But I could hang outside for moral support. After, we'll go grab a bite somewhere quiet, and you can tell me everything. That way you'll be able to decompress."

"You think I'll need to decompress?"

"I would. My head is on backwards, and I'm not even the one who found—"

"Please don't say your head is on backwards." She freed her hand from his grasp. Clayton didn't mean to be insensitive, but comments like that did not help.

"Sorry." He grimaced. "Wasn't thinking."

In the distance, a wolf howled, and she nearly jumped out of her skin.

Not a wolf, only a coyote.

She hadn't ever seen an actual wolf in the neighborhood. And Clayton didn't mean anything by the head-on-backwards remark—she was overreacting on all counts. "I've been thinking about something. Mom and Dad both trusted Troy Laquay. And I always have, too. For as long as I can remember, he's been our family lawyer. But when I saw him shove Sandra into the back of Dad's town car, it was... disturbing."

"What does Sandra say?"

"I didn't get a chance to talk to her about it. At first, on our walk, we were discussing Becky. Then, once we saw the blood trail, that put an end to all conversation. In the back of the cop car, Sandra wanted to talk about finding the arm, but I was worried the police wouldn't want us to confer. I thought we might accidentally influence each other about the details. And of course, we didn't know then, about the head, or that it would turn out to be Troy."

He traced circles in her palm with his thumb. "I think it's important to find out what he and Sandra were arguing about. Or if they really were. It's possible you got it wrong. Maybe he was helping her into the car, not shoving her."

"I didn't get it wrong." She could no longer talk herself out of what she'd seen, even if she wanted to.

"So, you're going to report that to Detective Winthrop?"

"I have to." She ducked her chin. "But I don't *want* to. Because the minute I tell her Troy and Sandra had a physical altercation, Sandra will, probably, need to be ruled out in his murder. And obviously, she didn't do it. I don't want to put her through something like that."

"Are we sure it was a murder? Couldn't the same animal that mauled his arm have somehow... sorry in advance... bitten his head off?"

"Detective Winthrop says it's not official until the medical examiner reports his findings. It's premature to call it homicide, but she thinks it's a strong possibility."

He met her eyes. "You should steer clear of Sandra until we have more information about Troy Laquay's death."

"There's no way she had anything to do with it."

"I'm not saying she did. But we don't know her that well. We have to at least acknowledge the possibility she was involved in some way."

"She's my biological mother."

"We have no actual proof she's your birth mom yet. And birth mom or not, she could turn out to be a sociopath."

"Mrs. Winters thinks she's my biological mother. Mom was sure of it. Laquay was sure."

"But you're going to repeat the DNA test."

"I plan on it, yes. And I will ask her about that argument with Laquay. But right now, we're both traumatized. I don't want to pressure her. A second DNA test is just to cross my t's. It's not urgent, and this isn't the best moment to push the issue."

"I disagree. I think it's exactly the right time to press."

She'd almost driven Sandra away once before with her doubts, and something else, too, was holding her back. "What if Sandra takes the test, and, somehow, that gives the police access to her DNA? I heard the cops can check private genealogy data bases—that's how they caught the Golden State Killer."

"Whoa. That is *not* a good argument. First, if the cops want Sandra's DNA, I'm sure they'll figure out how to get it on their own—that's their job. And, second, what the hell are you thinking? If Sandra Steele's DNA is found on Troy Laquay's"—he paused and paled—"body parts, the police need to know. *We* need to know. Like I said before, even if she is your biological mother, we don't know what she's capable of doing."

THIRTY

KATHLEEN

After her interview with Ivy Pinnacle this morning, Kathleen was certain there was something fishy going on with the Kane family.

Once is nothing. Twice is a coincidence. Three times is a pattern.

Since childhood, Kathleen's father, a retired police detective, had drilled this canon into her head. At age six, he'd used it to solve the case of a stray cat, who'd adopted their family, and to extract Kathleen's confession.

One: Whenever she'd been outside, ostensibly playing on the porch swing, the door to the screened-in porch would be found open.

Two: She'd taken a sudden liking to sardines, sometimes going through three cans a week—all of them consumed, suspiciously, on the back porch.

Three: While vacuuming, Mom discovered a bag of catnip under Kathleen's bed.

The case, while circumstantial, became too strong to refute once he marched out the *three-is-a-pattern* rule.

It was a lesson she'd never forgotten.

Too bad criminal cases, especially ones that affected people's lives, weren't usually solved so easily. But she always tried her father's theorem to see if it fit the crime.

One: Patsy Kane died in a suspicious, one-car accident.

Two: Patsy Kane's daughter—Ivy Pinnacle—was one of the two women who'd discovered a mangled arm that then led to the discovery of a mangled head.

Three: The head belonged to an attorney, Troy Laquay, who happened to work, almost exclusively, for Richard Kane.

But the so-called coincidences didn't end there. They extended well beyond the three-is-a-pattern rule.

She'd also learned, from Ivy, that Sandra Steele, the woman who was with her, was her biological mother. And this Sandra Steele had turned up out of the blue, after, *get this,* the *headless lawyer* dug her up.

Laquay said he'd verified her kinship through DNA, but, according to Ivy, he hadn't shown her any records prior to his untimely death.

Naturally, the DNA could be redone. Kathleen was keen to see the results, once the old records were located, or new testing came in. But what piqued her interest most was the story Ivy told her about a certain incident she'd witnessed.

According to Ivy, Laquay and Steele got into an altercation on the street, after which, Steele suddenly leaves town, and then, just as suddenly, returns. A beloved housekeeper "retires", also vanishing without warning, and then boom! Laquay loses his head.

And the money!

She'd almost forgotten about all that Kane family money.

Unless Kathleen's father's favorite theorem was wrong— and it had never let her down before—someone, possibly more than one someone, connected to this family had a secret worth killing for.

Kathleen was determined to find out who—and fast.
Before anyone else in the cursed Kane clan turned up dead.

THIRTY-ONE
SANDRA

Sandra carefully applied her lipstick. The shade was red enough to please, but soft enough to seem natural—if you'd just sipped a cherry slushy. Then, she brushed her auburn hair until it shone and finished off by spraying Sugar Blush body spray into the air and sashaying through it. Not that she expected Richard Kane to be susceptible to her feminine wiles, but it didn't hurt to make an effort. She wanted everything about her appearance to support her new pitch to the patriarch: *We're in this together*.

On a deep breath, she knocked at the door to his study, waiting, politely, for him to invite her inside. "Richard, it's me."

A full minute, maybe more, passed.

"Come in."

Finally.

No doubt leaving her standing there so long was his way of gaining the upper hand.

Fine. Her way of taking the power back was to pretend to let him be in control. Meekly, she approached his massive desk, looking to him for permission, waiting for his nod before seating herself in that awful un-cushioned thing he called a chair. "I hope I'm not disturbing you. You must have a lot on your mind."

"Indeed."

"I'm sorry for your loss. I know Troy Laquay was close with your family."

He unclenched the pen in his hand and looked at her, his expression not friendly, but not poisonous either. "What's on your mind?"

"I wanted to thank you for letting me stay here, in your home. You've been more than generous, and I don't want you to think I'm ungrateful."

"I thought we had an agreement, so I'm not sure why you came back. But frankly"—he raked a hand through his hair—"I was glad to see you. I didn't expect Becky Winters to pack her bags and leave. That's going to be very hard on Ivy, and Clayton seems to think her mental health is already an issue. So, when you showed up again, I wondered if slowly easing you out of the picture would be a safer choice for Ivy."

That's why he never gave Ivy the letter. This was going better than she'd expected.

He shook his head. "Unfortunately, though, things have changed. It may be too late for all that, now—Troy's death has knocked the wind out of me."

Could that be true? To her, Richard looked ready to take on any fight, take down anything or anyone who got in his way, but that might have more to do with his stature. Even seated, Richard Kane towered above her.

"Finding that bloody arm—I've never experienced anything like that. You'd think it would've been horrifying, and it was, but more than that, it was profoundly sad. I hope Ivy is doing okay. I feel awful about what she's been through."

"I *am* sorry you had to experience something like that, but I find it hard to believe you suddenly care about my daughter's welfare."

"It's true." She swallowed the lump in her throat. "I admit I've been looking out for myself up until now. But I don't want to cause Ivy any more pain. I was hoping we could sit down and hash out the best path forward, together."

"Whatever we agree on, you disregard. You don't keep your word. Whereas, with me, my word is my bond."

"That's not fair."

"Sure it is. I didn't renege on our bargain. I did exactly what I promised to do. And you keep on taking advantage."

"What are you saying?"

"I've been thinking about this a lot—I wonder if we've reached the end of the road. We may have to come clean to the police and to Ivy."

Her teeth clenched.

"Ivy *saw* Troy force you into my car. There'll be a record of me transferring a great deal of money from my account to yours. And now Troy is dead—under highly suspicious circumstances. I don't know who would benefit, if he had enemies in his work or personal life, but I'm certain the police will insist on a full accounting of your association with Troy and me. I believe our secret, and *your* blackmail scheme, are finished. It's going to come out. So, if you mean what you say about not wanting to cause Ivy any more pain, you'll allow *me* to tell her before you do. Patsy's betrayal will crush her. I don't know if she'll ever forgive either her mother or me, but I'd like a chance to explain it to her."

No.

No. No. No.

She'd always known the truth would come out sooner or later, but up until now, she hadn't much cared when—as long as she got her money.

But now, the stakes were much higher. "We don't have to *volunteer* the information. You paid me because you wanted to *protect* Ivy from finding out what her mother did. Has that changed?"

He narrowed his eyes. "Not in the least. Ivy's welfare is and always has been my only concern—that's the God's honest truth."

This was tricky. She had to make him think he could trust her. "You love Ivy more than anything in the world. I can see that. Which is why we have to keep our arrangement secret. Why not let her go on believing I'm her birth mother? I'll stay a little while longer, and then make an excuse to leave. I can fade from her life *gradually*. Eventually, we'll devolve into sending birthday and Christmas cards. I foresee a painless process that leaves Ivy no worse off—just like Patsy intended in the first place."

"That might've worked before, but now, a man is dead. Are you really suggesting we lie to the *police*?"

"We'll tell them I temporarily got cold feet about getting to know my daughter. So you and Laquay gave me a ride to the airport."

"And what about the pushing and shoving?"

"There was no argument. Ivy was mistaken."

"And the payoff? How will we explain that?"

"We won't. They'll need warrants to look into our personal accounts. They won't suspect a connection between you and me... unless one of us breaks. You and I are the only people who know the truth—that Patsy hired me to play Ivy's birth mother." She was hardly going to remind him about Dalton. And, thank goodness, he didn't know about Becky's involvement.

He leaned forward, planting his elbows on the desk.

"If we stick together, no one *ever* has to know." Surely he'd see reason.

His gaze locked onto hers. "The only way I'll trust you is if you tell me the truth. You're not doing this for my daughter's sake. If you expect me to conceal information from the police, you need to tell me what's in it for you. And if you have any skeletons in your closet, now's the time to come clean."

That last remark turned her blood cold.

It meant Richard suspected there was more to her story. And the more he dug around in Sandra's past, the more of a threat he became, not only to her, but to Becky and to Dalton.

THIRTY-TWO

SANDRA

The last thing Sandra intended to do was drag her skeletons out of the closet and parade them around for Richard's amusement. She'd already explained that she didn't want to hurt Ivy. Which was true, she didn't—not unless it was absolutely necessary to protect her own family.

But it was too dangerous to allow him to learn the truth.

So, if Richard wasn't buying her new-found concern for his daughter, she'd just have to work harder to convince him. "As I've said, I feel terrible for what Ivy's been through..."

"And?"

"And if we admit what we've done, it makes us both look like terrible people."

"That's true. And it might ruin my relationship with Ivy forever. What's more, it could worsen her mental health—Clayton thinks she might be on the verge of a total breakdown. But what do *you* care if Ivy thinks you're the devil herself?"

"Oh, come on. No one wants to be thought of as evil. But I admit there's a selfish aspect. My arrangement with Laquay, on top of that little scene on the street, could be twisted into something it's not. The cops might think our deal went sour. That

I've got a motive for murder. Once I'm established as a liar, anything I said in my defense would automatically be questioned."

He frowned. "Laquay pushed you around. Ivy witnessed it. Perhaps other people on the street did, too. But that's hardly motive for murder."

"The police might not agree."

The look on his face told her he wasn't convinced, but she had another angle. "Come to think of it, *your* motive to get rid of Laquay is *much* stronger than mine. He knew what Patsy did, and how you tried to cover it up. By your own admission, if Ivy finds out, it could ruin your relationship, not to mention it could push her over the edge. You paid me off easily enough, and I agreed to leave quietly. But Laquay? Suppose he wanted more than $100,000. Suppose he wanted more than you were willing to pay." She turned her palms up. "I'm only showing you how someone could spin it."

"So, I *murdered* him? My lifelong friend?"

"Did you, Richard?" The argument she'd made sounded convincing—even to her.

He closed his eyes, breathing heavily for a moment, and then looked squarely at her. "I had nothing to do with his death. I have nothing to fear from a police investigation. I think we should tell the truth—I don't want to, but it's the right thing to do."

"What about the loss of your reputation? Even if they clear you, there will always be those who suspect you. That's the way it works when there's a lot of publicity surrounding a pillar of the community. Think what the press would do with the story. And given all the lies you've told, even Ivy might doubt your innocence. It would hurt everyone, and help no one."

Another heavy sigh from Richard.

Dammit. It shouldn't be this hard to persuade a man with so much to lose to cover his tracks. A tiny voice in her head was whispering she might've underestimated his sense of honor. Would he insist on doing "the right thing"?

She hoped not.

Because if Richard Kane told the truth, if the police started digging into the fake family scheme, they would learn that Becky Winters offered up her own daughter and grandson to play the role of Ivy's birth mother and half-brother. They might put the pieces together and decide that if Troy Laquay threatened to reveal her involvement to his boss, she might have been kicked to the curb, left with nothing, after all her years of service. Or they might suspect that Becky Winters became furious when she heard about the way Laquay had treated Sandra. They might find out that the night he was killed, the very same night her mother left town, Becky argued with Laquay.

When she was on the phone with Becky, she'd heard a man's voice in the background—for a heartbeat, she'd thought it was Dalton. But Dalton was in Texas, so it couldn't have been him. And then she'd heard some sort of scuffle. The more she replayed it in her head, the more she came to believe the other voice in the room belonged to Troy Laquay.

So, no. Sandra absolutely could not let Richard confess the fake family scheme to the police, and she'd do *whatever* it took to stop him.

The reason was simple: It might lead the cops to Troy Laquay's murderer.

And as much as she hoped she was wrong, that murderer just *might* be her mother.

THIRTY-THREE
IVY

After a brief interview with Detective Winthrop, Ivy ditched Clayton and drove to the ranch. She felt obligated to let Sandra know what she'd told the detective, as it might cast suspicion her way.

When she arrived, Sandra and Dad were huddled in his study, and per Felicia, he'd left instructions not to be disturbed.

Ivy decided to wait in Becky's old room.

She paced its short length, then plopped down on the bed —there was nowhere else to sit—and suddenly, the bleakness of the bare floors, the stark white walls, unadorned save the lone cross hanging above the bed, struck her like a blow to the chest.

As a child, this room had seemed full of warmth; because in it, she always found comfort.

But now, she had to wonder *why* Mrs. Winters had chosen to live this way.

She went to church regularly, but she wasn't the type to constantly spout religion. She wasn't a zealot or especially pious. From her drawings, the sketches of dresses and gowns she made, Ivy knew she loved pretty things. She'd pick out vivid clothes and scrunchies in every color of the rainbow for Ivy, but dress herself in muted tones.

Gray, gray and more gray.

It was almost as if Becky was paying penance.

Yet, Ivy couldn't imagine what a person as selfless and loving as Rebecca Winters had done that she needed to atone for.

She closed her eyes, allowing memories of Mrs. Winters and Mom to tighten around her heart—it was so lonely here, without them. Then, sensing a shift in the atmosphere, another presence in the room, she opened her eyes and let out a small gasp.

Sandra stood before her.

It was crazy to be so jumpy around her, but after going over things with the detective, she couldn't help questioning what that tussle between Laquay and Sandra had been about.

"I didn't mean to startle you. Am I intruding?"

"Not at all. I'm glad to see you. I hope you're comfortable here at the ranch." Ivy got her breath and her common sense back. Sandra would never hurt her, and she couldn't have killed Laquay—she was on a plane to New York City... Although, upon reflection, she wasn't sure anyone could say exactly when the poor man was killed.

"More than comfortable. This is such a beautiful home," Sandra said.

"That's nice of you. Listen, I know, when you first arrived, I wasn't exactly welcoming, but I want to do better. My house isn't as luxurious as the ranch—but Clayton and I do have a guest room. You're more than welcome to it."

"I'm settled in here, so I think I'll stay put." Sandra inclined her head. "Less pressure on us, that way. We can get to know each other at our own pace."

Sandra was probably right about that. If only she had considered the pressure she was putting on Ivy, by appearing on her doorstep, out of the blue, they might have gotten off to a better beginning. Ivy had been thinking about what Clayton said last night. They didn't know Sandra, or her true character, yet. "I'm glad we have this chance to talk. I stopped by to let you know something—I gave a statement to the police this morning. I think it's okay for the two of us to talk now."

"I can't imagine why not. It's not like we're conspiring to keep something from the cops." A muscle below Sandra's eye twitched.

Ivy frowned.

She wanted, so badly, to trust her, but she sensed she was hiding something. Her head was warning her to be careful.

But her heart... With Mom gone and Mrs. Winters abandoning her, she wasn't ready to cast Sandra aside.

Not without giving her a chance.

"The day you left town, I saw you on the street with Troy," she said. "He pushed you into Dad's town car. It seemed very *unpleasant*. I mentioned it to Detective Winthrop, this morning. I thought she should know... under the circumstances, and I thought I should tell you that I told her."

Sandra's eye twitched again. "I don't expect you to keep anything from the police. Tell them everything you know. But you're mistaken. He didn't push me."

"Then what happened?"

"Nothing. Your dad and he pulled over when they saw me on the street. I told Troy I'd just called for a ride-share to the airport. He offered to give me a lift, instead. That's all there was to it."

"But I *saw* him shove you."

"I was running late, afraid of missing my plane. Laquay told me to hustle up, and he put his hand on my back. I *jumped* into the car—he didn't shove me, but I can understand how it might've looked that way. It's a misunderstanding."

Apart from the eye twitch, Sandra's face gave nothing away.

But Ivy knew what she'd seen. Laquay not only pushed her into the car, he'd grabbed her by the neck. Sandra was definitely hiding something about her relationship with Laquay. "Was my father in the car?"

A beat passed.

"Yes."

"And he rode with you all the way to Phoenix?"

"Yes. He said he had an appointment with a Hermès sales associate... We dropped him off on the way to Sky Harbor."

"If you were late, why drop Dad *first*?"

"It was on the way, Ivy." Sandra wiped her palms on her trousers. "A man you're close to has been murdered. It may not be official yet, but that's how it looks. I totally understand how upsetting this is, and I will answer any questions you like. I have absolutely nothing to hide. Not from you or from the police. Your family lawyer tracked me down at Patsy's request. Our interactions were brief and professional. There was no ill will or bad blood between us. I wish I had more information. That I knew something, anything, that could help the police find his killer—if in fact he was murdered. Do you have any more questions for me?"

"No." She took a deep breath. Either Sandra was lying, or Ivy couldn't trust her own eyes.

THIRTY-FOUR

IVY

Ivy's conversation with Sandra, yesterday, left her uneasy, despite the fact Dad later confirmed Sandra's version of events. The story was the same, from a perfectly pleasant offer to take Sandra to the airport, right down to dropping him off along the way.

She wished she could say all her doubts had been put to rest, and she'd slept well last night, but that wasn't the case. This morning her dreams had awakened her well before dawn and she'd called Dad, suggesting they revive one of her old childhood rituals.

Riding the ranch together before breakfast.

She'd considered inviting Sandra along, since she was right here, at the ranch, but the truth was she wanted this time with her father. And it would be easy enough to claim she simply hadn't wanted to wake Sandra.

Now, at half-past sunrise, the east pasture smelled of dew and grass and new beginnings.

Dad had already ground tied his horse.

Ivy dismounted her mother's favorite, John Muir, and let the reins fall, knowing Johnny would go nowhere without her.

The pine dropseed was in especially fine form—tall, loosely flowered and swaying in the barest of breezes. She plucked a handful and offered the slender green stalks to the horse, all the while stroking his nose and whispering, "Good boy."

"You're gonna spoil him," Dad muttered, his wistful tone belying the criticism.

She remembered her parents' frequent disagreements about handfeeding the horses.

You'll ruin that stallion. He'll get pushy and bite, Dad would say.

Johnny would never bite the hand that feeds him—unless its owner deserved it, Mom would clap back.

"Pish posh," Ivy answered, using her mother's old-fashioned expression. "Mom's been hand-feeding him since forever. And he's the best tempered of the herd."

"You're entitled to your view. But he's already nudging you for more. Pushy, I tell you."

Ivy clucked her tongue a few times to signal to Johnny treat time was over. "He misses Mom."

"You should ride him more often." Dad pushed his Stetson up and surveyed the pasture. "Be a good chance to clear your mind—and your heart, too."

She drew her brows together, uncertain of what he was getting at.

"Clayton tells me your nightmares are rearing up. Why not go back to your doctor? See if she can switch your prescription."

"I don't want to rely on pills to help me sleep—besides, they give me brain fog and only seem to make my nightmares worse."

"We're worried about you, honey—Clayton and I. I think you could benefit from more sleep, and maybe some anti-depressants. That's my two cents, but I realize I have to honor your decision if you don't want to go that route. I'm not trying to treat you like a little kid."

That was exactly how she thought he'd been treating her of

late—but she hadn't complained about it... to *him*. Clayton must've mentioned it. Her chest tightened, knowing Clayton had good intentions, but still feeling a flash of anger that her husband had betrayed her confidence.

"Anyhow, nothing cures the blues like a morning ride with your father," Dad said.

"Who says I have the blues?" She was about to ask him what else Clayton had been saying about her when a bunch of beer cans and cigarette butts, arranged into a smiley-face, caught her eye. "Must be deer season."

She pointed.

Dad strode over to the fence line, then bent and picked up a broken arrow nock, complete with colorful feathers. "Damn poachers."

In Arizona, it was legal to hunt on private property, *unless* otherwise posted. So, Dad had put up "no hunting" signs at every entrance and quarter mile post on the ranch.

"Is this a regular thing?" she asked. Most poachers did their best not to leave clues of their illegal activities behind. But whoever crafted that beer-can smiley face, and left a broken arrow nock with brightly colored fletchings, seemed eager to make their presence known. It was almost as if they were taunting them.

"Second time since the season opened I've found a smiley-face."

"You should report it to Game and Fish."

"Damn smartasses. Probably just kids." He turned his back to the fence, extending his arms to heaven.

Behind her, Johnny clomped and let out a loud neigh. A split second later, an arrow sliced the air, and her world contracted down to a single focus. "Dad! Lookout!"

His body jerked. Stumbling forward, he grabbed his arm.

Her legs, supercharged with adrenaline, pumped hard and fast, carrying her toward her father, toward the fence, toward danger. It was one of those moments where the actions you take don't come from logic—they come from deep within, from decisions made long ago about what matters most.

"Get down, Ivy! Get down!"

She had to get to Dad. Had to help him.

A heartbeat later, he slammed his weight against her, forcing her to the ground, covering her body with his. She lay, panting, her face smashed sideways in the dirt. Her vibrating skull made her ears hum, and she covered them with her hands. She saw red splotches in the dirt, and then, as if day had turned to night, everything went dark.

That voice again: *Get back inside, Ivy. Hurry!*

"Daddy! Daddy!" she cried out.

"Ivy, snap out of it. The arrow only grazed me." Dad touched the side of her face with a gentle hand, bringing her back to reality. "Crawl back to your horse and mount up as fast as you can. Keep your head down. Don't look back." He rolled off her. "Go! Go! Go!"

She dug her elbows into the damp ground, nauseous from the scent of blood. The thought of leaving her father, lying in the dirt, injured, was too much. "Not without you."

"I promise I'll be right behind you. Keep low to the ground and move *now*. Get the hell out of here before those damn fools fire off more arrows."

THIRTY-FIVE

IVY

While Ivy tended him, Dad sat shirtless in the kitchen chair. He didn't so much as wince as she poured stinging antiseptic over his raw wound.

The arrow had made contact with his upper arm, tearing off a small swath of skin and exposing a patch of shiny, pale-pink tissue beneath. "It's wide, but not deep. We should get you to the E.R. though, to be sure you don't need stitches."

"It's barely bleeding at this point. I don't need them to sew it up to make it look pretty. I'd rather let it heal on its own. I've got a box of antibiotic capsules upstairs, left over from the last time Mom had a sinus infection. Probably not even expired."

She wound a roll of gauze around his upper arm, securing a nonstick pad in place. He could've been killed, and instead, he was going to get by with a bandage. Thank heavens. But she couldn't shake it off so easily. "I won't take you to the E.R. if you promise you'll make an appointment with your doctor. You might need a tetanus shot."

"I'll call first thing tomorrow. And if I do need a shot, I won't put up a fuss. I'd do it now but Game and Fish should be here any minute."

Felicia appeared with a man in tow, proving Dad's point.

"Ron Larsson. Game and Fish." The man was tall and tan with an anemic attempt at a beard. His wispy blond hair and boyish features made him look like somebody's kid brother dressed up in a ranger uniform.

Dad rose and shook his hand.

Up until now, she'd been composed. In charge, even, as she tended to Dad. But with the ranger here, she could hand over the reins. As soon as she did, the anxiety she'd been holding at bay returned in full force.

Suddenly, she was on the ground, again, heart pounding in her chest.

The scent of blood and dirt filling her nostrils.

Her lungs collapsed as she struggled to draw her breath—the world around her dimming, fading.

Get back inside, Ivy!

The voice in her head, the same voice that haunted her dreams, was a warning sign. She was spiraling dangerously close to the edge of something she didn't dare acknowledge. Time to pull herself together, get back to reality before it was too late.

Focus on something concrete; find an anchor.

She fixed her gaze on a porcelain pitcher filled with daisies, and the room, the kitchen table, the men sitting around it, gradually came back into focus. "Someone shot my father with an arrow."

Ron Sable, from Game and Fish, removed his hat. "Arrow's out in my truck. I retrieved it from the east pasture on my way up to the house. I assume that's the one that hit you. Were there multiple arrows fired?"

"No," Dad said. "I'm sure it was an accident."

"You don't know that." Her voice sounded calm, reasonable—she hoped it didn't reveal the terror that had gripped her mere seconds ago.

"I know we've got poachers. This is the second time this season I've seen their beer cans."

"Saw those," Ron said. "That arrow's heavy carbon with a broad head. Used for hunting. I notice your signage is obvious and plentiful, so your poachers are in clear violation of the law."

"They *shot* him. That's against the law no matter what the signage." Ivy did her best to keep her voice controlled.

"It is. But unfortunately, we see hunting accidents every season. Since your father isn't seriously hurt—"

She nodded, realizing he didn't have the full picture because neither she nor her father had given him a critical piece of information. "You should know someone close to our family recently died under suspicious circumstances. He was found in the woods near Hidden Rock Trail."

Ron's eyebrows jumped up. "You knew that guy?"

"He was our family lawyer and a friend." Dad's voice had a catch in it. "My daughter discovered his arm. She's understandably on edge."

"That does put a different light on things. But the fact remains, this is deer season. Your land is adjacent to forest service property, where archery hunting is permitted, with a proper license—and it's permitted on private property unless posted. Not everyone follows the rules the way they should."

"So, your working theory is someone confused my father with a deer?"

"You don't hunt, do you, ma'am? All I'm saying is that most hunting deaths are accidental. Things happen. People are careless, foolish, ill prepared and, dare I say, ignorant. We had a case two years ago where a hunter mistook a woman hanging clothes on the line for a deer. Luckily, she survived."

Dad put his good arm around her. "Honey, you worry too much. This man's talking sense. If someone wanted to take me out, they would have used a rifle, not a bow and arrow."

Ivy sank into a kitchen chair, holding back her protests.

Between her father's need to shield her from anything that might cause her anxiety, and the ranger's pre-determined conclusions, she knew she'd be wasting her breath. But if Game and Fish didn't do their job, at least she'd have somewhere else to turn.

Kathleen Winthrop.

"Ma'am, I promise you I am going to run *all* the possibilities. I've got some questions for you, if you're both up for it."

Ivy looked to her father, whose face was paler than she'd seen it since her mother's funeral. But if he didn't feel well enough to talk, he'd never admit it.

"Fire away," Dad said.

Ron pulled out a notebook. "Let's start with the obvious. Mr. Kane, sir, can you think of anyone who might want you dead?"

Despite his unwavering expression, his lips went white. Then he lifted his arm to push back his hair. When he did, Ivy caught the finest tremor in his hand—and that made her heart clutch.

She'd seen her father get mad as hell, be buoyed by joy, brought to his knees by grief—but never in her life had she seen him tremble with fear.

THIRTY-SIX

SANDRA

In Flagstaff, even summer nights could get chilly. Sandra was grateful tonight was such a night. It made her dark jacket and sweats less conspicuous—a perfect night for a stake-out. She tightened her hoodie to better conceal her face.

Then something creaked, and she ducked her head in the nick of time to avoid a slew of gravel tumbling off the roof of the shed she was leaning against. She'd set up shop here, because of its excellent view of the entrance to the Canyon Creek Club.

In the few days since the "poacher incident", Richard had stayed close to home, with Ivy stopping by frequently to make a big fuss over his minor injury. No one had outright accused Sandra of anything, but she could sense their uneasiness, feel their eyes trained on her, as they followed her from room to room.

Well, tonight, she was turning the tables.

This morning, Richard had finally left her unattended in the house, and Sandra had taken the opportunity to go snooping in his office. When she'd found the door unlocked, it had disappointed her a little. Partly because she'd invested time in an internet search on how to bump a lock, but mostly because she figured that meant he didn't keep anything important lying around.

As it turned out, she was wrong.

In a desk drawer, she'd found a box of caramels, a bottle of whiskey... and a diary.

Not the kind young girls write their secrets in.

A daily planner.

The old-fashioned type where you scribble in your meetings on lined pages.

She'd flipped through Richard's diary, snapping pictures of all his appointments, both past and future.

Under today's entry, after a number of business meetings, he'd scribbled <u>CANYON CREEK CLUB</u> in the 10 p.m. time slot.

There was nothing particularly suspicious about meeting someone for late drinks at a popular nightspot. But he'd written the entry in all caps and underlined it twice—indicating its importance. She was certainly not above spying on the man to find out what he was up to, and she had to admit a small part of her dared hope it might be Becky he was meeting.

Grasping at straws? Possibly, but she'd still had no word from her mother, and the longer that went on, the more worried she got.

Becky might be in real danger, and Sandra was not leaving any stone unturned until she found her.

Another slew of gravel slid off the roof. Her back hurt from pressing against the aluminum siding. She'd been staking out the club for over an hour, and still no sign of Richard.

What if he wasn't coming?

Five more minutes and if he doesn't show... Oh man.

There he was, at last, entering the club with *Clayton*. Only Clayton was supposed to be out of town. Ivy had mentioned it specifically. She'd seemed anxious about being alone in the house—said she'd been having nightmares.

Even though it was after 11 p.m., Sandra decided to call and check in with Ivy. She wanted to make sure she was okay and find out what was up with Clayton. Maybe she'd misremembered about his business trip, or maybe he'd had a change of plans.

Ivy picked up the call right away.

"Hey, hope I'm not bothering you," Sandra said.

"Not at all," Ivy replied. "I'm bored. And with Clayton gone, I'm jumpy. Every time I hear a house noise, I do a walk-through with a baseball bat."

"When's Clayton due back?"

"Tomorrow."

Really? If he wasn't going home to Ivy after meeting with Richard, then where was he planning to spend the night? "I could stay with you tonight if you're nervous."

"Thanks, but I'm not that big of a baby. I think I'll just turn in."

"Okay, but call me if you change your mind. Anytime at all —doesn't matter. I mean it." They disconnected.

Interesting.

She considered following Richard and Clayton into the club, but there was little point. It would be too loud to overhear their conversation. And if they spotted her, she'd have to explain herself. It was time to pack it in for the night. She'd gotten all the information she could from her undercover mission—and it turned out to be more than she'd bargained for.

Clayton was lying to his wife, and Richard, apparently, knew about it.

THIRTY-SEVEN

IVY

Even for Flagstaff, the summer night was surprisingly chilly—at least her *undercover* outfit was warm.

Ivy tightened her hoodie around her face and cast a wary glance over her shoulder. Checked behind the bushes lining the sidewalk—she could've sworn she heard someone breathing quietly back there.

But she found nothing. No one.

No doubt her guilty conscience was making her paranoid.

Spying didn't come naturally to her, and she couldn't help thinking about the dread she'd felt creeping over her, only seconds ago, when she'd sensed she was being watched.

She wasn't proud of sneaking around behind Sandra's back. But as it turned out she'd been right to be wary of her. She'd hoped Sandra's behavior would be above reproach.

But that didn't pan out.

Ivy had spent the evening tailing Sandra, and Sandra had spent the evening staking out the Canyon Creek Club. She'd also called Ivy, pretending not to know where Clayton was, even though she'd obviously seen him entering the club with Dad.

Ivy's stomach dropped—Clayton was supposed to be in Phoenix. And Dad was well aware. Her own family, the people who were supposed to love her and have her back, all lied to her. The only person who hadn't was Becky Winters, and Ivy had no idea where she'd gone, or whether she was ever coming back.

Then, Sandra turned, stood staring in Ivy's direction.

Dammit.

Had she spotted Ivy?

Heart pounding, she shrank deeper into her hoodie and hurried off in the opposite direction.

How had things gotten so tangled?

Ivy had resorted to spying on Sandra.

Sandra was spying on Dad and Clayton. Everyone was claiming to be somewhere other than where they actually were.

Tomorrow morning, first thing, Ivy would go see Detective Winthrop to report Sandra's unusual behavior. Except... what if Sandra was in some kind of trouble?

If only she could ask Mom or Mrs. Winters for advice.

The wind picked up, and she quickened her step.

As soon as she got home, she'd pour herself a big glass of wine and crawl under the covers with a good book. If she could distract her mind, salvage a bit of sleep from what was left of the night, perhaps she'd wake up with an answer about how to proceed.

No doubt Buddha was right when he said "Three things cannot be long hidden: the sun, the moon and the truth".

But total honesty might be too simplistic an approach when people could get hurt.

She rounded the corner, hopping impatiently from one foot to the other, waiting for the light on the crosswalk to turn green. The cold wind cut through her hoodie, chilling her to the bone. The damn traffic signal was taking too long. It might be out of order. She looked both ways. No cars. No cop around to ticket her for crossing against the light.

She stepped into the street.

Another foot forward, and then she heard it.

An engine revving. The screech of tires.

She tried to run, but her feet rooted to the ground—she couldn't move, couldn't scream, couldn't breathe.

Time stretched, bent, slipped from her grasp, as the dark SUV barreled toward her.

Her body lifted, slammed backwards, hit the pavement with a loud thud, sending pain knifing up her back and legs.

And then, she heard it again... an engine revving.

They're coming back!

"Ivy! Ivy! Do not move!" Gloved hands cradled her head.

Someone hovered over her—restraining her. Despite her confusion and the sticky liquid dripping in her eyes, casting a red filter across the night, she recognized that face—*Sandra*.

Since the day Sandra Steele showed up on her doorstep, the world had gotten more dangerous.

"Ivy, do not move!"

Sandra had been there, at the ranch, when someone shot Dad with a crossbow. Ivy had to get up, had to get away. "You lied to me! You tried to kill me! Let me go! Let me go!"

"Sweetheart, *please*, you have to lie still until the paramedics get here."

She wanted to keep fighting, but her body refused to cooperate. And Sandra was strong—too strong for her to resist. It was no use; she felt her muscles go limp.

"That's a good girl. Don't fight it."

"Am I going to die?" she whispered.

"No. No. No." Sandra pressed a quick kiss to Ivy's cheek.

It had a strange effect—quieted her.

"That's it. Just take it easy until help arrives. You've had a close call, Ivy, but you're going to be okay. You stepped into the path of an oncoming car. I yanked you back, and you landed hard. You were unconscious for a minute or so."

"You saved me?"

"Thank heavens that Yukon didn't hit you."

Sirens blared.

Louder.

Closer.

Think, Ivy, think.

Sandra hadn't followed Ivy tonight. *She* had followed *Sandra.* That's why Sandra was here.

Sandra *saved* her—she hadn't tried to kill her.

But someone had.

THIRTY-EIGHT

SANDRA

Sandra left the curtained-off area in the emergency department to give the doctor privacy to examine Ivy. It was up to him whether or not to admit her. But the nurse had said, earlier, she thought that would be the plan.

Ivy had a headache, trouble balancing, she didn't know the day of the week—all signs of a concussion.

At 2 a.m., the security grilles were rolled down over the hot food line in the hospital cafeteria. But the rest of the room was open, allowing patients and visitors the use of tables and chairs, napkins and assorted condiments. Sandra swept her gaze around the big empty space and spotted vending machines on the back wall.

She fed a five-dollar bill into one featuring a graphic of a cup topped with swirling steam. Coffee, bitter and black, was just what she needed. A wave of nausea hit her as her mind flashed back to an image of Ivy in the middle of the road, a black Yukon roaring straight at her.

Sandra's arms and thighs felt sore, as if she'd worked out too hard at the gym. She must've strained them when she ran into the street. Though her body felt the results, she didn't remember the actual rescue.

Only the seconds before and after.

Ivy falling to the ground.

Blood streaming down Ivy's face, her eyes closed, her chest still.

The blast of relief when she felt Ivy's breath on her cheek.

It had happened so fast, and afterwards, she'd focused only on keeping Ivy still until the paramedics arrived.

She sipped her coffee, letting it burn her tongue. Relishing the pain. She deserved it, for all the lies she'd told. A big gulp this time, scalding the back of her throat. Making her cough. And then, she looked up to find Kathleen Winthrop marching her way.

The detective joined her without asking permission. "I was hoping to find you here. I wanted to speak with you while the doc's finishing up with Ivy."

"You've seen her already?"

"Just to let her know I'm here. The hospital called me. Ivy claims someone deliberately tried to run her down in the street. You witnessed the incident?" Winthrop slipped a notebook from her pocket.

"I jerked her out of the way—or pushed her. I don't actually remember."

"Go slow. Relax and tell me everything you can recall." The detective scratched pen against paper until the ink marks became visible.

"I was headed home—I'd been downtown, earlier."

"Where, exactly, had you been?"

"Walking around. I thought I might go into the Canyon Creek Club for a drink, but I changed my mind. I was enjoying the night air."

Winthrop arched an eyebrow. "That's quite a walk from the main drag. Other than the club, there's nothing but cheap motels and industrial buildings. I don't think I'd go for a stroll on that particular street."

"I like to wander around at night. It's almost a form of meditation for me."

"Okay."

"Anyway, I was about to set up a ride-share when I saw a woman step off the curb. At first, I didn't realize it was Ivy. I heard a loud engine. Tires screeching. I remember a dark vehicle. I think it was a Yukon. I saw her eyes, and that's when I recognized her. Next thing I remember I was kneeling over her on the sidewalk, praying she was alive. I made sure she was breathing, and then I called nine-one-one."

"What color was the Yukon?"

"I think black. But it was dark. So, I suppose it could've been blue."

"Did you see the plates? Even partially?"

"No."

"What about the driver? Male or female?"

"I couldn't say. I didn't see. Or if I did, I don't recall."

"So, to be clear, you were out walking, no particular destination, and just happened to be on the sidewalk at the exact moment a speeding Yukon narrowly missed hitting Ivy. You hadn't planned to meet Ivy on your walk. It was a *coincidence*?"

"Right. I didn't plan to meet her. In fact, we'd just gotten off the phone." Ivy might provide this information and it would seem odd if Sandra held that back. Besides, there was no reason not to be as truthful as possible about this particular incident.

"How long before the event did that conversation take place?"

"Gosh. I'm not sure. Not long though." She waited a beat. She didn't love where this was headed. She'd been on the ranch the day of the "poacher incident" and now, here she was at the scene of another freak accident the very same week. It didn't make her look good, but there was someone else who looked even worse. "I called to check on her, because I thought she might be lonely—what with her husband being out-of-town. Clayton was supposed to be in Phoenix."

"What do you mean supposed to be?"

Sandra shrugged. "That's what he told Ivy. But I saw him earlier, going into the club. You might want to ask him what he was doing there. Why he lied to his wife."

Kathleen's brow furrowed. "Will do. I appreciate the information. But to be clear, on what *you* were doing. You say you and Ivy were both walking at night in the same area. Even though you'd been talking on the phone, you didn't realize you were near each other. It was all coincidental. I'd say that's a very lucky break."

"Me too." And that was the rub.

Ivy *lied* to her.

Of course, it might have been an innocent lie. Ivy didn't owe her an explanation as to her whereabouts. Suppose she didn't want Sandra to know she was going for a drink? She might've wanted to be alone, and anticipated Sandra might ask to join her. Ivy's clubbing habits were none of Sandra's business. But, like Detective Winthrop, she couldn't help wondering about the coincidence.

Had Ivy been following her?

If so, what was Sandra going to do about it?

THIRTY-NINE

IVY

Ivy!

She was on the ground, the smell of blood in her nostrils.

No!

She thrashed beneath the sheets. The back of her head throbbed, like someone was chipping away at a block of ice. Hushed voices floated, drifting around her, seemingly from all sides. Her eyelids were leaden doors, closing her off from the rest of the world. Flinging them open, she grunted.

White walls.

Worried faces.

"Where am I?"

On one side of the bed, Dad stood, back straight, his five o'clock shadow giving him a good start on a beard. His fists clenched and unclenched at his side. There was a mustard stain on the collar of his white shirt. His cherished Stetson was tossed carelessly on a bedside chair.

His eyes fixed on her face. "You're okay, honey. You're in the hospital. But everything's fine."

She slid her gaze to the other side of the bed, where Clayton hovered in a rumpled shirt bearing a mustard stain above the third button. "Did you guys get burgers?"

"What?" Clayton looked confused, then he grinned. "Oh, yeah. We had sliders at the Canyon Creek Club."

"Tonight?" She grasped a white cord dangling from the bed and fished for the attached remote. Her fingers fumbled at first, but with a little trial and error she managed to raise the head of her bed and sit up. "You told me you were in Phoenix."

"Don't worry about that now," Dad answered for Clayton. "The important thing is you're going to be absolutely fine."

Her husband lied to her. But, hey, don't worry about it. Everything's perfectly swell.

She shook her head and instantly regretted it—she'd set the icepick back in motion. "Someone tried to run over me."

"The police don't think so," Clayton said mildly.

She couldn't tell if he was actually calm or only pretending for her benefit.

"Detective Winthrop is looking into it. What we know is that you walked into the street at the same moment a black SUV, Sandra says a Yukon, sped toward you. Sandra, thank heaven, pushed you out of the way. You hit your head on the pavement. You have some scrapes and a mild concussion— they're keeping you overnight as a precaution—and they gave you something for pain."

More meds. That's why it was hard to keep her eyes open. That's why she couldn't think straight. And that dream... "Someone tried to kill me."

Clayton reached for her hand. "The most likely scenario is that it was accidental. But like I said, the detective is looking into it."

"How did you know I was in the hospital?"

"Sandra called us. I'm so grateful she was there. We owe her your life, hon. We owe her *everything*," Dad said.

The icepick had subsided enough for her to risk a nod. She rubbed her stiff, sore neck. There was no denying it. Sandra saved her life. But... she'd also lied. And she wasn't the only one. "Why aren't you in Phoenix, Clayton?"

"Richard and I are going to leave you be and let you get your rest. We just wanted to see you with our own eyes to make sure you were okay. We should've waited until tomorrow. We didn't mean to wake you. You can barely hold those gorgeous brown eyes open. So get a good night's sleep, and I promise we'll talk tomorrow."

"I want to talk now."

"He's right, sweetheart. You need your rest." Dad grabbed his hat.

"No. I need an answer. From *both* of you. You were together eating sliders at the Canyon Creek Club when Clayton was supposedly away on business. Clayton lied to me, and Dad, you lied by omission. Why didn't you tell me you were meeting Clayton when you knew I thought he was out-of-town?"

"I was in Phoenix, like I said. I had meetings all day and one scheduled for tomorrow morning. But Richard called and asked me to meet him, and I agreed. I was going to spend the night at home, after I met with Richard, and then head back to Phoenix bright and early. You're more important than business."

"But we talked on the phone tonight. Why didn't you tell me?"

"Because I asked him not to," Dad said. "The truth is, I'm worried about you. Ever since Mom died, you've been moping around, neglecting your garden, avoiding your friends. And then Becky leaving, the terrible incident with Laquay, my accident on the ranch—I can't even name all the troubles without running out of breath. I wanted to check in with Clayton on how you're holding up."

"You mean mentally."

"Yes."

"And what did he say?"

"Clayton thinks... *we* think it might be a good idea for you to go to therapy. Not only to get more medications. I'm talking about *counseling*. Clayton's willing to go with you, and, hell, I'll even show up if you want me there."

"Wow. I know how you feel about 'head shrinkers', Dad. You must think I'm off my rocker, big time."

"Clayton and I want to support you—that's all."

"When Mom died, I was in bad shape—I'll own that. I'll even admit my grief was sliding into depression. But I'm stronger now."

She was definitely groggy, but the explanation Clayton and Dad gave baffled her. Neither were fans of counseling, and, in her own opinion, she was getting slowly back to normal. Finding a detached arm in the woods had set her back, but it would upset anyone with regular human feelings. Dad's close call had shaken her, but he was the one who'd almost been killed—not her. There were the nightmares, problems sleeping, but those weren't new. And they'd arranged their clandestine meeting to discuss her mental state *before* an SUV tried to run her down.

So, what had gotten Dad concerned enough to call a secret meeting, on this particular night?

She glared at Clayton. "What stories have you been feeding Dad about me?"

"No stories. I haven't said anything to him I haven't said to you many times over." Clayton sighed, as if he was explaining something for the umpteenth time, when, in fact, it was the first time she'd confronted him with his tattling.

"Don't get mad at Clayton. No one's trying to force you into counseling if you don't want to go." Dad planted a kiss on her cheek.

She folded her arms across her chest. "I appreciate the concern, but I think I'll pass on therapy."

Because her problems were definitely *not* in her head.

And one way or another, she was going to get to the bottom of things.

FORTY

IVY

Ivy's boots glided across the floor, the sawdust, soft and slippery, beneath her steps. The Canyon Creek Club had been Mom and Dad's favorite Saturday night hang-out. As a girl, Ivy would watch wistfully as Mom dressed for the evening, painting on fire-engine red lips, sweeping dark mascara across her long lashes.

"Can I go? Please, please, please," she'd beg.

Mom would answer with a shake of her head and then offer her a swipe of lipstick as consolation.

As a girl, Ivy could only imagine her mother and father twirling and two-stepping, while a mustached cowboy fiddled his heart out.

But as a young woman, she and Clayton, her one and only forever beau, often joined them. Sometimes, they'd switch partners and Clayton would twirl Mom, allowing Dad to take a turn around the dance floor with Ivy, her heart thrumming in time to the music. Dad spinning her breathless. Then there'd be cold beer hitting her tongue, followed by a feast of barbeque ribs, fried okra, and plenty of laughter.

As often as she'd come here to dance, she'd never set foot in the club during daylight hours. Never seen the sunlight sweeping over tables, illuminating the nicks, and those stains no amount of scrubbing could wash away. The stage was vacant save for a drum set, speakers and empty guitar stands.

The place still smelled like barbeque though.

Collin "Cougar" Maddox must already have the meat slow-cooking in the back.

"Mr. Maddox," she called out. "It's me, Ivy."

Cougar was a family friend. But he'd always been closest to Mom. He and Dad were friendly enough, but Ivy noticed the way his eyes lit and his voice softened when he was around her mother. They'd been on a date or two in high school, and according to Dad, Cougar still had a thing for Mom. Mom always protested he was being silly, and besides, no one in the wide world held a candle to Richard Kane.

Out of loyalty to her father, Ivy had always kept a bit of distance between herself and Cougar Maddox. But now, as Patsy's daughter, she suspected he'd be willing to grant her a favor.

"Ivy, darlin'." Cougar ambled out of the kitchen, his graying blond hair puffing in the breeze of a circulating fan. He halted, a respectful distance in front of her, his grin deepening the crinkles around his blue eyes. "How many times I gotta tell you to call me Cougar? We don't open until four, but if you like I can get you something to drink."

"I'm sorry to bother you, Mr. Maddox—Cougar," she said. "I hope it's alright I let myself in—the door wasn't locked." Everyone knew he didn't lock the door to his club when he was there, cooking. And he was pretty much always there, cooking.

"Of course. I'm glad to see you. How you been doing? I heard about that business with Troy Laquay. I guess everyone has. I been thinking of you. I don't mean to be presumptuous, but I know you been through a lot this past year and it hurt my heart, for your mother's sake, to hear you were the one discovered that arm."

"Thank you, I'm holding up fine."

"Really? How about that drink. Something on tap? Or I can fix you up a cosmopolitan if you prefer."

She was about to decline, but decided it might be friendlier to accept. "A beer would be great. You choose. Will you have one with me?"

His eyebrows lowered. "I will."

She settled herself at the bar, placing her purse on the counter and stretching her toes to find the stool's foot rest. Meanwhile, Cougar filled two glasses from the tap and placed one in front of her. "This is a local IPA—one of my favorites. It's on the lighter side. Not too hoppy."

She reached for her purse.

Cougar swatted her arm with a beer-chilled hand. "On the house."

"But I wanted to get both of these."

"No, darlin'. It's on me."

"Are you sure?"

"Now I'm insulted."

"Oh, no. I don't mean to. I didn't want you to feel obligated because..." She was going to say *because my mother died*, but stopped herself.

"Let's not make a big thing of me buying a friend a beer. Now, I'm more than happy to drink with you until the doors open, but you're here for something important."

"How did you know?"

"Because you've never come here alone before. I think this is the first time you and I ever had our very own conversation, just us."

She sipped her beer and wiped her upper lip with her

sleeve. He was right. And she felt bad about that. This shouldn't be all about her. "So, everything good with you?"

"I'm still sad about Patsy. I cared for her a great deal." This time he didn't look down or apologize for being presumptuous. "Man, do I miss her."

"Me too."

A beat or two passed and while she might have expected the silence to be awkward, it was just the opposite. She felt somehow closer to Cougar. More natural around him because of his obvious attachment to her mother. She would probably never know the exact nature of his feelings, but what counted, to her, was that they were real.

"Cougar," she said, finally.

"I'm listening."

"Something happened the other night, outside the club. I was nearly hit by a car."

"Oh my God. Are you hurt?"

"I'm fine. The car didn't hit me. But I banged my head on the pavement. Anyway, I was wondering if you have surveillance cameras that might catch the street."

"You want to see my surveillance footage."

"Yes, I mean if you haven't erased it or handed it over to the police."

"The police?"

"Have they been by, asking questions?"

"No." He rested his mug on the counter. "I'm confused, Ivy. If the car didn't hit you, why would the police want the footage?"

"I think someone deliberately tried to run me down. I'd like to check it out for myself. Do you have the tapes from Saturday night?"

"The security footage self-deletes after either three or four days. Can't remember which. But there's a good chance I still have it. If I do, we can watch it together."

"If you don't mind, I'd like to screen it alone." She had an ache in the pit of her stomach, not knowing what she might discover. If the driver of that Yukon turned out to be someone she knew, someone she trusted... she didn't want to fall apart in front of Cougar.

FORTY-ONE

Kathleen sat side by side with Ivy Pinnacle at a metal desk bolted to the floor of a small interrogation room. Given her recent hospitalization, she'd planned to take Ivy's follow-up statement at her home, where she would be more comfortable. It was Ivy who'd insisted on meeting her at the station.

On its own, that wouldn't have been enough to raise anything up the flagpole for Kathleen, but add to it the fact she'd come armed with security footage—footage she'd sought out on her own—and the red flag was soaring.

She pivoted in her chair so that she could look Ivy directly in the eyes, and was taken aback by the burst of sympathy she felt for this woman. Then she glanced at the two-way mirror, where the captain was observing, and her professional persona quickly resurfaced.

Cool-headed.

Empathetic but not sympathetic.

On your side one minute, intimidating another, depending on what the situation called for.

"To review, you understand you're making this statement

voluntarily. You're free to leave at any time. Just routine. Same instructions as last time, remember?"

"Yes, right." Ivy touched her temples, as if she had a headache, which might be expected given her recent concussion.

Last week, during Ivy's first interview, they'd gone over the details of Ivy finding the arm in the woods, as well as the possible altercation she'd witnessed between Laquay and Sandra Steele. Today was about the incident outside the Canyon Creek Club.

"Let's get down to it." Kathleen uncrossed her arms. "First, I've got to say it's highly unusual for a victim to bring in security footage on her own. I mean, unless it's from her own cameras. Why did you approach Collin Maddox?"

Ivy's lips tightened. "Why *didn't* you?"

"We would've gotten around to it." As a matter of fact, she'd been on her way to visit Maddox when Ivy called and told her she had the footage. She'd paid him a visit anyway, and obtained an official copy. Just in case Ivy attempted to edit it.

Not that she suspected she would, but chain of custody was imperative for any potential evidence. Especially since this most recent accident made the third in a row for the Kane family. The mother's car crash, the father getting shot with an arrow, and now this near miss with Ivy.

Then, of course, there was the deceased family lawyer.

There was definitely a pattern here. Kathleen just needed to fill in enough details to be able to decipher it.

"The footage might've self-erased by the time you requested it," Ivy said.

"This only happened Saturday. I'm not sure how fast you think routine investigations move." The expression on Ivy's face told Kathleen her soft voice hadn't been enough to mitigate her words.

"It's routine to you, but not to me. Someone tried to kill me, and possibly my father, too, but no one seems to be taking these things seriously."

"I promise I take them seriously, Ivy." One way to communicate that was by assuming an empathetic tone. The other was to spell it out. "Game and Fish is diligently looking into the incident with your father—we'll coordinate with them and share information on an as-needed basis. And if someone did deliberately try to run you down, I'm going to find them and hold them accountable. You did well, getting a hold of this footage. Let's roll it, now, if you're ready."

"I'm ready." Ivy powered on her tablet and navigated to the footage.

Kathleen slipped on her reading glasses.

Together, they watched the grainy, jerky image of a black Yukon barreling toward a slight figure. Then another figure burst into view, pushing the first out of danger. A hoodie fell from figure number two. The facial features were unclear, but the profile suggested a woman, and in particular, Sandra Steele. Figure number two checked figure number one for breathing and pulse. Then pulled a phone from their pocket. No clear view of a plate.

"Even if we enhance this, I doubt we can get the plate number. But we should be able to get make and model on the vehicle. Looks like a Yukon to me. I'll confirm and get back to you," Kathleen said.

"You can see it was intentional—that he tried to run me down."

"Motive—intentionality isn't something we can see, Ivy. It can only be inferred. And by the way, with those tinted windows at night, we can't tell if a man or woman was driving, or how many people were in the vehicle. I wouldn't assume the driver is a 'he'."

"Sure, but you can *infer* it was deliberate. That's obvious from the footage."

She hesitated. Her gut told her Ivy was right. But she operated on facts. "It's suspicious."

"He never slowed down!"

Kathleen nodded. "Agreed. But it's possible that he—let's call the driver 'he' for the sake of convenience—maybe he didn't see you."

"You can't be serious."

"You were dressed in black. *All* black. Including a black hoodie. Including your shoes. May I ask why?"

Ivy covered her mouth, then lowered her hand—a common tell when someone is lying. "That's just what I put on. I didn't think about it. I wasn't expecting to be run down on the street."

"Okay. But when you're out at night, it pays to be visible. I'd advise reflective clothing if you're going for a run or a walk."

"Are you blaming me?"

"No. I'm trying to get the facts. The driver was speeding. He might've been impaired—happens a lot on a Saturday night at that hour. It's the driver's responsibility to watch out for pedestrians. I asked why you dressed in black because if there's a reason, I need to know. I'm also pointing out why this *might* not have been an attempt on your life. Given your dark clothing, and the poor lighting—it is possible you weren't seen. And you haven't told me yet what motive you think someone would have for trying to kill you."

Nor had anyone offered a theory as to why someone would want Patsy Kane and Richard Kane dead.

But Kathleen had one. "Let me ask you, Ivy. Is there someone who would benefit financially from your death? Or from the death of your parents? Do you have, say, a family trust?"

"There is a trust. But I don't think that's relevant."

"When you die, who does your money pass to?"

"My husband. And I believe Becky Winters is included in

my father's will... but you're getting off track. Clayton didn't do this."

Kathleen couldn't help noticing how quickly Ivy jumped to her husband's defense—when all she'd done was ask a general question about a family trust. "Not accusing him. These questions are routine. I have to ask them—and one more housekeeping item. I read the preliminary statements you and your father gave Game and Fish. I didn't see mention of who, if anyone, in your family or close circle of friends is a bowhunter."

"Clayton hunts. So do half the men in Coconino County." Ivy's shoulders hunched high, nearly hiding her ears.

It seemed Kathleen had touched a nerve, yet again. "To be clear, your husband hunts with a crossbow?"

"Yes. He's in a club."

"Anyone else you know, personally?"

Ivy's hunched shoulders relaxed. "Most of the ranch hands. Our neighbor's son, and his father. A few of the men Dad plays poker with. It's a long list. You'll have to get the names from him."

"Thanks, I'll check with your father. Now, can you think of anyone who might have a reason to harm you?"

"I have to admit, my head has been spinning trying to figure out the answer to that question. Dad and Clayton think I'm confused, paranoid even. And I can understand why. But they're wrong. I might not know *who* wants me dead, but I think I've figured out *why*." Ivy leaned forward, her eyes darting around the room. "I'm the one who found Troy Laquay's arm. *Sandra* and I found it. She could be in danger, too."

"That's plausible." The connection was, in fact, at the forefront of Kathleen's mind. "But you say you don't know anything about Laquay's death. That it was mere happenstance you found the arm."

"Yes, but the killer doesn't know that. What if the killer

thinks we know too much? That we saw something, and now he's trying to stop us from talking?"

"By 'us' you mean you and Sandra."

"Yes."

"Speaking of happenstance. The two of you happened to be on the same block at the same time on Saturday night, but you weren't together. These are a lot of coincidences. I can't help you, Ivy, if you aren't truthful."

Ivy looked up defiantly. "You'll have to ask Sandra what she was doing at the club. But our being in the same place at the same time was no coincidence. I followed her because I wasn't sure I could trust her."

"Okay." Kathleen sucked her teeth. "*Now* we're getting somewhere."

Ivy's head snapped back, and her voice bristled. "But she proved to me I can. Watch the footage again, Detective. If it weren't for Sandra, I'd be dead."

FORTY-TWO
KATHLEEN

The rain was falling so fast and thick it looked like the window behind the captain's desk was melting. Kathleen hoped Ivy had made it home safely before the sudden downpour.

Ivy's upturned nose, those innocent brown eyes—even some of her mannerisms—reminded Kathleen of her younger sister. Plus, Ivy's obvious bereavement tugged at Kathleen's heart. But one thing she'd learned from being a cop—no matter how much you might like a witness, a victim or even a suspect, they were not your friend. A certain amount of distance was necessary. Without objectivity, an investigation could slide into the ditch quicker than a car on an icy road.

"Sit down, Kathleen."

Captain Boswell wasn't one for long chats. He generally kept things short and to the point. Inviting his detectives to "sit" wasn't his M.O. She planted her hands on her hips. "I'm okay, sir."

"Suit yourself." He yanked the rolling chair behind his desk, and Kathleen watched one wheel catch on the plastic protective floor mat. He took his seat, arranged the picture of his wife and son, fiddled with the height of the chair.

He was definitely getting comfortable. She might as well, too. She sat down across from him, practicing her best posture. "I'd like to track down Becky Winters. I think she might be able to shed light on Ivy Pinnacle's family situation."

"No."

"Excuse me?"

"You heard me."

"But, sir, you watched from behind the mirror. Did you hear the entire conversation?"

"I did. Which is why I want to be clear on this. Troy Laquay's death is your priority. It's obvious you feel protective of Ivy Pinnacle. But Ivy and her family are not your concern."

"Respectfully, Captain, the safety of each one of our citizens is my concern. *Our* concern."

"In a broad sense, yes. But right now, you have one job and one job only. We need to determine if a murder took place, and if one did, we have to solve it. You shouldn't go delving into matters that are better left for a family, a prominent family I might add, to work out on their own. From what I can see, this woman, Ivy Pinnacle, is depressed. She needs therapy. There's absolutely no evidence that anyone is trying to kill her."

"The car never braked. Never slowed."

"And as you pointed out, she was dressed in black. There was very little light."

"There was enough. And the car's headlights illuminated her."

"At the last minute. But by then it might have been too late to slow down, and as you also pointed out, the driver might have been impaired. We don't have unlimited resources. Stick to the Laquay case."

"Ivy Pinnacle is part of that case. She found the arm."

"And yet, you talked about going hunting for the housekeeper, to find out more about Ivy's family situation. You asked questions relating to the crossbow incident—a matter that's in the hands of Game and Fish. Yes, you needed Ivy's statement regarding the near miss on the street in order to close her complaint. But none of it is relevant to Troy Laquay's death."

"Ivy is a witness, and now, someone might have tried to murder her."

"No evidence of that."

"And no evidence the close call was *not* an attempt on her life. Respectfully, sir, I think it's important to find Mrs. Winters, pull on a few more threads. The timing of her departure seems suspicious. Someone might have murdered Laquay to prevent him from revealing what he knows."

"About?"

"The Kane family. Rebecca Winters might know something as well. It's too coincidental—she left right after I questioned Ivy and her about Mrs. Kane's accident. Shortly after that, Laquay's remains were found. I think she might tie things together for us."

"Is that some kind of woman's intuition you're going on? Because I see nothing to point to that other than a wild imagination."

It would be easy to get her back up. Point out that the male detectives in this department, which would be all of them except her, regularly played their hunches. That he'd called her "protective" and dismissed Ivy's own concerns about her safety. Wasn't the implication, in saying Ivy needed therapy, that she was being a hysterical female? And that Kathleen was letting her emotions and a wild imagination mislead her?

She could give him an earful about how he was letting his assumptions about women get in the way of the investigation. But that would only make him dig in. The captain was old school, but he wasn't malicious in his machismo. He was a smart man who could be reasoned with.

So, Kathleen had a choice.

She could get mad, or she could lay it out logically for him.

"If you don't mind me thinking out loud, I'd like to review some facts, along with what the witness, Ivy Pinnacle, just revealed in her interview."

The captain lifted one shoulder, then spread his hands. "I don't mind. I'm all about the facts."

"Fact one: Our victim, Troy Laquay, was employed by the Kane family for decades. He'd recently handled a very sensitive matter—locating Ivy's birth parents. Fact two: Patsy Kane died in a one-car accident. There was a bottle of whiskey beside her, but no alcohol was found in her bloodstream."

"Which amounts to nothing. The bottle was probably a gift for a friend. It's presence in the car—"

"Misled the officers on scene into assuming she'd been drinking. Made them less likely to suspect foul play."

"Patsy's accident is being investigated. We're not turning away from any evidence that may still come to light," the captain countered.

"Fact number three: The housekeeper, who was a confidante of Mrs. Kane, suddenly goes missing in action."

"She left a letter of resignation. *No one* has suggested she's a missing person or that she met with foul play."

"But like Laquay, she worked for the family for decades. She *knows* things only someone living in that house could know. So why, all of a sudden, does she take off without leaving a forwarding address?" She took a breath. "Fact number four: The birth mother, Sandra Steele, shows up and just so happens to lead Ivy to the location of Laquay's severed limb."

The captain grimaced. "I believe Ivy said *she* chose the location of the hike. And let's not get carried away with numbering the facts or we'll be here all day. Just say your piece, and get on with it."

"I'll double-check whose idea it was to go hiking. I'm just thinking out loud. But you heard what Ivy said in our interview. She admitted, in the end, that being on the same street at the same time as Sandra Steele was no coincidence. She *followed* her, because she had a gut feeling that Sandra was lying to her."

"Like I said from the get go, Ivy Pinnacle needs therapy. Sandra Steele saved her life. That's the one thing we saw for sure on that footage. I understand Ivy thinks someone wants to kill her, and her father, too. But the simplest, and best, explanation is that all this upheaval in her life has made our young lady paranoid."

"Someone shot her father with a crossbow—"

"Almost certainly accidental." The captain tipped back in his chair.

"And on Saturday night, she was nearly killed. You know that tired old chestnut: Just because you're paranoid..."

FORTY-THREE

SANDRA

Sandra arrived, fifteen minutes early, for her scheduled brunch with Ivy at Brandy's bakery. Once seated, she smiled at a young mother who was attempting to corral a vibrant, willful toddler. He reminded her of Dalton as a little boy. That started her playing back her own experiences as a young mom and got her chipping away at the hardened perceptions she'd held about her own childhood.

Still no word from Becky.

Unless, and her heart picked up speed at the thought, she'd contacted Ivy. If she had, maybe she could manage to subtly get it out of her without giving away their connection.

Even if Becky were lying low, Sandra couldn't see her completely cutting ties with Ivy. Not unless something had happened to her. Or she really was involved in Laquay's death.

It was almost impossible for her to believe Becky was a *murderer*, though.

If she had done it, it must've been self-defense.

And there was no way she could've or would've dismembered his body. That had to have been wildlife... except who really knew what *anyone* was capable of when the stakes were high enough?

"Are you ready to order?" a lanky young man, wearing a gray T-shirt and skintight purple jeans, asked.

"I'm waiting for someone," she said, pointing to the second menu the hostess had provided.

"I can bring you a mimosa while you wait. The all-you-can-eat brunch includes up to three mimosas."

"But does it include cab fare home?" She smiled.

He jerked his head, clearing away a few hanks of brown hair that had fallen over his dark eyes. "Between you and me, they're mostly orange juice."

She spotted Ivy and waved. "My friend's arrived. We'll take two—and see what you can do to get us an extra splash of champagne—I'll handle the cab fare."

Ivy was wearing a scoop-neck pastel-green cashmere top and jeans. She glanced at her smart watch, which she'd dressed up today by switching the sporty band she normally wore for one with gold links.

Sandra had priced both the watch and a similar band—as a Christmas gift for Dalton—and decided she couldn't afford it. Naturally, that was before she'd come into one hundred grand, courtesy of Richard Kane.

"I'm not late, am I?" Ivy sounded short of breath. It seemed she still hadn't fully found her footing around Sandra.

"Not at all. We're both early." Sandra stood and embraced her pretend daughter. She felt soft and smelled fresh. Hugging Ivy was like hugging a rain cloud. "I ordered us mimosas."

Ivy seemed like the sort of person who drank mimosas at brunch. Sandra never drank mimosas, nor did she brunch.

That was a life for other women.

Women with money in their pockets and time for friends.

"Sounds amazing," Ivy said.

"It's okay for you to have alcohol?" Ivy looked pale today,

and Sandra suddenly worried the mimosas had been a bad decision. There was something about Ivy that brought out her maternal instincts. Even though she was only pretending to be Ivy's mother, she was, after all, a mom in real life—not a perfect one, but she did her best. "So soon after a concussion?"

"I suppose not. But a mimosa hardly qualifies." Sending her a sheepish smile, Ivy swished into her seat.

"Our server recommends the brunch. What do you think?" she asked.

"You definitely should have the buffet—it's on me," Ivy said.

The server reappeared with the drinks.

"Brunch, please." Sandra held up two fingers. After saving someone's life, there was no shame in letting them pick up the check.

Ivy touched her stomach. "Erm. Hang on. I'll just have an English muffin and a side of cottage cheese."

The server was gone before Sandra could cajole Ivy into changing her mind. "Is your stomach bothering you? Nausea might be a sign of a worsening concussion."

"A little, but not to worry, I'm practically good as new." She took a sip of her drink and then smiled, as if that proved it. "Thanks to you."

Sandra ran her fingers up and down the stem of her glass. "It's so lucky I was there."

"Yes, well. About that. I want to come clean about something."

"Oh?" She already knew Ivy had lied about being at home that evening. Now, she hoped she would explain why.

"I didn't trust you, so I asked Felicia to keep an eye on you. She gave me a heads up before she dropped you off at the Suds Factory on Route 66. I followed you, on foot, from there to the Canyon Creek Club."

Sandra swilled a bit of her frothy drink and swallowed slowly, allowing this to sink in. They kept eye contact, not in a threatening game of chicken, but in an open, nothing-to-hide kind of way.

Except Sandra had plenty to hide.

And more reason than ever. Ivy's honesty made her *wish* she could tell her everything. "You *didn't* trust me. What about now?"

"I've thought about it a lot. And I believe you're holding something back—this is me not holding anything back from you, so please don't take offense. But you risked your life, running out in front of that car, to save me. If that's not proof of trustworthiness *when it counts*, nothing is."

"You saying so means the world to me, and I know trust is something that has to be earned. I give you my word I'm not holding anything back." She wasn't lying to Ivy for her own amusement—it was, unfortunately, a necessity. "In time, I hope you'll come to believe me. Is there something in particular you want to ask?"

"Only a million things."

"Why don't I grab something from the buffet while you decide where to start. Answering a million questions is going to require sustenance," she quipped.

When Sandra returned, her plate overflowed with breakfast meats, fruit, muffins and eggs. More than enough to soak up the three mimosas she planned on consuming.

Ivy stopped nibbling at the plate the server had brought her. "Before I start, is there anything you want to confess? If you haven't been one hundred percent honest, now's your chance. I've got a get-out-of-jail-free card in my pocket."

She wanted to come clean about *everything*. That wasn't an option, but there were some things she might safely reveal. "I don't live in Paris. I made that up to provide distance in case things didn't work out between us. The truth is, I live in Fort Worth, Texas, in a duplex apartment in a modest part of town. Dalton is living with me for the time being—he recently lost his job, and I'm helping him get back on his feet. He attends Tarrant County Junior college, but he's been accepted to UT— the University of Texas at Austin. Until I came here, I worked as a waitress at night, and a teacher's aide during the day." She felt like she'd just lost twenty pounds.

Ivy pursed her lips. "I can understand the Paris story—why you'd want an easy out. Is there anything else?"

"Not that I can think of," she said. "Is there a chance that get-out-of-jail-free card is good for another round? In case I remember something later?"

Ivy arched an eyebrow. "So, there is more."

"If I'm being honest, and I want to be, I might've overlooked something—only because so much has happened. But I promise I'm not holding anything back on purpose."

Ivy nodded, her face inscrutable.

"I don't know if you believe me or not," Sandra added.

"And if I'm being honest, I don't know either."

"Fair enough. Now, it's your turn. Ask your first question." *Make it a hard one. I deserve to squirm.*

Ivy took a sip of her mimosa. "You are my biological mother? You took a test, and you're willing to take another if I want?"

"Yes. Next question." That was easy. She couldn't possibly refuse a DNA test without giving the game away.

Ivy drained her glass. It clinked against her plate when she set it down. "Who is my biological father? Does he know I exist?"

FORTY-FOUR

IVY

"Who is my biological father? Does he know I exist?" Ivy repeated.

Sandra smoothed her hand across her face, wiping away her reaction like an incriminating fingerprint. "You want to know your biological father's name. Of course you do. And I'm happy to tell you."

Ivy wanted to believe in Sandra, but she was making it hard.

When had trusting someone become so complicated?

Until recently, it had seemed like an all or nothing matter. Any deviation from the truth would render an individual unworthy of trust. But she was beginning to think it was far more intricate.

Dad and Clayton had lied to her about meeting at the Canyon Creek Club, but she *knew* they loved her.

And then there was Sandra.

Ivy could sense something wasn't right about the way she'd appeared at her door, the stories she'd told, and yet she'd run into the street, risking life and limb, in order to save Ivy. Even though she'd admitted to lying about Paris, even though she was clearly hiding something more, on the *deepest* level, Ivy trusted her. Just like she did Dad and Clayton.

But that didn't mean she believed every word out of their mouths.

From now on, she was implementing a new policy—trust the *person* but not necessarily their words. From now on everything had to be verified. "I do want us to get another DNA test. But I need time to do some research and find out how to go about that."

"Whenever you want." Sandra looked around and, apparently catching the waiter's eye, raised her empty mimosa glass and two fingers.

Fine with Ivy—she could use another one.

Sandra tapped her nails on the tabletop.

Ivy pulled out her phone. "Do you mind if I record this? I want to give you my full attention, but I also want notes."

"No problem." More tapping.

Sandra seemed to be waiting for the server to come and go, but that shouldn't take long. The restaurant was busy, but most customers were ordering the buffet, and mimosas were lined up in preparation at the bar. Moments later, the server had come and gone and Sandra was left with no more excuses.

Moment of truth—hopefully she was about to find out her bio dad's name. Ivy's hand wobbled as she lifted her glass. "Shall we toast to us?"

"To us." Sandra clinked her champagne flute against Ivy's. "And to building trust."

Trust.

That tricky concept, again.

"Your father's name is... Mike—Michael," Sandra said, then lifted her fork. "This eggs Benedict is fabulous. You could have a bite of mine, or I can get you a fresh one from the buffet if you want to try it."

Seriously? Was she going to have to bring out the dental pliers? "Mike who?"

"Mike Smith."

It was hard not to roll her eyes. There must be millions of Michael Smiths on the planet. Had Sandra made that up on the spot? "That's a very common name."

"And it's his, so what else can I tell you?"

"How did you meet?"

"At a dance. You know how sometimes there's a wallflower off in a corner pressed against the wall?"

"Uh huh."

"Mike was that wallflower. I went to the sophomore dance with a bunch of girls, and I spotted him over in the corner. He was something else, so handsome. Huge brown eyes—a lot like yours—anyway, I went over to ask him to dance, and I saw tears on his face. A big strong hulking guy crying at a school dance."

Ivy closed her eyes, trying her best to suspend disbelief—it wasn't easy. A handsome boy alone at the dance. It sounded like something you'd read in a romance novel.

"It turned out Mike's girlfriend broke up with him that night. She'd been seeing his best friend behind his back for weeks."

She couldn't help sounding as incredulous as she felt. "So, he just spilled his guts? Told you that the very first time you met? At a dance, in front of everyone?"

"Yes, except it was a private conversation. He had a bottle of tequila, so we went out to his car. We climbed inside and got to know each other well. The way two drunk, lonely teenagers do."

"So, I was conceived in the back of a car. A one-night stand."

"Not a one-night stand. And it wasn't in a car—I don't think. I guess it could've been in his backseat, but we mostly did it at my house after school while my mother was at work." Sandra looked down at her busy, tapping fingers.

Something in her expression, the way her smile had disappeared, made Ivy begin to believe her story. "Did your mother leave you alone a lot?"

"All the time. She was a single mom—you're not the only one who doesn't know who your father is."

Ivy reached her hand across the table, but Sandra didn't take it.

"So, that's how I met your father. What else do you want to know?"

"When you found out you were pregnant, did you tell him?"

"Yes. I loved him."

Ivy waited. Expecting to hear the cliché. That when he found out Sandra was pregnant, he'd wanted nothing to do with her or the baby, and he'd bounced.

"He was nervous. I was too. But we were in love. Or at least I thought so. We decided to get married."

"You got married? Is he Dalton's father, too?"

"No and no."

This time, before Sandra looked away, Ivy was sure she saw moisture in her eyes.

"We were both below the age of consent, and his mother refused to give it. I didn't bother asking my mom, since his had already said 'no'. We came up with a plan to get fake I.D.s and elope, but then we realized it wouldn't be legal so there was no point. I wanted to run away, but Mike said he wouldn't be able to get a decent job. His mother kept pounding away at him, putting it into his head that a baby would ruin both our lives. Eventually, she convinced him."

"What happened next?" By now, Ivy was all in. Sandra's expression, her voice, her body language—she had to be telling the truth.

"He took off. He said he wasn't ready for the responsibility, and he never wanted to see me again. I tried to find out from his mother where he went, but she claimed she didn't know. I was too scared to have a baby on my own. So, when I couldn't hide my pregnancy from my own mother anymore, she helped me arrange the adoption."

"A closed adoption."

"Yes. I was the one who wanted it that way. I was afraid if I knew where to find my baby, if the adoptive parents sent photos and such, it would be too hard to let her go."

"Do you know where Mike Smith is now?" Ivy held her breath, hoping, but not expecting.

"I haven't heard from him since I was fifteen."

"What about his mother?" That seemed like a promising lead.

"Don't know where she is either. She moved away, too. I wish I could help, but I don't know anything. And I'll be honest, I'm not sure I could handle it if I did. If you want to track down your biological father, you'll have to do it on your own."

FORTY-FIVE
SANDRA

Sandra hurriedly climbed into Ivy's Mazda SUV and slammed the passenger door, just as the heavens upped their setting from *gentle-mist* to *turbo-blast*. That made two blinding rainstorms this week.

Lunch had been rough, and Sandra was glad it was over, but hopefully she'd comported herself well.

Ivy's voice seemed softer, her shoulders more relaxed, her smile genuine. She'd asked Sandra lots of questions, and in her own estimation, her answers had been believable. By the time they'd paid the check, Ivy *seemed* to buy into the story.

But the more time she spent with Ivy, the harder it was to go on lying to her.

And the more Ivy trusted her, the more Sandra's heart hurt.

Don't beat yourself up. You had to make her believe you.

Until she knew for certain that Becky was alive and well, what she'd gotten herself into and how deep, she was going to keep on lying—and do whatever else it took to make sure her *own* family was safe.

Not *everything* she'd told Ivy had been a lie. Take the story of Mike Smith. That wasn't his real name, of course, and he was not Ivy's father. Sandra didn't meet Dalton's father at a dance—but they had gone to dances together. The beating heart of the story—two young kids in love, dealing with a surprise pregnancy—that was true. So true it'd been tough going for Sandra. She hadn't been able to get through it without tearing up.

Until recently, she'd believed those youthful choices of hers were the most foolish ones she'd ever make.

But now, she'd topped herself—showing up at Ivy's door, conning money out of Richard Kane. The only saving grace was that, so far, Dalton's role had remained peripheral. He hadn't done anything other than lend his name to the fictious long-lost half-brother, thus filling out Ivy's family tree.

This game was proving not only foolish, but dangerous—she couldn't believe she would ever think such a thing, but the $100,000 payoff she'd conned out of Richard wasn't worth the damage she'd wrought. Not that she was solely responsible for this disaster. Plenty of other people had a hand in it.

Patsy was the one who'd plotted it.

Laquay had executed her ill-conceived intrigue.

Richard had allowed the deception to continue, albeit under a bit of duress.

Troy Laquay was dead, and her own mother might be responsible.

She shuddered at the thought.

Thank goodness Dalton was safely tucked away in Fort Worth, oblivious to what was happening out here in Flagstaff.

If she weren't so worried about Becky, she'd curse her for dragging Dalton into this mess. When Ivy asked who her bio dad was, Sandra wanted to tell her the flat-out truth.

I have no earthly idea, because I am not your mother.

But she couldn't.

She hoped Richard would steer Ivy away from hiring a real investigator, and keep quiet about their deal. If the scheme were exposed, it wasn't only Sandra who would pay a price.

Becky would have to answer for her part in all of it.

"Thanks for the lift," Sandra said. "I hate it that you drove out of your way in this weather. I should've called a cab."

"There's no way I'd let you do that. Besides, I want to ask Dad to re-engage the investigator Laquay was using. If I hire someone new to find Mike Smith, they'll have to start from scratch."

Sandra took in a deep, relieved breath. As long as Ivy didn't try to find an investigator on her own, as long as she relied on her father to find someone, their secret was safe... unless Richard decided to do the right thing.

But what were the chances of that?

Low, but definitely not zero.

If he let scruples win out over common sense, they'd all be in a lot of trouble.

Which was why it was important to keep Dalton as far away as possible.

If it had been up to her, he wouldn't have been involved at all. But Becky had convinced Dalton to go along with the scheme first, and then Dalton had convinced Sandra. He couldn't make it happen without her, and, of course, they needed that money.

Foolish wasn't the only word she'd used to describe her recent decisions—*irresponsible, inexcusable, reprehensible* also came to mind.

What kind of woman commits fraud with her son and her mother?

She should have talked Dalton out of it and told Becky to forget about it.

The closer Ivy got to finding her true family of origin, the more dangerous the situation became. "Why not let the dust settle before looking for your father? You've been through a lot, and even though it's selfish of me, I'd like a chance to work on *our* relationship before bringing Mike back into the picture." She paused and decided to play what she thought was her best card. "I don't know how I'd feel about sticking around if Mike came back."

Ivy hit the brakes so hard the car slid into the next lane.

"Careful!"

"Sorry. I thought I saw something in the road," Ivy said.

The ensuing vacuum in the conversation accentuated the swish of the windshield wipers and the roar of the wind against the glass.

She kept her eyes on the road, white knuckling the steering wheel.

"How do you feel about what I just said?"

Ivy sighed. "Sorry, I'm gathering my thoughts. I hear you. But it's important to me to get the whole picture of who I am, and where I came from."

"But surely you understand that would open up old wounds for me." The catch in her voice wasn't an act. The pain of being abandoned at fifteen by the boy she'd loved had never gone away. It remained a hidden scar—one she'd never shown *anyone* before today.

"Sandra, I respect your feelings. I don't want to disregard them," Ivy said.

"But?"

"I need to know the truth. Besides, I don't expect the investigator will find him quickly. If it were easy, Laquay would have found him. But if I am fortunate enough to locate him, you won't have to see him. I can travel to meet him on his own turf, and if at some point he wants to come here, to Flagstaff, I'll give you plenty of warning so you can—"

"Get out of the way?" That sounded petulant, and petulant wasn't going to get the job done.

Maybe the best thing to do was to let this whole business play out.

Let Ivy ask for Richard's help. Let Richard steer her in the wrong direction.

Richard might regret paying her off, but he was in too deep to go telling the truth now.

If only things weren't so complicated.

And where the hell was Becky?

She checked her phone—no messages from her mother, but there were three missed calls from Dalton.

Shielding her phone, she typed out a message to him.

Everything's fine here. I'll update you soon.

Hopefully, that would be enough to keep him at arm's length. If Dalton found out Becky was MIA, he'd insist on coming out here, and she couldn't have that. It was too dangerous.

Between Laquay's mangled corpse, Becky vanishing, and Ivy's close call, one thing had become clear:

The stakes in this diabolical game she was playing had officially been raised to life and death.

FORTY-SIX

IVY

Michael Smith.

I know his name.

The rain stopped, just as Ivy turned into her father's private drive.

From her peripheral vision she caught sight of Sandra's creased brow, her lower lip pulled tightly between her teeth, the way she jabbed her phone as she typed out a message.

"Here we are," she said, trying to keep the excitement out of her voice. It'd been difficult for Sandra to talk about the past—about Ivy's biological father. And she wanted to show respect for Sandra's feelings, even while her own heart fluttered in her throat.

A common name like Michael Smith wasn't much to go on, but it was a start. Ivy wheeled the car around the circular drive, parking it near the front entrance, behind a sky-blue Ford Explorer she didn't recognize.

Sandra didn't look up from her phone.

Texas plates.

Ivy's fingers prickled, like a bee sting.

Ivy didn't know anyone from the state of Texas, or she hadn't. But Sandra just confessed she didn't live in France.

Sandra lived in Texas.

Her heart was racing. She took a big breath, while admonishing herself not to get her hopes up. There were a million reasons a car with Texas plates could be parked at Dad's house. What were the odds? She squeezed her eyes shut, trying to prolong the moment. Afraid to open them and find the Explorer had mysteriously vanished.

"Dalton!" Sandra exclaimed.

Ivy's eyes flew open.

A young man, even taller than Dad, with Sandra's exact shade of auburn hair, toed down the steps. How had she missed seeing him, standing there? Perhaps he'd been around the side of the house or lurking behind a pillar.

"Is-is that my brother?" she managed.

Sandra nodded, her face a shade whiter than porcelain.

And where Ivy would've expected a smile, Sandra's mouth tugged down at the corners. "Are you feeling ill?" she asked.

"I'm fine. The winding roads made my stomach a bit wonky, but I'm not sick or anything." Suddenly, she brightened. "Hurry up. I can't wait to introduce you to Dalton."

Ivy didn't need encouragement. She popped out of the car and ran around for a hug.

A few weeks ago, she had no idea she had a sibling, and now here he was, grinning at her, and hugging her back.

"I'm Ivy."

"I figured. I'm Dalton Steele—your half-brother. Great meeting you."

She turned her head away, tears suddenly flooding her eyes. "I'm sorry for getting emotional."

"I'm sorry for surprising you." He approached Sandra for a side hug. "I've been calling you all morning, Mother."

"I saw some missed calls a few minutes ago when I took my

phone off focus mode. But you could've texted or left a voice-mail. And why didn't you call *before* you left? I'm sure you didn't drive all the way from Fort Worth in one morning."

"Busted. I figured you might try to stop me," Dalton said.

That made no sense to Ivy. Why would Dalton assume Sandra didn't want him here?

Ivy was certainly glad he'd come.

"I don't like you missing school." Sandra blew out a hard breath.

He shrugged. "I got permission to take my exams early. I'm officially on summer break."

"Oh, that's amazing. So, you're here for a while?" Ivy opened the door, and Dalton and Sandra trailed her inside. "You can stay here, at my father's ranch, or you're welcome to the guest room at my place. Whichever you like."

"Mom, you're here, right?" Dalton asked.

"For the moment," Sandra said.

"Then if it's okay, I'll bunk at the ranch."

"It's definitely okay." Dad's voice preceded him down the hall. He extended his hand to Dalton. "Richard Kane. We spoke on the phone."

"Dalton Steele." The men surveyed each other, genially.

Now Sandra went full-on ghost white.

"Mom, are you okay?" Dalton grabbed her beneath the elbow.

She wobbled, and then folded down onto the stairs. "Those darn, winding roads. I'm a little carsick. That's all."

"Felicia! Bring Mrs. Steele a water bottle a.s.a.p." Richard lowered himself beside her and lifted her wrist. "Pulse is fast."

Sandra scoffed. "I'm fine. Just give me a minute."

Richard stood and offered Sandra a hand up. "Whenever you're ready then."

Felicia delivered the water, and they all wandered into the living room. Sandra's small episode, a near faint, Ivy would call it, had brought Ivy back to earth. Which was a good thing, because she wanted to concentrate on every word her half-brother had to say.

Naturally, she'd been wanting to meet him, and she'd expected to do so at some point.

But he'd gotten permission to take his exams early rather than wait the short time until the end of the term. Ivy couldn't help wondering what had happened that made Dalton Steele jump in his car and drive nearly 1,000 miles to be here *now*.

She watched him, out of her peripheral vision, trying not to be too obvious about it.

The way Dalton was greedily eyeballing the Ansel Adams photographs on the wall and Dad's collection of Frederic Remington table-top sculptures made her uneasy. He was either a true fan of western art or he was calculating their dollar value in his head.

Sandra's reaction to his sudden appearance was too strange to ignore. The more Ivy thought about it, the more certain she felt that Sandra was not the least bit happy to see him. After saving her life, Ivy owed Sandra everything. But that didn't mean she had to close her eyes and ears.

Sandra was definitely hiding something.

What if that something was Dalton?

FORTY-SEVEN

SANDRA

As she sipped her water, Sandra could not prevent her hand from trembling, giving away her nerves.

Coming to Flagstaff had been the worst idea ever. But what was done was done, and she'd be damned if she'd let Dalton suffer because of her mistake.

Mothers are supposed to protect their children.

Not fall apart in the face of danger.

No more collapsing in stairwells.

This fake family charade might be a ticking time bomb, but she wasn't going to light the fuse by giving up the game now. She needed time to sort this out before a DNA test result or finding Ivy's real father exposed the truth.

And the first order of business was to get Dalton the hell out of here.

The only way to minimize the damage was to keep her cool.

She pulled her shoulders back and smiled, when what she really wanted to do was shake Dalton until his teeth rattled. "I was so excited to see you, I nearly fainted. Next time you decide to surprise me, try to remember that your mother is a delicate creature."

Richard scoffed. "Funny, I didn't take you for being the least bit fragile. Your son called me about an hour ago—he was trying to reach you. I would've worked harder to get the message to you if I'd known the surprise would literally knock you off your feet."

She took another sip of water. Her hand was rock-steady, and from here on out, it would remain that way.

"Dad, thank you so much for welcoming Dalton. It means the world to me." Ivy had tears in her eyes.

"That's right," Sandra chimed in. "The way you've extended your hospitality to me and now my son—out of love for Ivy. It's heartwarming. If only every parent could be like you."

"Okay, enough." He waved off the compliments. "A man doesn't need thanks for the things he does for his daughter. And now that I've gotten to know you a little, I realize what a great addition you... and your son will make to our family."

His syrupy words turned her stomach.

She didn't buy his one-big-happy-family act for a minute— but she hoped Ivy would.

"Speaking of the things you do for me," Ivy said. "I've decided I'd like to search for my biological father. But you don't need to foot the bill. I only need the name of Laquay's investigator and any records to date."

The excited look on Ivy's face about broke Sandra's heart. She didn't know if Laquay had created a phony paper trail, or counted on Ivy taking him at his word, but she doubted there were any "records to date" or even an investigator.

Which meant Ivy was in for more lies.

And it was going to be up to Sandra and Richard to tell them.

FORTY-EIGHT

IVY

Ivy almost didn't venture out today. She'd awoken with a doozy of a hangover, from the single cosmopolitan Clayton whipped up for her before bed, and a bone-deep sense of foreboding. But she was determined not to cloister herself at home.

She'd be damned if a hunter with a crossbow, or a bogeyman behind the wheel of a Yukon, was going to stop her from living.

Besides, the Sunday farmer's market, set up on the greens behind the library, was one of Ivy's favorite things in life. The small size of the park limited the number of vendors, so it wasn't the big production you'd find in, say, Phoenix, where mini-versions of popular restaurants and shops had elbowed their way in to the mix.

Flagstaff's version had stayed true to the concept of locals offering up homemade jams and hand-painted crafts. The food trucks sold burgers and frybread covered in clouds of powdered sugar and the like. All save one very special truck, manned by Chef Robby. Robby had been head chef at a Michelin top-rated restaurant in Vegas, until he broke down sobbing one day under the weight of a food critic's complaint that his béarnaise sauce was too creamy. He now owned a cabin on the outskirts of town and cooked whenever and whatever he damn well wanted.

Ivy was glad to see that today, he damn well wanted to make chicken schnitzel and almond roulade. "How much for the roulade?"

"Twenty-nine ninety-nine for the entire roll or six fifty for a slice."

"I'll take a slice, please."

A man of few words, Robby somberly plated the spongy delicacy and handed her a plastic spoon.

Stared past her, frowning.

She turned to see what had caught his eye, and spied a dog off-leash and two teens bounding after it.

Gina Crenshaw bumped Ivy's elbow, nearly capsizing the roulade. "Sorry. Sorry. Sorry."

"No worries," Ivy said. She didn't know the woman well, but she recognized her from the photography booth she set up most weeks at the market. "Looks like they've apprehended the outlaw."

Gina shaded her eyes. "So they have. How's the cake?"

Ivy spooned her first bite into her mouth and let it melt deliciously. "Highly recommend."

"I'll have to get some before Robby runs out." Gina tilted her head, hesitating. "You're Ivy Pinnacle. We've met before."

Ivy had bought three photos from Gina over the past few years. Two of Antelope Canyon and one the Wupatki ruins. "We have. I've got several of your pieces in my home. I love your work."

Gina's face flushed. "Thanks." She shifted her weight, gazing past Ivy, much as Chef Robby had done. "Are you here alone?"

Ivy stepped back. That was borderline inappropriate. If a man had asked her the same question, she would've ended the conversation and turned on her heels. But coming from a woman who sold nature photography, it was probably innocuous. "I love this market. It's such a beautiful day and I didn't want to miss it."

"But you usually come with your husband."

Okay, this was getting weird. "He couldn't make it today."

Gina shaded her eyes again, still looking past Ivy. "Well, then, nice bumping into you—that didn't come out right. I didn't mean that literally."

"No harm done from the bump!" Ivy lifted her plate and gazed at the picnic tables on the other side of the park. "See you later, then."

"See you later." Gina didn't move from her spot.

Heat rose to Ivy's cheeks. Strange how both Robby and Gina had stared past her rather than looking directly at her. It was like she had spinach in her teeth or her shirt on inside out. She glanced down to verify there was no wardrobe malfunction before heading for an empty table on the other side of the park.

Sensing someone behind her, she stopped and turned, but no one was nearby.

Why did you come alone?

This was a public park in the middle of the day.

This was *Flagstaff*.

But it had been just outside of town, in the middle of a sunny day like today, that she and Sandra had stumbled onto Troy Laquay's detached arm.

And no more than a mile down the road, someone had tried to mow her down with an SUV.

She looked left, then right.

A few more steps and a creepy sensation raised the hairs on the back of her neck.

The park was crowded with people, so naturally, she heard branches snapping, leaves crackling underfoot. Yet whenever she stopped, no one else was around.

She slipped her hand in her pocket, feeling for her car keys.

No.

She wasn't leaving yet. She would not allow recent events to stop her from enjoying the farmer's market.

She sighed, and then her wrist slipped.

As her roulade began to slide off the plate, someone bumped her elbow, and all was lost.

The cake splattered onto the grass, and Gina's dog, now safely on-leash, cleaned up the icing.

"No! Scout!" Gina jerked the leash. "I'm so sorry."

Ivy fanned the empty plate in front of her. "It's fine."

Gina tugged her dog close to her side, her eyes darting all around. Landing everywhere but on Ivy.

Ivy's mouth went dry. "Is everything okay, Gina?"

Gina's knuckles were white as she gripped the leash.

"Because, honestly, you seem distracted," Ivy said.

"I don't want to frighten you. But I can't *not* say something. It's probably nothing." She lowered her voice to a whisper. "I noticed a man earlier, when you were at the food truck. Everywhere you go, it seems he's not far behind, only I think he's trying to stay out of sight. See that guy leaning against that tree over there—I'm sure he's been following you."

Ivy's legs threatened to give way but she stood her ground. Forced herself to breathe. She had to face the situation with a modicum of courage. Yes, this might be the very person who'd tried to run her over.

But there were a number of explanations, and virtually all of them were more likely than the one playing in her brain like a skip on an old record—that she was being stalked by a killer.

In broad daylight at a crowded venue.

"Do you want me to speak to him? I'll tell him to go away, or we could call the police," Gina whispered.

Ivy shook her head, at last working up the nerve to look in the direction Gina was pointing.

FORTY-NINE

IVY

Dalton.

The tingling in her fingers subsided. Her tight chest relaxed, and she let out a breath. "I know him. Everything's fine."

Gina reached out, touched her shoulder. "How well do you know him? The way he was watching you, sneaking around, was very strange."

"Thank you, so much, for having my back. I do appreciate it. But that's my brother. There's absolutely nothing to worry about."

Gina's face flushed. "Oh, gosh. So sorry. I'll go round up my girls. And feel free to stop by the booth later. I'd love to give you a photo—to make up for scaring you like that. I feel terrible. I never meant to insult you or your family."

"Don't apologize. The world would be a better place if everyone looked out for their neighbor. I appreciate what you did." Gina barely knew her, and yet she'd cared enough to chase her down and warn her. On impulse, Ivy gave her a quick hug.

Gina flashed her a sweet smile, followed by a frown when Dalton waved. As he sauntered toward them, she made a beeline in the direction of her daughters, leaving Ivy on her own.

Ivy threw a quick glance after Gina, surprised by how much her words had affected her.

She'd asked, *How well do you know him?*

And the truthful answer was, *Not at all.*

"Hey there, lovely. Fancy meeting you here." Dalton reached his arms out, offering her an embrace.

She stepped into it, but stiffened at his touch.

Throwing his hands up, he stepped back. "Too presumptuous?"

She'd hugged him the first time she'd seen him, and nothing had changed since then. "It's fine."

A vein bulged in his forehead.

It seemed she'd annoyed him.

"Anyway, this is a nice little market," he said. "A bit quaint, but I don't mind. We should check out that food truck. I think I saw cake."

Dalton was behaving as if he'd just now spotted her, when in fact he'd been trailing her since she'd gotten here. If she wanted to build a relationship with him, she should let him know she was aware of it. Tell him she promised to be honest with him, and that she expected the same in return.

"I had the roulade—the cake—already. It was delicious..." She was about to add that she knew he'd seen her, when he interrupted.

"Oh, too bad. Honestly, I don't even like sweets, but I thought you might enjoy it. If you've already sampled the wares, I'm out."

So, he was going to double down on a completely unnecessary lie.

Even if he acknowledged he'd seen her before, and had been hanging back, it wouldn't have made him seem stalkerish—it was the lying that accomplished that.

"Did you know I was going to be here?" Ivy asked.

He lifted one shoulder. "How would I? But I'm glad we ran into each other. I've been wanting to talk to you without Mom or Richard around."

"Oh? I don't believe in keeping secrets from my father."

"Too bad he doesn't feel the same way."

"What are you implying?"

"Nothing. I'm saying straight out he's keeping secrets from you."

"Well, then. I can certainly see why you didn't want to say that in front of him."

"Don't get defensive. He lied to you about your adoption. So I don't think I'm speaking out of turn."

"That may be, but he's also been there for me my whole life. Loving me, looking out for me. Which is certainly more than…"

"More than Sandra did?"

"She had her reasons, and I don't blame her. I've had a wonderful life."

"I wish I could say the same."

Her chest tightened. This wasn't the relaxing morning she'd hoped for. And Dalton wasn't the man she'd expected him to be. All that excitement she'd been feeling about meeting her brother was rapidly being replaced by distrust, dislike even. "We seem to have gotten off on the wrong foot."

"Not my intent. But I don't believe in sugar-coating. Sandra hasn't always been the greatest mother. She's made a lot of mistakes—then again, we all have."

She couldn't help wondering what kind of mistakes *he'd* made. "You said you wanted to talk to me about something."

"I was wondering if you could loan me some money—so I can start looking into finding your bio dad."

"My father said he'd handle the investigation."

"We should do it on our own. And frankly, I'm broke. I'm not sure I have enough to cover the expenses."

She crossed her arms. "What expenses?"

"Travel. Greasing palms. Almond roulade in the park."

"I thought you didn't like sweets."

"I lied."

You sure did.

But he was right about one thing—Dad was keeping secrets. He and Clayton met behind her back. They discounted her fears about her close call with the Yukon. Dad admitted that after Mom died, he'd decided not to tell her about her adoption —*ever.*

If Sandra hadn't shown up, Ivy still wouldn't know.

So, the idea of finding her biological father, without relying on Dad, did hold appeal. If she partnered with Dalton, they could get to know each other better in the process.

The only trouble was, after catching Dalton eyeing the valuables at the ranch, and now stalking her—every bone in her body was screaming: *Don't trust him!*

FIFTY

IVY

Commanding her hands not to shake, Ivy snipped the bright-red top off a gerbera daisy stem, then poked it in between cubes of smoked cheddar cheese and purple cauliflower florets.

It's going to be fine.

You can do this.

No one will suspect a thing.

She pulled in a shaky breath, stood back, and surveyed the vegetarian "charcuterie board" she'd recreated from an online article.

Entertaining was hardly her forte, but it was part of the subterfuge, and a nice place to focus her nervous energy. It'd taken her the better part of the morning to arrange the fare onto a piece of butcher paper that stretched nearly the full length of Dad's buffet table. The hard and soft cheeses included both mild varieties for the faint of heart and strong ones for the connoisseurs. For fruit, she'd chosen familiar grapes and berries paired with a touch of the exotic—dragon fruit that she'd cut into chunks and then replaced in its own scooped-out skin. She'd thrown in various nuts, pickles, baguettes, dips and even sweets.

No question she'd gone overboard. There was absolutely no way the five of them—Dad, Clayton, Sandra, Dalton and Ivy—would be able to eat all of this. And though she'd carefully followed the instructions for "how to assemble the perfect charcuterie", hers, though colorful, turned out a bit sloppier than she'd hoped.

But it was almost time for the guests to arrive—it would have to do.

She had a plan, and even if it, like her charcuterie, was imperfect, she was determined to carry it out.

Since none of the people about to gather in this room had been one hundred percent honest with her, she no longer felt obliged to be one hundred percent honest with them.

She wanted them all together in one place, so she could sneak away safely and search Dalton's room. She'd suggested they gather at the ranch and insisted on preparing the food herself, to give the household staff the day off.

"Wow. Honey, this is really something." Dad came up behind her—she hadn't heard him come in. "I don't know why you wouldn't let Felicia help you, but obviously you've done a great job."

"I wanted this to be special for Sandra and Dalton, and I had an itch to do something creative."

"Mission accomplished."

Dad was wearing his favorite uniform—a white T-shirt and jeans. She couldn't help noticing something was missing. "Where's your bandage?"

"Don't need it." He pushed up his short sleeve, revealing a ragged, pink scar. "See here, there's hardly even a mark left. I told you it was nothing to worry over."

Right. Unless the poacher who shot him was *not* a kid with bad aim and worse judgment.

Unless he wasn't a poacher at all.

But there was no convincing him, and when she'd told

Detective Winthrop about Dad's "accident", she'd been assured Game and Fish were doing a thorough investigation.

Ivy had no choice but to drop the subject. Still, it remained at the top of her mind, along with her own close call and Laquay's death. "Who's worried? Check out the spread I made."

One side of Dad's face quirked up. "Don't take this as a criticism, but where's the meat? I thought these things included salami and whatnot."

"Dalton is a vegetarian."

"I hope you won't take offense when I pass up the purple cauliflower and that spotted thing over there." He frowned. "Are we supposed to eat the flowers, too?"

"Ha ha. No. And no one's going to force you to try anything you don't like. Feel free to fill up on cheddar cheese and cookies, but please be nice. No jokes about Dalton's dietary habits. I want him to feel comfortable."

"And I want you to be happy. That's why I rolled out the red carpet for both of them. Your family is my family. I mean that, honey."

She felt her throat closing around potential tears. Dad was a good man, and she wanted to believe him. But as Dalton had rightly pointed out, her father had lied to her about some very important things.

She *hoped* he wasn't lying now.

That he truly wanted them to be a family. "Thanks, Dad. That means more than you know."

"Whatever you need from me, I'm here."

"Me too." Sandra was in the doorway. "I couldn't help overhearing. Thanks again for your hospitality, Richard."

"We're both grateful," Dalton popped in, with Clayton trailing behind.

Clayton had been touring Dalton around the ranch.

"And we're all hungry." Clayton grabbed a fistful of pistachios, simultaneously knocking a bowl of tzatziki with his elbow and spilling half of it onto the butcher paper. "Uh oh, I messed up your fancy dip."

"Fingerpaint with it if you want. As long as you're having fun. Please, everyone, enjoy." The spilled dip was a perfect distraction. "Load up your plates. I'll be right back with extra tzatziki. I think we'll need more."

"I can go," Sandra said. "You relax."

"Thanks, but I actually have to whip more up. It's homemade." She held her breath, waiting for more objections. Surely someone would say she shouldn't bother. That their hostess should sit down with the rest of them. But no one did.

This was her chance.

Now was the moment she'd hoped for.

But it had come sooner than she'd anticipated—she hadn't had time yet to psych herself up.

Her stomach felt fizzy, her legs weak. Manipulating her own family didn't feel right.

Her whole life, she'd believed honesty was the key to good relationships.

She'd always strived to be a truthful, forthright person, and to believe in the goodness of those around her.

But she was beginning to see that turning a blind eye to the flaws in others wasn't simply naïve.

It was sometimes dangerous.

She slipped out of the room, through the kitchen, and up the backstairs.

On a deep breath, she turned the knob to Dalton's room.

Locked. Dammit!

FIFTY-ONE

IVY

Ivy would not give up this easily.

She'd come prepared in many ways, but she hadn't expected Dalton's door to be locked. Her father's ranch was a home—not Fort Knox. Though a state-of-the-art alarm system had been installed outside to protect the house and grounds from intruders, there was no indoor security. That would've been an intrusion on the privacy of family and staff.

What was the point of locking his bedroom?

The room's simple privacy lock, designed to keep children from bursting in on their parents, and vice versa, could hardly be counted upon to keep a determined intruder out.

And she was determined.

Then again, simple privacy might be all Dalton was after. Perhaps he had nothing to hide.

She'd love to believe that.

For a moment, she let that soak in. She had a whole new set of people to learn to love and care for, who would, in turn, learn to love and care for her: a birth mother, a half-brother, and somewhere out there, a biological father. In her *it's-possible* world, no one was trying to hurt her. All the lies were designed to *protect*—either her or the liars themselves—but not to destroy or cause harm.

People lie all the time to save themselves from embarrassment or gain a social advantage.

None of us are perfect.

If she caught Dalton or Sandra in one of those common lies, she wouldn't consider it disqualifying, any more than she'd been willing to kick Dad and Clayton to the curb for meeting behind her back.

On a deep breath, she tiptoed up and stretched her hand as high as she could, patting her fingers along the ledge atop the bedroom door. After two sweeps, she decided the key wasn't there. Which made sense. Dalton would have kept it on him. He needed the key to get back into his room.

No problem.

Mom's study was two doors down, the place where she'd gone to think and read. The very room where she'd written that children's book for Ivy. Where she'd typed her famous "Flagstaff Wave" op-ed for the *Gazette*. Like most rooms in the main house, it had a privacy lock. The generic key should be above the door, where all the keys had been kept since Ivy's childhood, so she couldn't accidentally lock herself inside.

In two shakes, Ivy located the key on the ledge above the study door. As predicted, it fit perfectly into Dalton's doorknob, and just that quickly, she was in her half-brother's lair.

So far, this had been easy.

But she knew the difficult part awaited in the form of that laptop, carelessly left lying at the foot of the bed.

She kept the door cracked—if someone was coming, she wanted to be able to hear their approach. She fished in her pocket for the thumb drive she'd brought along and opened the laptop.

Please don't let it be password protected.

A password screen popped up.

Unlike the locked door, she'd thought of this obstacle ahead of time and come prepared. But who knew if her advance strategizing would be enough. Realistically, if Dalton used a high security password, she wouldn't be able to hack it. But if he was like most people when it came to cybersecurity, she had a shot.

Earlier this morning, she'd done a search and made a list of the fifty most commonly used passwords. They varied from the most obvious, such as *123456* to the head-scratching *qwerty*—which it turns out reflects the first six letters on a keyboard.

Lots of sports terms like *football* and finally nerd words like *startrek*.

She tried all fifty.

The thumb drive felt slick in her hand. She rubbed the sweat off with her shirttail and made a wish, like it was a magic lamp, before giving it one last go.

According to the internet, fifty-nine percent of people use birthdays as passwords.

Dalton was twenty-seven years old.

She didn't know his birthday, but she could narrow the year down to two—depending on which month he'd been born.

Neither year worked.

Her own password was her birthyear, only backwards.

She typed in the first year backwards.

The screen flashed.

A tone sounded.

With a racing heart and fumbling fingers, she inserted the drive, quickly opened a search engine and went to the history—deleted.

Dammit.

In the distance, she heard quiet footfalls.

No. No. No.

She hadn't gone to all this trouble only to get caught... or to walk away empty-handed.

As fast as her trembling hand allowed, she dragged all the

folders on the desktop into the open drive, hit eject, then yanked the drive out, while simultaneously slamming the laptop shut.

She made it to the hallway, just as Dalton appeared at the top of the stairs.

Their eyes locked.

Had he seen her duck out of his room?

She recalled pressing the button to relock the door, but had she remembered to actually *close* the door?

She threw a glance behind her and let out a big breath.

His bedroom door was shut, but she couldn't be sure he hadn't seen her.

"Hey," he said, neutrally.

"Hey, yourself." Should she try to explain what she was doing upstairs when she was supposed to be making dip?

No way.

This was her father's house, after all. She didn't need to explain. It wasn't like he'd caught her in his room with the computer open. She followed his gaze, down to her right hand, and realized she still had the key in it.

"I thought you were making dip," he said.

"Yeah. Can you believe I forgot the list of ingredients?"

"Isn't it just cucumber and yogurt?"

"I'm impressed you know what goes into tzatziki."

"Vegetarians know these things."

"Still impressed. But there're spices, too."

"Uh huh. What are you doing up here?"

There was an edge in his voice that raised the hairs on her arms. She palmed the key. No use pocketing it now, after he'd seen it. Besides, he might find it suspicious, but unless he'd seen her coming out of his room, there was no way for him to know for sure she'd been snooping.

Any other time, if a guest in her father's house had spoken

to her like this, she'd have told them off, and then Dad would've sent them packing.

But Dalton had a right to be wary of her, just as she had a right to be wary of him.

"My mother kept her recipes in a file cabinet in her study. I needed to check the list of secret spices in the tzatziki." She inclined her head toward the study door. "If you want, we can come back up after brunch, and I'll grab her recipe file for you— you can make copies if you like."

"Of your mother's *secret* recipes?"

"All families have secrets, Dalton. Maybe it's time ours stopped keeping them from each other."

FIFTY-TWO

SANDRA

Sandra had been itching to get inside Patsy Kane's study. If she could search every inch of this ranch she would, but that wasn't going to happen. It would take a team of cops, armed with a warrant, weeks to get through all the nooks and crannies. But she had no such advantage. She had to be careful sneaking around under the watchful eye of Richard and his staff.

Her best chance to find clues that might lead her to her mother, or shed light on what really happened to Troy Laquay, was to concentrate on likely high-yield areas.

Patsy Kane's study topped that list.

As luck would have it, at brunch this morning, Ivy had promised Dalton she'd return to the study to retrieve her mother's secret recipe file. An offer that had first perplexed him, and later made him suspicious enough to pull Sandra aside and suggest that Ivy was up to something. That the *recipe file* was some sort of awkward ruse.

But from what Sandra had seen, Ivy was too honest, too naïve, to be capable of subterfuge. If Ivy had been acting strangely around her newfound "brother" it was probably just a case of nerves.

Then, Ivy had returned to Patsy's study as promised.

The good news was that gave Sandra a legitimate excuse to enter the study and have a look-see.

The bad news was that Ivy's presence also presented an obstacle to outright searching. Sandra would have to be subtle with her snooping and hope an opportunity would organically present itself.

"Knock, knock." Sandra slipped through the half-opened doorway, her eyes darting about, cataloguing information as quickly as possible in case Ivy preemptively dismissed her. "May I come in?" she asked belatedly. "Dalton mentioned something about secret recipes. He's not terribly interested, but I am. That dip you served was to die for. Tzatziki is usually so blah."

Ivy wiped her cheek with the back of her hand and looked up from her spot on the couch.

Even if she hadn't known this was Patsy's study, Sandra would've gotten it from the vibe. The floral-patterned chintz sofa with a rolled camel back. The woodsy wallpaper that appeared to be hand-painted. The glass birds perched atop bookcases, one of which was entirely filled with children's books, well-loved, judging by their creased spines.

This was clearly not Richard's domain.

This must've been where Patsy came to reflect and study.

Her happy place—perhaps it had been Ivy's happy place, too.

"I didn't hear you coming," Ivy murmured.

Because she'd been tiptoeing up the hallway. She'd wanted to catch Ivy off guard, and clearly, she had. "Oh, honey. You're crying."

Ivy didn't deny it—how could she given her melting, red face?

"I'll be fine in a minute." Ivy sniffled into a crumpled tissue.

"May I sit down?" Sandra managed to snuggle up to Ivy and

rest her arm around her shoulder before she completed her sentence, giving Ivy no opportunity to refuse.

More sniffling.

Ivy trembled against her, bringing out misplaced maternal instincts, when the instincts that would've best served were of the killer variety. She was getting soft. "What's wrong? Talk to me, honey."

"I'm sorry." Ivy wiped another tear.

"Oh, no. Nothing to be sorry for. I snuck up on you in a private moment—but I'm glad I did. Whatever it is, I want to help."

"I'm just feeling overwhelmed. I came in here to get Mom's recipes and found this book, lying open, face down on the table, as if Mom had just been here reading. I can't imagine who would've taken *this* book off the shelf. I considered whether I might've done it myself—I have absolutely no memory of it if I did. Anyway, the next thing I knew I was sitting here reading our special story and sobbing like a loon."

Sandra touched the open book on Ivy's lap—*Ivy Makes a Friend*. She remembered it from Patsy's obituary, but she couldn't let on she'd researched the family before her arrival. "What's this?"

"A story my mom wrote when I was six. As you can probably guess from the title, I had a hard time making friends."

"She wrote this for you?" The book was impressive. Hardbound with lively drawings of children jumping rope, playing hide and go seek, carrying trays to a lunch table.

"She did the illustrations, too. One afternoon, when I came home, stinging from the way Julie Dickey teased me over my hair—mine was curly, and almost red, back then—she slipped it into our after-school story-time. Mom read to me almost every day, sometimes twice a day. She used to do these funny voices for the characters."

Patsy Kane was a saint—something tickled a doubt Sandra

had had earlier but soon forgot in the midst of all the chaos. If Patsy loved Ivy so totally, so selflessly, would she really have planned to keep her biological family away from her? Even if it meant losing her, wouldn't she have wanted what was best for Ivy?

"I'll never forget the crushed look on Mom's face when I told her I was too big for story-time." Ivy's voice cracked. "I'd give anything to have that time again."

"Children grow up, Ivy. I'm sure your mom was sad to see the end of story time, but I'll bet she was also proud of you. And you'll always have your very own book—what a wonderful gift she gave you." Sandra felt achy, hot tears welling behind her eyes.

If Becky had ever read to Sandra, she didn't recall it.

Most of her memories of Becky were of her hurrying off somewhere, with her purse swinging at her side.

No. That wasn't fair.

Not *somewhere*.

Becky always had a job to get to. "Not every mother gets the chance to have those special moments with her child."

Ivy lifted her chin. "I'm incredibly lucky. You might say I had two mothers. Whenever Mom couldn't be there for me, Mrs. Winters filled in, helping me with my homework or reading to me. I don't think I ever had a sitter in my entire life."

For a moment, Sandra couldn't catch her breath, thinking of Becky, doting on Ivy, whereas Sandra had only gotten scraps of her attention. You'd think Ivy would be more worried about Becky, after all the love she'd showered on her. "But Mrs. Winters *was* a sitter."

"Oh, well, technically, I suppose. But, to me, she was family." Ivy's voice dipped. "It hurts that she left without a saying goodbye, but she's given so much of herself to me over the years, I don't want to be selfish. I'm afraid if I try to find her, she'll feel pressure to come back to work. She deserves to take time for herself."

"Mm hm." *Enough already.*

Apparently, Becky, too, was a saint—except when it came to her own flesh and blood. When Sandra had needed her mother the most, that was exactly the time Becky had moved in with the Kane family to help them care for *Ivy.*

Sandra had yet to get over that.

Her maternal instincts toward Ivy were now officially quashed.

She dug her nails into her palms—Ivy Pinnacle did not need Sandra taking her under her wing.

Sandra had her own kid to look out for, and her own mother.

However imperfect they might be, Dalton and Becky were her responsibility—Ivy was not. "So, did you get the recipes?"

Ivy frowned. "No. I got sidetracked."

The sudden change of subject might have been jarring, but Sandra didn't care. "I'll get them. What about keys to the filing cabinet?"

"In her desk, I think."

"That doesn't sound secure."

"Mom didn't keep anything of value in there. I doubt she was worried anyone would try to steal her children's book ideas or her secret recipes. And heaven knows Dad never set foot in here."

Sandra retrieved the key and, working quickly, began rummaging in the filing cabinet. Ivy came up behind her and peered over her shoulder.

The shift in mood was palpable.

Maybe she'd been too obvious. She'd practically jumped over Ivy to get to the file cabinet. "I found them. Patsy filed them under S for *Secret Recipes.* I guess you were right—she wasn't worried about anyone stealing them."

Too bad she hadn't had more time to search. But Sandra now knew where they kept the key to the file cabinet. She could come back later on the pretext of a lost earring or some such to peruse the rest of the files...

Ivy reached past her.

"Look at this." Ivy pulled out a thin envelope with feminine handwriting on the front. "It says 'For Ivy' on it."

"Funny you didn't find that before." Sandra resisted the urge to snatch the manilla envelope from Ivy's grasp.

"Before?"

"Weren't you in the file cabinet this morning? Checking the recipes."

"Oh, of course! But this was stuck in the very back of the cabinet."

Sandra had to admit it could've been easily missed. But the way Ivy was blushing seemed off. Dalton might've been right. Maybe Ivy hadn't really been recipe hunting earlier. That could've been a cover story. But for what crime? "Do you want some privacy, or would you like me to stay with you while you open that?"

Ivy wandered back to the sofa. "I suspect this has to do with my adoption. So, it might concern you, too. I think we should open it together."

FIFTY-THREE

IVY

With eager fingers, Ivy opened the envelope and pulled out the papers. Any worries she'd had about Sandra realizing she'd lied about looking for recipes were instantly supplanted by the wonder of what she held in her hands.

A letter from Mom.

Her pulse thumped in her ears. This missive might contain answers to many of her questions... or to none of them. But one thing was certain, this was Mom's handwriting. She recognized it from every note tucked into her school lunches, every birthday card, every shopping list. The mere sight of it was enough to make her heart squeeze, her eyes film with moisture.

"You don't have to let me read it." Sandra's voice was nearly inaudible.

Ivy looked up. That world-by-the-tail look Sandra usually wore had been replaced by something child-like, something far more vulnerable. For the first time, Ivy felt as though they were in this thing together.

Part of her wanted to keep this letter private, between herself and Mom. But here was a chance to share an intimate moment with Sandra, and her gut was telling her that's what Mom would've wanted.

"I know I don't have to. But I want to." She cleared her throat and began to read out loud.

Sweetest Ivy,

You were only four days old when your father handed you to me for the first time. I remember a clock chimed "one". Your brown eyes popped open, and, in that instant, I fell in love with you.

I had never loved anyone that much, and I was terrified.

My arms shook so hard I nearly dropped you. My knees threatened to give way, but I wouldn't let them. I made it to the safety of the rocking chair. And as I cradled you, I whispered a promise that I would always protect you. That I would fight for your happiness until my dying breath.

I know I haven't been a perfect mother, but I've done my very best. I've made mistakes, but I've always acted from love, and I hope you will forgive me for them.

Here is the truth:

I am your mother, but I did not give birth to you.

I will sit down with you tonight, to answer any questions you may have. But I thought, first, I'd gather my thoughts on paper—you know me, I always think better with a pen in my hand.

It's good to put things in writing.

I want you to have all the information you need in case you want to find your birth parents.

So here it is.

FIFTY-FOUR

SANDRA

Sandra's head felt light. As if all the blood had drained to her feet. Her fingertips tingled. She closed her eyes, then opened them again, testing to see if this was real or a nightmare.

She'd known all along this game couldn't continue forever.

But now, her mother's fate was in her hands, and perhaps Dalton's, too. *Why* had he defied her wishes and shown up unannounced? What if Becky had dragged him into something deeper? Sandra could *not* allow her cover to be blown until she found out what was really going on behind the scenes.

Still, Ivy was no longer a mere face in a photograph.

She was a living, breathing woman.

A person Sandra had grown to care about.

This letter might reveal nothing.

Or it could destroy Sandra—and not only Sandra, but her family, too.

She forced herself to smile encouragement as Ivy read on.

When Dad and I adopted you, the process was closed at your birth mother's request. All we knew of her, at the time, was that she was fifteen when she got pregnant—sixteen when she gave birth to you. We were told she was in good health, with no physical or mental impairments, and that she requested that your adoptive parents be college educated. It seems this was quite important to her.

We were also told your biological father was sixteen, in good physical and mental health. He left town shortly after learning of your birth mother's pregnancy, and did not provide financial or emotional support.

Importantly: Because his whereabouts were unknown, he could not give consent to the adoption. It seems this situation is not uncommon, and there are legal means around it. All the necessary steps were taken to contact him, and when they failed, we were able to move forward with the adoption.

I wish I could tell you more about him. But I'm afraid that's all I know.

But I do have other news.

A few months ago, I wanted to bring everything out in the open and leave it to you to decide if you wanted to know more.

In the end, your father and I decided it would be best to find your family of origin, first, so that we could assure ourselves they wouldn't bring any danger into your life, in case they were criminals, or drug addicts or such.

I asked Troy Laquay to look into the matter, and he was able to locate your birth mother and a half-brother. So far, he's had no luck finding your biological father.

Your birth mother's name is Sandra Steele. She has a twenty-seven-year-old son, named Dalton Steele. She has no criminal record, and passed a thorough background check. She's agreed to meet with you online if you're interested.

Sandra could feel her fingers again, her heart beating in her chest, her breath flowing in and out of her lungs.

Everything was okay, at least for now.

Then Ivy turned over the page.

I'm also enclosing your birth certificate.

I'm nervous but excited to find out how you want to proceed.

Love you always and forever,

Mom

FIFTY-FIVE
SANDRA

The clock in the hallway chimed one.

"It's a sign," Ivy said.

Sandra shook out her hands. There was nothing to worry about. The letter would only serve to convince Ivy that Sandra was indeed her birth mother.

Looking at Ivy now, with her innocent, hopeful expression, Sandra wished, with all her heart, that it were true.

But she had not given birth to this young woman.

Therefore, the birth certificate Patsy placed in that envelope couldn't possibly be the original. The original would have the names of Ivy's actual biological parents, whomever they might be, and that would've revealed the whole, misguided scheme.

"What's a sign?" She cocked her head at Ivy.

"The clock chiming. That's how the letter started. My mother remembered the clock chimed 'one' when she held me for the first time."

"You're right. This is such a special moment. Thank you for sharing it with me."

Ivy didn't respond; instead she frowned at the official-looking paper in her hand—the birth certificate.

"Everything okay?" Sandra asked.

"I don't understand." Ivy passed the certificate to Sandra.

She'd expected the document to be a fake, created by Laquay, and listing Sandra as the birth mother. But of course, she hadn't gotten that lucky. Instead, the certificate appeared to be authentic, listing the parents as Richard and Patsy Kane.

"I thought it would name you as the mother and Michael Smith as the father. But this looks identical to the one Mom gave me a long time ago."

Sandra had researched adoptions at length. She understood the situation. "This must be your amended birth certificate. That's the way closed adoptions work. The adoptive parents' names are substituted for those of the biological parents. The amended certificate can then be used for legal matters just like an original—without revealing the adoption."

"But I was hoping—there must be a record of my *actual* birth parents *somewhere*."

"As I understand it, there is. But that original birth certificate is sealed." She hesitated. There was no use trying to hide what could easily be found with an internet search. "It can be unsealed by court order, or if the birth parents allow it."

"So, if *you* give permission, it could be unsealed."

"Without your birth father's consent, I'm not sure I could. The law is complicated—it could get sticky."

"But Mom's letter says that after some legal maneuvers, the adoption was allowed to proceed without him, so surely a birth certificate could be unsealed without him, too."

"Who knows? I suppose you could hire another attorney. But why bother with all that when you know I'm your birth mother, and I've already told you your father's name?"

Ivy pivoted so that they fully faced one another. She reached for Sandra's hand. "You saved my life. I wouldn't be here right now if you hadn't pushed me out of the way of that car."

Sandra felt a knot forming in her stomach. She could anticipate the "but" that was coming.

"But... without the original birth certificate, without having been part of Laquay's original investigation, I would love to do what we discussed. You remember I said I would research how to get another DNA test."

Sandra smiled, like this was the best news ever, because what choice did she have? "Uh huh."

"It turns out it's super easy. I found a company online and they sent me a kit. I was going to bring it up at brunch, but then I decided I didn't want the rest of the family there for something this private. Just you and me."

"I agree. It should be a mother–daughter thing. When things settle down, we'll go away for a weekend together. Take the test, and then crack open a bottle of champagne to celebrate." Hopefully she could keep stalling. Put off the DNA test as long as possible. She needed time to find Becky. Time to find out what happened to Troy Laquay. Even if her mother had nothing to do with his death, either she or Sandra would probably be considered a suspect.

Ivy shook her head. "Let's save the champagne for when the results come back. I have the DNA test kits and a same-day express envelope in my bag."

"You brought it with you? You want to do this now?" Sandra managed to choke out the words.

"Don't look so worried. It won't hurt at all." Ivy reached for the tote that had been resting by her side. "All we have to do is swab our cheeks and mail it in to the company."

"How long until we get the results?" Hopefully it would take weeks, months if she were lucky.

"The website promises to get the answer back to us in five days."

She swallowed a curse. If she refused, the reason would be obvious, and Ivy would have her answer: that Sandra was a complete and total fraud. "Let's do it. I can't wait to put this whole thing behind us."

Ivy passed her a swab.

Sandra straightened her back, peeled off the plastic and jabbed the swab into her mouth.

How had it come to this?

She wasn't a criminal—at least she hadn't been in the past.

And she certainly wasn't a detective.

But now, she had a mere five days to find her mother and solve the mystery of who killed Troy Laquay.

FIFTY-SIX

KATHLEEN

After a quick survey of the Pinnacles' living room, Kathleen had a decision to make. If she remained standing, it would create pressure to terminate the interview quickly. But her seating choices were not conducive to squeezing information out of Ivy and Clayton Pinnacle.

That fancy white sectional, for example.

So deep that even someone of her considerable stature—she was half an inch shy of six feet—could not sit with their back supported and their feet on the floor at the same time. You would have to either recline with your legs stretched across the cushions, or perch on the edge like a damn bird.

Either posture would undermine her authority.

The blue accent chairs would've worked, but they were both currently occupied by the home owners. Ivy on the left, Clayton on the right.

That travertine coffee table looked sturdy enough to support her weight.

Like the couch, it would require her to perch on the edge, but it would put her so close to them, she'd seem more bird of prey than dove. She eyeballed the midpoint between Ivy and Clayton, then lowered herself onto the coffee table, facing them.

Ivy's eyes widened.

Clayton coughed.

But neither issued a reprimand for desecrating their beautiful table.

They'd been the ones to summon her, but, with her bold seating choice, Kathleen had now, officially, taken charge. "Thanks for getting in touch."

"Have you had a chance to review the photos we sent over?" Clayton asked.

Kathleen slipped out a group of prints from a manilla envelope. She had, in fact, reviewed them earlier, but she was here to ask the questions, not answer them. "Tell me about these."

"Are you sure you wouldn't like something to drink? Water or soda? I can make coffee." Ivy fidgeted in her chair.

Kathleen had declined refreshments upon her arrival. Ivy seemed to be stalling. Which was odd since she'd been the one to initiate the encounter. "I'm fine. But I'll let you know if I get thirsty. Tell me about these photographs."

"They were taken by Dalton Steele," Ivy said.

"Your half-brother."

"Yes. I think so."

"You think he took the photos, or you think he's your half-brother? Which one?"

"Both. He's Sandra Steele's son—you know that story already. DNA is pending."

"You never found Laquay's records?" Ivy had previously mentioned that testing had been done. Sandra Steele's DNA was on Kathleen's list of items to follow up. The captain didn't think the Kanes' family history was relevant to Laquay's death, but Kathleen wasn't so sure.

"No. And I wanted to repeat it. We used a private company I found online. Mr. Laquay's staff never found the records we requested after his death. His assistant said he must've done the work off books."

"Does that bother you?" It did Kathleen. Even if Laquay was working off books, he should've provided paperwork to document his findings. Unless, of course, his findings weren't what he purported them to be.

"I understand why he might not have put it on record. I do believe Sandra Steele is my biological mother. I'm simply verifying... in case."

"In case Troy Laquay was lying to your mother and father?"

"He had no reason to lie about my birth family."

"But we can't ask him now, can we? Since he's deceased."

Ivy's face was growing whiter and Clayton's redder.

"I hadn't thought about that. I've always trusted him, but considering his sudden, terrible demise, I suppose we have reason to question whether or not he was concealing things in his business or personal life. Has the M.E. determined his manner of death?" Ivy asked.

"We invited her here to talk about the photographs, honey," Clayton said. "You're getting sidetracked."

"Yes, but it's relevant. If Laquay's death wasn't an accident, then—"

Kathleen held up her hand. She did have news. And given the distraught look on Ivy Pinnacle's face, she didn't want to withhold it—she wasn't that cruel—even though her gut was telling her something was off about the M.E.'s conclusions. "This is not for public information, yet. So keep it under your hat for now. The M.E. hasn't finalized his report, but he plans to note the official cause of death as exsanguination due to a bear attack and the manner of death as accidental. Park rangers confirmed bear tracks in the area, and the wounds on the back of the neck, the dismemberment and eating of entrails are consistent with a bear mauling."

"I read, in the papers, his skull was fractured. How does that fit with a bear attack?" Ivy asked.

"That could've been from the mauling, but the theory is Laquay fell, while hiking, and hit his head on a rock. Later, a black bear came across him incapacitated and unconscious. Black bear attacks aren't usually fatal, but they can be—you remember that fatal encounter in Prescott a few years back."

Clayton dusted his hands. "This is great news. I don't mean to sound cold—it's just such a relief to know there's not a killer on the loose out there. I'm sorry for Troy, but at least he didn't leave a family behind."

"No wife or kids, but his mother lost her only son. He had a sister. And friends." Kathleen wasn't one to pull punches. "But you're right, about one thing. You do sound cold."

He narrowed his eyes. "I'm just being honest. I'm sorry the man is dead—but at least he wasn't murdered. Let's get back to the photographs."

"Happy to. You were saying you think Dalton Steele took them. But you're not sure? Have you asked him?"

"No. He doesn't know we have them," Ivy said. "I copied them from his computer onto a zip drive, and then Clayton printed them out for me."

"You must think these are evidence of some sort of crime or you wouldn't have called me. But I'm not sure what you want me to make of them." Kathleen had an opinion, but Ivy clearly had her own ideas, and she wanted to hear them.

"Detective, it's obvious he's been stalking my wife. There are nearly one hundred photographs of Ivy around town. All of them taken without her knowledge. Dalton Steele is bad news."

"I understand your concern, but there's nothing illegal about taking photographs of a person in a public place where there is no expectation of privacy. And if he hasn't approached or harassed you, Ivy, we can't do anything."

Ivy twisted her hands together. "I might be imagining it, but there have been many times I've felt someone's eyes on me, then I'd turn and find no one there. Once, I caught Dalton in the act, following me around, at the farmer's market, but I can't say he harassed me. I've been with him a little since then—since he's staying at my father's ranch. He hasn't done or said anything threatening. Which is why I hesitated to call you. But Clayton thought it was important."

Clayton stood up, then sat down again. "Ivy's been a bit paranoid of late—especially about that Yukon. But when I saw these photographs, I got concerned. Dalton has been following her—call it stalking or don't, the guy is trouble."

"Have you considered what it must be like for him? Suddenly finding out he has a half-sister. Maybe he's checking you out, the same way your parents had Laquay check Sandra Steele out before letting her into your lives."

Ivy bit her lip.

Kathleen would bet she was withholding something.

"If it makes you feel better, I'll look into Dalton's background. In the meantime, if you don't feel safe around him, you should avoid him. Have your father tell him to move off the ranch."

"I don't want to say anything to Dad, or do anything to jeopardize my relationship with Sandra. But I would appreciate you looking into him. Did you notice the time-stamps on these photographs?"

She'd definitely noticed.

"The first one was taken two days before we found Troy Laquay's arm—but Dalton told us he only got to town a few days ago."

Kathleen didn't have to wonder why Dalton lied about when he arrived in Flagstaff. He lied because he was hiding something.

She just didn't know what.

"And there's one other thing." Ivy lowered her voice.

"Those pictures of me, dressed in black, walking on a street near the Canyon Creek Club. Those were taken the night someone tried to run me over. Which means Dalton was there."

"Are you saying he was the driver?" Kathleen asked, keeping her face and voice neutral.

"I'm saying he was there."

"And even though I've informed you Troy Laquay's death will be ruled accidental, not the result of foul play, you're still convinced someone tried to kill you?"

"Someone drove an SUV straight at me." Ivy pivoted and looked pleadingly at her husband. "I might have a concussion, I might wake up screaming at night, but I am not crazy. Whoever was behind the wheel of that Yukon wants me dead."

FIFTY-SEVEN
SANDRA

"Slow down, Dalton. We'll never spot Becky's car at this speed." Sandra reached for the passenger side grab bar.

"This is a waste of time." Dalton made a sharp left and zoomed over the railroad tracks, rattling Sandra's teeth. "No matter how slowly I drive, if she's left Flagstaff, we're not going to find her."

If she'd left town.

Sandra was convinced the text she'd received from her mother, that story about Becky retiring to live her best life, was baloney. "I don't believe she would up and leave without giving notice. When I asked to see the letter she left Richard, he couldn't produce it. Said he threw it away. Very convenient if you ask me. The last time I spoke to her, she begged me to come back to Flagstaff. Why would she do that if she was planning to leave? And there's something else. I didn't mention it because I didn't want to alarm you, but I found this on the floor, in her old room."

She handed Dalton a small pearl earring.

He held it up between his thumb and index finger, then quickly passed it back before returning his gaze to the road, a deep furrow in his brow. "That looks like part of the pair I sent her for Christmas. Anyone can lose an earring."

"She's meticulous with her things. And a gift from you, I'm sure she'd guard with her life. Did you see that it's cracked? What if someone ripped it out of her ear?"

"She probably just stepped on it. Take it easy, okay? But... it's high time we filed a missing person report. You've got that detective's number."

"We can't report her missing, and you know the reason why."

"You could do it anonymously. Say you're a friend, and she hasn't returned your calls. You don't have to tell them you're her daughter to file a report."

"I won't have to tell them. If they go digging into Becky, they'll find out who I am... and who you are, on their own. This whole scheme will be exposed and we'll *all* be in jeopardy. But that's not my main concern."

"Oh, right, I forgot. You think she's hiding out because she killed that lawyer." Dalton scoffed. "If I wasn't so worried about her, I'd be laughing my head off instead of cruising Flagstaff searching for Becky's old clunker."

"I know it sounds crazy—but the last time I talked to her on the phone, when I heard that scuffle, I swear I heard Laquay's voice in the background. The call disconnects. Becky disappears, and Laquay's dead body turns up. Your grandmother is a fighter. If he threatened her, or one of us... no telling what she'd be capable of doing."

Dalton wasn't making things any easier on her. Now she had to worry about both Becky and him. "But if she didn't do it, that means there's a killer on the loose. *Someone* tried to mow Ivy down in the street. It's like there's a big target on the backs of anyone close to this family. Which is exactly why I don't want you here. You should go home."

"I'm not a kid, Mother—you don't get to tell me where I can

and cannot be. Becky usually calls me several times a week. It's annoying, but when I stopped hearing from her, I got worried. *That's* why I came, and I have every right to be here."

"No, you're not a kid. You're a twenty-seven-year-old man who still lives with his mother." She immediately regretted the words. In fairness to him, it'd been her idea for him to move back home after he got fired. On the other hand, if he hadn't gotten into a fist fight at work, he'd still have his job.

That vein in his forehead was doing its thing. The one that turned blue and bulged whenever he was about to lose his cool. She needed to take the temperature down.

She flipped the station on the radio, searching for a soothing song, or some classical music. But this damn town was loaded with country stations and rap music. "You should've paid for satellite radio. These stations are crap."

"This isn't a rental car."

"What?" Dalton had been wanting to buy another car. His old one was always breaking down. She'd just assumed he'd rented a safer vehicle to make the drive from Texas. It was obviously used, but it was still more than Dalton could afford. "How did you pay for an Explorer?"

"Don't worry. I didn't skim from our ill-gotten gains to buy myself a sweet ride. I used a car share service. It's cheaper than a regular rental and a lot less hassle." He slowed up, pointing out the window. "We're coming up on the bus station. I'll make a lap through the parking lot."

The stress was getting to them both. She shouldn't be snapping at him, or jumping to conclusions. "Sorry about what I said before. I know it's hard on you, not having your own place."

"I'm sorry, too. Let's try to remember we're on the same team—just until we find Becky. Then we can go back to our usual stand-off."

She shifted in her seat. Dalton might be right. It was unlikely they would spot Becky's car. But if she'd left town, it might be parked at the bus station or the airport. "If you've got any other ideas, I'd like to hear them—besides going to the cops."

"Grandmother had nothing to do with Laquay's death. I wish you'd trust me on that," he said. "But I see how the cops might suspect her if they knew they were scheming together."

"We were *all* scheming. Thank goodness *you* were nowhere near Flagstaff when Laquay was killed. At least that makes one of us with an alibi."

"Of the three of us, I'd be the first one the cops would try to pin it on. A young guy with a record." He pulled out of the bus station lot. "Her car's not here. Where to next?"

"Airport." She punched another button. The radio played more static. An idea was floating around in her head, but hadn't yet come in for a landing. "Dalton, explain this car share thing to me. How does that work?"

"It's like rideshare except instead of people driving you around in their car, they loan you their car for money. Like those vacation rental sites, but for cars. You do it all online or through an app. They message you where and how to pick up the vehicle."

"An app? So, you don't have to meet anyone face to face to pick up the car?"

"I guess you could meet the owner before picking up the car, but people usually don't. That's part of the appeal. In my case, I checked in via the app and the owner unlocked the car remotely. I never saw them."

"And there are no stickers or anything that make it obvious it's not your own car?"

"I don't see anything on this one."

"Pull over at the library," she said.

"You think her car will be at the public library? She's been hiding in the bathroom reading those Tessa Dare novels she loves so much this whole time?"

"I wouldn't put it past her, but no. I want to use the computers—I've got an idea." If Sandra were going to run someone over, she wouldn't use her own vehicle. And if she had a choice, she wouldn't show her face at the rental car counter either.

While Dalton cruised downtown, his eyes peeled for Becky's car, Sandra hit the library computers.

It was a long shot, but this wasn't The Big Apple.

She was counting on the number of folks offering to loan out their personal cars, in a small city like Flagstaff, being manageable.

After logging on and conducting a quick internet search, she found the one and only active car-share site in Flagstaff— "Caro".

A grand total of twenty-two vehicles were currently available in Flagstaff and the surrounding areas.

Always take your shot—even if it's a long one.

Of those twenty-two vehicles—exactly *one* was a black Yukon.

FIFTY-EIGHT

SANDRA

Sandra had gotten all she could from the vehicle and was now ready to return the black Yukon. Its owner had been suspiciously hesitant to meet Sandra in person—like they had something to hide. But Sandra had convinced them, and, for her own safety, she'd suggested a public place for the drop off.

The little park behind the library was the perfect spot.

There's nothing to worry about.

She had pepper spray in her purse and Dalton was using their location-sharing app to track her phone. Pulling in a long, shaky breath, she tried to beat back the nagging voice in her head.

The one that kept insisting she shouldn't be here alone.

Who was to say the owner had loaned the Yukon out to someone else that night?

Maybe *they'd* been the one driving, and she was about to come face to face with a killer.

She looked behind her, then side to side, trying to shake the eerie feeling she was being watched, but there was no one around.

Stay calm. Don't blow this.

Sandra flounced the ends of a bright-purple scarf she'd wound around her neck in order to make herself easy to spot. But the owner should be able to recognize her from her driver's license photo. She'd uploaded that, along with a selfie, at check in. The host had given her zilch by way of identifiers in return, and she hadn't pressed.

Maybe he'd had a bad experience in the past with a guest user, or maybe he was just the cautious type. Neither scenario would work in her favor. Sandra had to be careful not to spook him if she was going to get the information she needed.

She looked over her shoulder again, checking out the lay of the land. Looking for the best escape routes in case she had to make a run for it.

It was definitely the same black Yukon.

And now, she had the evidence to prove it.

After picking up the Yukon from the Safeway parking lot, Sandra had sat in the vehicle and, with the help of an internet search, thoroughly educated herself on the Yukon's navigation system.

Then she'd pulled up its recent history.

On Saturday June 4, someone had input the following:

From: current location West Mountain Parkway

To: Canyon Creek Club 7200 Hidden Hills Highway

Was the evidence circumstantial? Sure. Enough to hold up in a courtroom? Maybe not. But it was enough for her.

Oh, crap.

A few yards ahead, she recognized Gina Crenshaw. Hopefully, she wouldn't remember Sandra. They'd only bumped into each other that one time on the street. Other than that, they hadn't seen one another since high school, and they'd never been friends. With any luck, Gina would walk right by.

Or not.

Gina was waving at her. But this was Flagstaff. So probably just the good-ole *Flagstaff wave.*

She raised her hand in return.

Dammit. No. No. No.

Go away, Gina!

"Sandra, it's me. Gina Crenshaw. This is something. We keep bumping into each other."

"Hey. Yeah. It's great, but I'm meeting someone..."

Gina sat down on the bench, looking at her expectantly.

"It's a private meeting, so I'm sorry but I don't have time to chat."

"What? Oh, my bad. I thought you understood when I said *it's me.* I meant I'm your Caro host. You rented my Yukon. Did you leave the keys in the car?"

They were in her pocket. She tightened her grip around them. Hanging on to the keys was a means of keeping her host captive until she got the information she was after. If she'd left them in the car, or if she handed them over right now, there would be nothing to prevent Gina from walking away.

She huffed out a breath.

How stupid of her to assume the owner of the Yukon would be a man.

And how extraordinarily unlucky for her that it turned out to be a woman she knew from high school.

Thank goodness Gina didn't seem to remember *that.* If she had, she wouldn't have been skittish about meeting up with Sandra.

She felt her tight jaw relax—it didn't seem likely this was the person who tried to run Ivy down.

Maybe this wasn't so unlucky after all.

Gina held the key to finding the killer and, maybe, to finding Becky.

Sandra wasn't going to let her walk out of this park until she pried the information she needed out of her.

"I was so nervous when you said you wanted to return the vehicle in person. That never happens. And Caro doesn't recommend it for safety reasons," Gina said.

"Well, thank you. I'm glad you took a chance."

"Me too. You looked nice enough in your selfie, but I was still worried about meeting up until I remembered you."

From bumping into her the other day, she hoped. "How are your girls?"

"Still not watching where they're going. But Sandra, that's not what I meant. You don't remember *me*?"

She decided to bluff. If she kept up the lie, it would be believed. That's the way lies work. It's called gaslighting. You just gotta stick with it. "Yes. Your girls ran into me on the sidewalk, and you made them apologize. Which they did quite nicely. We chatted for a minute."

"Don't you remember me from high school? We had gym class together. It was only one semester. But after staring at your selfie, it all came back to me. My last name was Jordan back then. Yours was different, too. Not Steele. I think that's why it took me so long to put things together. What was your maiden name? I've been racking my brain. Was it Summers?"

"You've got me mixed up with someone else. I grew up in Texas."

"But you look and sound just like her... You don't have a Texas twang."

She forced a laugh. "I'm sorry I'm not your old friend, but I promise I'm a nice person. Not dangerous or a criminal. Thank you again for agreeing to break your rule and meet face to face."

Gina's head was tilted, her nose bunched up, but she didn't say anything—she was going to take Sandra's word for it. Gina was far too polite to call her a liar. Hopefully, she was far too polite to *think* it.

"The resemblance is uncanny. Okay, well, hopefully you

had a five-star experience. If you did, I hope you'll leave a review. I can message you a link."

Of course, that's why she'd agreed to meet even though she didn't want to. That five-star review was important to Gina. It would help her business. And she must need money or she wouldn't be renting out her personal car. Here was something to work with. "I definitely will leave a review. And you have gone above and beyond. But I have a few questions, if you don't mind."

"Sure. I hope nothing went wrong. Sometimes the passenger door sticks a little. You just have to jiggle it. But I have a part on order. I'm taking care of it."

"No. The car is great."

"Was it clean enough? I know there's a stain on the back mat. I wash it before every rental. Maybe I should replace the mat."

"Oh, that didn't bother me. I wanted to ask about the car's history."

"It hasn't ever been in an accident, if that's what you're getting at." Her tone was growing defensive. The last thing Sandra wanted to do was to antagonize her.

"My review is five stars all the way. I loved the car. It was spotless. The ride was so smooth. I don't know any other way to do this but to be honest with you. Is it okay if I tell you something personal?"

Gina nodded. "Sure."

"I think someone who rented your car might be the same person who stole my backpack at a bar the other night. I noticed it missing, and I ran outside just in time to see them jump into a black Yukon. I called the police, but they said if I didn't get the license plate, they couldn't help me."

"I'm so, so sorry that happened to you. But why on earth do you think it was someone who rented my car? There are a lot of Yukons on the road."

"I guess I got lucky. I needed to rent a car for my errands, and when I logged onto Caro and saw your Yukon, I thought *that's it! That's the same car.*"

"I don't think it was *my* black Yukon."

"It would be an amazing coincidence, I know. But can you help me figure it out? Did you rent out the car on June fourth?" She didn't want to admit she'd hacked the navigation system. She suspected that would put an end to this conversation pronto.

"I'd have to check my messages."

"Do you mind?"

"Now?"

"You could give me the information, or I could have the police bring you in for an interview instead." *Too aggressive. Tone it down.*

"I'm not supposed to give out any information about my guests."

"But if you check, and it wasn't rented out that day, I can scratch your car off the list."

She scrolled through her phone. "Oh my God."

"I knew it! Who rented it that night?"

"I can't tell you. I could get kicked out of the Caro program."

She shrugged and slipped the keys out of her pocket. "I understand. I don't want to get you in trouble. It's just that this person is out there, and they might hurt someone." That much was true. "And I don't think the police are trying very hard to find them." Also true. "But if I can give them a name, they'll have to check it out."

Gina was studying her with her head tilted again, as if she were still trying to figure out if she was "Sandra Summers".

"Like I said, I'm not that girl you knew in high school. But what if I were? Would you help me then?"

Gina looked away, then began typing on her phone. After

several moments she inched closer and held the phone so Sandra could see the selfie and the driver's license photo the renter had uploaded at check-in on the night of June 4.

Sandra turned her head and stifled the urge to vomit.

FIFTY-NINE
SANDRA

Troy Laquay rented the black Yukon on June 4.

Only he couldn't have because his severed head was found in the woods on June 1.

"You were right. We should go to the police and tell them everything." Sandra shifted her position on the park bench to face Dalton. His chin was tucked, and his eyes darted about, the way they used to do when he was a child and had been caught in a lie. Suddenly, she felt uneasy about how much of what she'd just learned to reveal to her son.

He crossed his arms over his chest. "I don't know about that. Besides, I never said tell them everything. I said file a missing person report on Becky. You're the one who pointed out we would all come under suspicion for Troy Laquay's murder if the police find out what we've been up to. And, now, you've convinced me we should lay low. I say we keep looking for her on our own."

"But everything has changed. I now know, for a fact, Becky didn't kill Laquay."

"I don't share your dim view of her—I've always known my

grandmother is no killer. But what makes *you* suddenly sure she had no part in that creep's murder?"

"Because the person who tried to run Ivy down has to be the same person who murdered Laquay. And Becky would *never* hurt Ivy. She loves Ivy more than she loves *us*, her own family. She's not running from the police. And if she's not hiding from the police, then where is she? What if she's hurt, or kidnapped or..."

"Maybe it's *you* she's running from. And who's to say the cops will be convinced Becky's feelings for Ivy exclude her from Laquay's murder. If that detective realizes our connection to Becky, we'll *all* be exposed. It will give me a motive for killing Laquay. If we go to the cops now... I don't want to go to prison." His teeth were clenched tight, and his voice sounded different, like someone she didn't even know.

"But you have an *alibi*. You were in Texas." Her heart flipped in her chest. "Unless... Dalton, is there something you're not telling me? When did you first get into town? Tell me the truth."

"You really are a piece of work, Mother. First, you suspect Becky of murder, and now you accuse me."

"I didn't accuse you."

"You questioned my alibi. And if my own mother doesn't believe me, the cops sure as hell won't. Especially not with my record."

"Your juvenile record is sealed."

"They'll unseal it. You may have faith in the justice system, but I don't."

She squeezed her eyes shut. Her head was pounding. Her chest aching. He was acting like a guilty man, but he couldn't be.

He's your son.

He has an alibi.

And a dead man used a Caro app to rent a Yukon.

"I'm trying to protect *everyone* in this family. But at the moment, I'm not sure how to accomplish that." She fought back the tears that threatened and stuck up her chin.

"Then stay chill. Going to the cops is not the best way to find Becky, and it sure as hell isn't the best way to protect me. You're so damn sure of yourself. You say whoever murdered Laquay tried to kill Ivy, but you have no proof. It's just a hunch."

"It's the only logical conclusion."

"Why? Just because the navigation system shows the Yukon going to the Canyon Creek Club that night? I think you know who the driver was. I think you're the one who's not telling the whole truth."

"Why are you looking at me like that? What are you so scared of? Were you or were you not in Texas when Laquay was killed?"

His hands clenched into fists. "If you don't tell me everything you know, that means you don't trust me. And if you don't trust me, the cops will definitely think I did it."

"All I know is that a *killer* rented the Yukon. They murdered Laquay, and later, they tried to kill Ivy. The Yukon was at the Canyon Creek Club on June fourth. That's not a coincidence."

She could tell, by the look in his eyes, he knew she was holding back. And it was that very look that terrified her. It was that very look that stopped her from telling him the whole truth.

How she knew Laquay's death was murder, and not a bizarre hiking accident.

She knew because the killer had Laquay's phone.

How else could they have uploaded a dead man's selfie into the Caro app?

SIXTY

KATHLEEN

Above Kathleen, a dead street light flickered back to life, drawing attention to the spot where she'd been surreptitiously monitoring Ivy and Clayton Pinnacle for a good twenty minutes. She pressed her back against the side of a grimy tin shed. Another favorite T-shirt lost to grease stains—price of being a cop.

The night hadn't started out as a stakeout.

She'd simply wanted to get another look at the road where the incident involving Ivy Pinnacle and a black Yukon occurred. Only this time, she wanted to check it out at night, to better replicate the event's conditions. Neither Ivy nor Sandra had mentioned a flickering street lamp, so she had to assume that, on the night in question, this one had been fully operational.

The street itself was wide and unobstructed. No construction in progress.

Crossing lights at the intersection ahead and behind.

Speed limit thirty miles per hour.

A law-abiding citizen would have little chance of narrowly missing a pedestrian under these conditions. Then again, the only open business at that time of night was the Canyon Creek Club. If the driver was inebriated, that would explain it.

And then there was the question of motive. Or rather lack thereof.

Ivy believed whoever murdered Troy Laquay mistakenly thought she had something on them. But if Laquay's death was an accident, as the M.E. had ruled, that hypothesis went out the window. Then there was Dalton Steele and his one hundred sneaky photographs. But he and his half-sister had never met until a couple of weeks ago. They weren't competing for an inheritance, and while he might resent her superior financial situation, he didn't stand to profit from her death.

Clayton Pinnacle, on the other hand, did.

If someone tried to kill Ivy, Kathleen couldn't rule out either Dalton or Clayton with what she knew so far. Dalton's photographs placed him near the scene that night, and Clayton admitted to leaving the Canyon Creek Club a few minutes before the incident.

"I've seen enough." Clayton hooked his arm through Ivy's. "Let's grab a drink while we're here."

Kathleen watched Ivy and Clayton enter the club, and then waited a couple of minutes before following. From what she'd seen and overheard tonight, Clayton had brought Ivy back to the scene in order to convince her no crime had occurred. While Kathleen observed, they'd paced the street, and had taken photos with their phones. When Ivy pointed out the clear conditions on the road, Clayton noted the driver was probably drunk. He'd further argued there'd been no moon that night.

He told Ivy he'd looked it up.

So, right there on the spot, Kathleen looked it up.

The moon had been full.

Either Clayton was lying, or he had his dates mixed up, or he was really bad at Google.

Kathleen tugged her sleeves, smoothed her hair back, and stepped inside the club.

A minute later, her favorite single-mom-putting-food-on-the-table server, Suzie Palopinto, tapped her shoulder and pressed a cold beer into her hand. "On the house."

Kathleen looked toward the bar, trying to catch Cougar's eye, but his back was turned. "Tell the boss I said thanks."

"Will do. Just signal when you want another."

She couldn't hear herself think in here, much less continue to eavesdrop on Ivy and Clayton, but at least she could enjoy the band and keep an eye out for anything strange—like someone else tailing Ivy.

Maybe a half-brother with a fancy camera—was that Dalton hulking in the shadows, near the club's back door?

SIXTY-ONE

IVY

The last thing Ivy wanted to do was relive the night she nearly died. But Clayton had insisted it would be therapeutic. So they'd done a re-enactment—minus the black Yukon, Sandra shoving her to the ground, and the trip to the hospital.

In other words, they walked the street, took some pics and Clayton reassured her she wasn't in danger—she was just crazy.

Oddly enough, she felt better.

Kathleen Winthrop had a part in that, too. Ivy could tell she was good at her job. And if a bona fide police detective didn't think her case against the driver of the black Yukon had merit, then it might be time to admit her memory wasn't as iron-clad as she thought.

Memory problems and confusion are hallmarks of a concussion.

And she had been concussed.

Cougar spotted her and came over. "What's your poison, Ivy?"

"Ha ha. I'll have a greyhound," she said.

"I'm easy. Beer, please. Whatever you recommend," Clayton said.

"You got it." And then Cougar was gone—this place was busy tonight.

Clayton frowned. "You sure you're okay to drink? Doctor said to avoid alcohol and caffeine."

She rolled her eyes. Clayton was the one who'd suggested coming to the club in the first place. If she'd been in charge, they'd be home in bed watching that new documentary on space. "My symptoms have been gone a few days. I don't think one drink will hurt me. And besides, I deserve a reward."

"What for?"

"For not obsessing over those photos we found on Dalton's computer."

Again, the detective didn't seem to think it was a big deal. And it made sense that Dalton would be curious about his half-sister.

She was certainly curious about him.

At the thought of what she'd done to Dalton, her shoulders shrank. Breaking into his laptop and then asking the detective to look into his background was every bit as bad as him taking surreptitious photographs of her.

And speaking of detectives, over Clayton's shoulder, Ivy spotted Kathleen Winthrop sitting at a corner table, all by herself. Ivy was tempted to go over and ask if she wanted company, but thought better of it. She was off duty. And she might be meeting someone. Regardless, it would be an intrusion. "Huh."

"What?" Clayton asked.

"Nothing. Mind my purse. I need the ladies' room." She didn't know why she didn't mention the detective. Except that there had been that tense moment between Kathleen and Clayton earlier today, when Kathleen had called him "cold".

When she returned from the ladies', Clayton was waiting for her, a greyhound in his outstretched hand. "Sorry if I was hovering earlier. About the drink—I trust your judgment, and if you feel up to it, I don't object. In fact, finish this, and I'll buy you another. The sky's the limit for my best girl."

She took the glass and raised it in the air. "To paranoia. I'd rather be crazy than dead."

"Don't!" Kathleen Winthrop charged at her. "Put down the drink!"

Ivy froze, but Clayton reacted right away, knocking her hand.

The greyhound went flying. Cold, sticky grapefruit juice doused her neck and blouse and seeped between her breasts. She looked down and saw shattered glass on the bar, and in her lap.

"Police! Clayton Pinnacle, on your feet!"

"What the hell, Detective?" His face was stony, his voice ice-cold.

"I said on your feet! Now! Turn around! Put your hands behind your head! You have the right to remain silent."

SIXTY-TWO

KATHLEEN

Right up until the moment Kathleen got him out to the parking lot, Clayton Pinnacle was cooperative.

"What did I do?" Like a snarling wolf, he bared his teeth at her when he spoke.

But now that they were out of public view, he was letting his true colors fly. "You tell me."

Clayton was both too smart and too proud to offer resistance in a crowded bar.

People in this town knew him.

Son-in-law to a wealthy rancher, investment analyst for a national brokerage firm, chairman of the board of the Better Business Bureau. It would be hard to paint himself as an innocent victim to her vindictive cop if he fought or fled.

He thought he had enough money and power to escape the consequences of his actions—and, sadly, he might be right.

"I haven't done a damn thing! And I won't stand here and play games. I'll sue for false arrest."

"I haven't officially arrested you." But that was the plan. "What did you put in your wife's drink?"

Ivy gasped and grabbed Clayton's sleeve.

He reached for Ivy's hand, brought it to his lips and then continued to hold it. "She's out of her tree. Better call a lawyer for me and a shrink for Detective Delusional while you're at it."

"You wanna keep it up? Call me crazy like you do your wife?" Kathleen would love to detain the husband. But with the sawdust on the barroom floor currently soaking up her proof, she doubted she'd be able to hold him unless Ivy got on board with the charges. "A security camera covers the entire length of the bar."

"So?" Clayton widened his stance.

"I can get a warrant for the footage. The more you lie to me, the worse you'll look to a jury."

"Even if I did put something in her drink, she's my wife. You can't arrest me for it."

Ivy slipped her trembling fingers from his grip and backed up a few steps.

Kathleen moved in on Clayton until she could smell the liquor on his breath. "Spiking your wife's drink is a felony—just the same as if she were a stranger."

"That assumes the use of an illegal substance."

It sure did. And she had nothing to test—the drink was spilled, the glass shattered. If this were a television show, the crack crime-scene team would grab a tox report off a shred of sawdust. But this was real life. The security footage would show Clayton spike the drink, if they were lucky, and that was all the evidence they were likely to get. No harm had come to Ivy. She hadn't taken a single sip, so without a confession, there was no way of knowing if Clayton intended to poison his wife or just dope her up for his own purposes.

She could drag him down to the station, but she couldn't hold him long.

"I confess." Clayton spread his arms, beckoning his wife.

"Ivy, please forgive me. I admit I put one of your allergy pills into your greyhound. But I swear my intentions were good. You are the love of my life. I would *never* do anything to hurt you. One Benadryl won't knock you out. I thought it would take the edge off, help you get a good night's sleep. Since the day you found that bloody arm, you haven't slept through the night once. You're healing from a concussion. You need rest."

Ivy's jaw was slack, her entire body shaking. Kathleen stepped away from Clayton and closer to Ivy, in case she fainted.

"She's not well, Detective. Can we wrap this thing up? I'd like to get her home."

"To me, she looks upset—not sick. And you're not going home." Kathleen could book him. He'd be arraigned and released within hours, but at least Ivy would have time to get out of the house if she chose to do so. Kathleen could only hope she was smart enough for that.

"Please, don't arrest him." For the first time since Kathleen shouted her warning, Ivy spoke.

"You're convinced someone wants you dead, and you think the police aren't paying attention. Now your husband spikes your drink and you beg me not to arrest him? Who's not paying attention? Trust your gut, Ivy. Don't let him get away with this."

"Oh, for God's sake. Ivy knows I would never hurt her."

"Do I?" Ivy drew herself into a taller stance. "You're always pushing medication on me. Take this tranquilizer, take that one, too, while you're at it. Don't forget your antihistamine. And when I refuse, you decide to put them in my drink? If you would drug me without my consent, how do I know what else you might do?"

"If you were in your right mind, you wouldn't question my love for a second, much less give credence to this absurd accusation." Clayton clenched his fists at his sides. "What this nut- job cop is implying is that I'm trying to *murder* you."

"Are you?"

"Honey, this isn't you. This is the concussion talking."

Ivy covered her face with her hands.

Kathleen decided not to butt in. This was between a husband and wife, and her money was on the wife.

A few beats later, Ivy stuck her hands in her pockets and looked up, dry-eyed. Calm as you please—like a different person. Like a person who'd finally seen the light. "No, Clayton. This is *me* talking. As much as I'd rather be misremembering, I'm not. I was diagnosed with a mild concussion, but that's over. Detective Winthrop is not crazy, out-of-her-tree, delusional, or a nut job—and neither am I. I'm not saying it was you who tried to run me down, but *someone* did. I'm not saying you poisoned my drink, but you put *something* in it."

"I promise you, my love, it was an antihistamine. If you check my glove compartment, you'll find the bottle of Benadryl capsules. Please, go see for yourself."

"I will look in a minute, but if I find that bottle, it doesn't prove you put allergy medicine instead of some other drug in my drink. And since you knocked the glass out of my hand, we'll never know what it was. After this, why would I trust you?"

"You know me, and you know how much I love you. I knocked the glass out of your hand because the detective screamed at you not to drink it. It was a reflex, my protective instincts kicking it."

"Except you were protecting yourself, not me. But let's suppose it was just allergy medicine. If you brought it with you, and it's in your glove compartment now, that means you *planned* to get me drinking, knowing the doctor advised me to avoid alcohol. I'll check the label, but I'm pretty sure you're not supposed to mix antihistamines with liquor."

"One Benadryl, baby. Please, you're not thinking straight."

She's got this. Kathleen was enjoying this more than she'd expected.

"So, now we're back to crazy? You spike my drink, but I'm the one in the wrong." Ivy jerked her head. "Go ahead, Detective. Arrest him."

SIXTY-THREE

KATHLEEN

Kathleen glanced at the wall-clock in the Pinnacles' living room. Past 10 a.m. already. Where the hell was Officer Wadley with that warrant? Ivy Pinnacle had already loaded a small suitcase into her Mazda and seemed as anxious to be on her way as Kathleen was to get her out of the house.

Clayton Pinnacle had hired an experienced criminal attorney, and as soon as all the paperwork was done, he'd be released on his own recognizance. Though Kathleen was confident the judge would grant her application for a search warrant for the Pinnacle residence, she'd prefer to execute it without the husband creating drama.

"Can I get you anything while we wait?" Ivy asked. "Coffee? Water?"

"No, thanks." Kathleen stretched one leg out in front—happy to be sitting in a comfortable chair, facing Ivy, rather than balancing on the coffee table or drowning in that monster sectional of theirs. She couldn't wait to pull the damn thing apart and toss its cushions—just for the fun of showing it who was boss. "You're headed to your father's ranch? I think that's wise."

"I'm not afraid of Clayton."

"If you are, there's no shame in that. It's smart to play it safe. You gotta take care of yourself."

"I'm not trying to hide, but after what he did, I don't want to have to look at him—not right now."

Kathleen learned a long time ago it was better not to mince words in these situations. "Does Clayton ever hit you, or threaten you in any way? Because we can do something about that, if he does."

"No."

"You're sure?"

"I promise you. We hardly ever argue. I can count the times he's raised his voice to me on my fingers. Clayton is not quick to anger." Ivy pulled her lower lip between her teeth. "He's always been protective, but until recently, I wouldn't have called him controlling." She shook her head. "But lately... it's stifling to be around him, and what he did last night doesn't feel real. I can't help thinking I'm going to wake up any minute from a terrible dream."

Kathleen made sure to look her directly in the eyes. "Last night happened. It was as real as it gets. When you do see your husband again, don't let him tell you different."

"I won't."

"Listen, if you'd like to get going, I can have Wadley deliver the warrant to you at the ranch. I'll hang around outside until then."

"I don't mind waiting until Officer Wadley gets here. I want you to search the house. I don't understand why you can't, since I'm giving permission."

"Supreme Court says one spouse can't consent to a search of the marital home without the other spouse's consent."

"I suppose that makes sense. You will let me know when you're done? I'll feel better knowing for certain there are no drugs in the house."

Or poisons—or other evidence your husband plans to kill you.

Once the husband attempted to dope his wife, whether with Benadryl or some other substance, the chance of that near miss with the Yukon being an accident all but evaporated in Kathleen's estimation. The captain felt differently, but even he had to admit they had reason to conduct a thorough investigation into Mrs. Pinnacle's recent string of bad luck.

Ivy inched forward in her chair. "Do you think you'll find something?"

"If we didn't have good reason to think so, we wouldn't have applied for a warrant."

Ivy nodded, then her lips parted, as if she wanted to say something, but hadn't yet made up her mind.

"What about you, Ivy? You were here all night. If I were in your shoes, I would've conducted my own search. Did you have a look around? Find anything concerning?"

"I—I didn't." Her voice faltered. "That's just it. It's not what I found. It's what I didn't find."

Ivy was at war with herself. Kathleen could see the battle written all over her face. In her experience, this kind of inner struggle usually preceded a major revelation. She waited, patiently, for Ivy to make a choice—protect her husband or tell the truth.

"His crossbow." Ivy met her gaze. "He keeps it in a locked cabinet in the garage. I opened that cabinet last night, and the hunting bow and all his arrows are gone."

SIXTY-FOUR

IVY

Ivy felt like she was on a precipice, staring down into a yawning, black canyon, about to slide over the edge. Last night and today had been one big amalgamated disaster, not separated, as they should've been, by a period of sleep.

Now, at the ranch house, she didn't bother to kick off her shoes before diving onto the bed in her childhood room. She hadn't been able to close her eyes knowing Clayton had slipped something into her drink. And, as if that wasn't suspicious enough, his crossbow was missing.

How could she protect herself if she didn't know who to trust? She really needed someone to talk things over with, get some perspective. Last night, she hadn't wanted to wake Dad, so she'd waited until morning to call. But he wasn't answering his phone. Which was all the more confusing, because she'd left him texts and voicemails asking him to get in touch. She'd said it was urgent.

She hadn't even had the chance to let him know she planned to move back to the ranch until she could sort things out with Clayton. Of course, Dad would welcome her home, but she wasn't so sure he would see the incident at the club the same way she did. Clayton and Dad were close. She could envision a scenario where Dad would tell her she was making too much of it. She could even envision a scenario where he'd side with Clayton, insisting that she needed her rest.

As for the crossbow... she shouldn't jump to crazy conclusions. It might be at Dad's cabin in Payson. Maybe Clayton had decided to store it there, instead of in the garage.

Her mind was racing. She couldn't quiet her thoughts— couldn't tell if her suspicions about Clayton were rational, or the result of sleep deprivation.

She needed a nap, badly.

Her eyelids were leaden, too heavy to keep fighting... and then came the rap on the door.

A familiar rhythmic tapping that mimicked the old jingle.

Shave and a haircut, two bits.

She bolted upright.

Their secret knock! Mrs. Winters!

"Becky! Is that you?" No. There was no one here. She must've dozed off for a second. It was a dream or... a hallucination, brought on by lack of sleep and wishful thinking. Like that time she thought she heard a music box playing in her closet after Mom died.

She checked her phone.

An hour had passed. Still no messages from Dad or the detective. Did that mean the search of her house was not yet complete, or that they hadn't found anything?

Of course they won't find anything.

Except what if they did?

She imagined Mrs. Winters' special knock again. How she wished she were standing outside the door, calling: *I'm here if you need to talk.*

Her mind drifted back to childhood nights, snuggled in the tiny room with Mrs. Winters. She still couldn't understand why she'd left without saying goodbye. It was so out of character.

What if something had happened to her?

With all the chaos swirling around her, Ivy hadn't dared let her mind go there, but now that it had... she couldn't stop thinking about it.

If Becky had decided to retire, even if she couldn't face telling Ivy in person, she would've contacted her by now. There was absolutely no way she'd go this long without reaching out. It was as if she'd simply vanished into thin air.

A chill crawled down her back.

This wasn't a simple matter of a woman suddenly deciding to retire.

She leaped out of bed.

Becky might be in danger, and here she was lying around feeling frightened and sorry for herself. It was time to do something. She was going to conduct a search of her own.

Starting with Mrs. Winters' old room.

The one with the secret door.

SIXTY-FIVE

SANDRA

It was the ruckus that drew Sandra to Becky's old room. She'd been making a sandwich in the kitchen when she'd heard thumps and bumps, loud enough to make her drop a mustard-covered knife onto the floor.

Then, while she was cleaning up the mess, she'd heard screeching and scraping—like someone was rearranging furniture. When she pinpointed the direction of the noise, her heart climbed to her throat.

It was coming from Becky's room.

Not the Mountain Room, but that tiny dump of a bedroom her mother had occupied for nearly thirty years.

"Becky?" The door was ajar so she walked straight in, and right away her heart sank. It was only Ivy, but what was she doing in here? "Sorry I didn't knock, but the door was open. I didn't know you were... I thought Becky was back."

Ivy's eyes were glassy and red around the rims. A blue and gold NAU sweatshirt was riding high, showing her flat belly above her jeans. Beads of perspiration dotted her upper lip. Her hair was mussed, and her jeans rumpled—like she'd slept in them.

"Are you okay?" Sandra was still reeling from the dashed hopes of finding Becky safe and sound, moving her things back into her old crappy bedroom.

Ivy tugged her shirt down and slumped against the tall chest of drawers, which for some reason jutted out into the room, perpendicular to the wall. "Not really."

"I'm here if you need to talk." Surprisingly, she meant that. Sandra's life had been rough, whereas Ivy's had been cushioned by wealth and privilege. But money hadn't turned Ivy into an entitled brat like it might've. Patsy and Becky deserved some of the credit for that, no doubt, but Ivy did, too. Sandra sensed an innate goodness about her—something born rather than bred into her.

"I could use someone to talk to. I... I hope I can trust you." Ivy had such a lost expression in her eyes.

Sandra's throat closed out of pure guilt. Who would take advantage of such an innocent young woman? She didn't like herself much at the moment. "How can you? You hardly know me."

"You saved my life, and frankly, I have no one else to turn to. Besides, I have a feeling it's the right thing to do."

"Why do you say you have no one else to turn to? I would think you could turn to your husband. Did something happen between you and Clayton? Is that why you're here instead of at home?" Sandra locked eyes with her, daring her to duck the question.

"It's a long story."

Sandra sat on the bed and patted the quilt—hoping Ivy would sit with her and they could have a real conversation. She might not deserve Ivy's trust, but she wanted to help. "Ivy, what's happened? Have you and Clayton argued?"

At last, Ivy settled down beside her. "Clayton's in jail."

The words jabbed, like an upper cut to the jaw. But she did

her best to keep her expression neutral, her voice even. "Tell me what happened. Take your time and go slow."

"I'm ashamed to say it, but my husband duped me. Last night, he put something in my drink at the Canyon Creek Club. Kathleen Winthrop was there. She saw the whole thing and arrested Clayton. Now I'm wondering if this is the first time he's done something like that—there have been times I've felt confused or woozy to the point I haven't been able to trust my memory. And there's more—I'm awfully worried about Mrs. Winters."

When Ivy finished her story, Sandra took her by the hand. "Thank you for trusting me with all of that. I'm honored."

"Thank you for hearing me out, and for not dismissing me. I can imagine what Clayton would say if I told him I think Becky might be in danger. He'd blame it on my pills or call me paranoid."

"Pills he's been feeding you. And if it helps, I don't think you're being paranoid about Mrs. Winters. I was surprised she left without notice. It never made sense." Sandra weighed her next words carefully. She'd always been uneasy about Clayton, but she hadn't pegged him as a bad husband. And if she'd been wrong about that, what else was he capable of? Could he be behind Laquay's murder? If so, that would let Dalton off the hook, but it made her all the more worried about her mother. If Clayton had killed Laquay, and Becky found out, somehow...

She drew in a sharp breath, noticing something she should've seen earlier.

Where the chest of drawers normally stood, a dingy line outlined a door in the wall. Her mouth dropped open. "Is that a door?"

"To a secret room," Ivy said. "I've known about it since I was a little girl. I was about to have a look inside when you came in. Should we go check it out together?"

"I just got chills. You know that book *The Lion, the Witch and the Wardrobe?*" Sandra crossed to her side.

Ivy's lost expression changed into something... dreamier. "Mom used to read it to me. But, unfortunately, that door is not the gateway to Narnia. It leads to a small room, a remnant from when they converted the old laundry area into a bedroom." She cranked the handle and pushed.

The door creaked open.

Ivy patted around on the wall, and suddenly an old glass light fixture came to life. Sandra blinked, then toed her way inside, wary of rats or bugs until she saw the relatively clean tile floor in what appeared to be a narrow hallway. They turned a corner, and her heart sped up.

Ivy gasped.

SIXTY-SIX

IVY

A pile of worn blankets.

A single pillow.

Water bottles stacked in the corner.

An empty box of granola bars.

There was even a broom leaning against one wall.

It had surprised Ivy to find the light working and the room free from cobwebs.

Now she understood.

Ivy picked up a gray fabric scrunchie, the kind Mrs. Winters wore on her wrist in case she needed to secure her hair for some chore or the other. "I think Mrs. Winters has been sleeping here. Why else would the room be tidy? Someone had to put a new bulb in that light fixture. No one except Mom, Becky and me knew about this room. And see that scrunchie? The trousers? Those are Becky's things."

"She's been hiding in here the whole time." Sandra's face was white, her voice a mere whisper. "I wonder if she comes out at night for supplies."

Hiding. "I suppose that's possible. When I moved the chest, out from the wall, I noticed there was already plenty of space—enough for a small person to squeeze behind." The chest had clearly been moved farther out than usual. Having once gotten stuck behind it, she would know. "The door opens toward the inside of the secret room. So if Becky wanted to, she could get in and out without having to move the chest. She knows this house and everyone's habits like the back of her hand. If anyone could sneak around without getting caught, it's her."

Their eyes met.

What was Becky afraid of? If she'd been sleeping in this hideaway, she must've been frightened of something, or *someone*. "It's a relief, in a way—I don't see any signs of a struggle, no blood... thank heavens! But it doesn't make sense. If she's in some sort of danger, why hide out in this room? Why not just leave?"

"I can think of two reasons." Sandra crumpled onto the pile of blankets. "First, she has no money and nowhere else to go."

Ivy felt sick at the idea of Becky, alone and frightened, with no means to escape whatever danger was chasing her. "Dad said he deposited a large bonus directly into her account."

"Obviously, your father lied."

She swallowed back her protest. She didn't think he'd lied. Becky left a note. Dad had no reason to think she was hiding from them. He probably put money in her account, but she didn't know. "What's the second reason?"

"She's sticking around to protect someone."

Her breath caught.

Me. She believes I'm in danger.

I am in danger—and Becky's been risking her own personal safety to watch over me.

Ivy lowered herself beside Sandra, and in the process banged her wrist against something hard. She dug under the blankets and extracted the offending object—a small mahogany box, inlaid with mother-of-pearl.

A secret box in a secret room.

This box might contain evidence or an important clue.

The question was, with so many people lying to her, could she face what she found if she opened it?

SIXTY-SEVEN

SANDRA

Sandra was in over her head and she knew it. In the beginning, she'd been so hungry for a better life for Dalton, so mad at the world over the things that had been unfairly ripped from her, she hadn't considered how her plan to con money out of Richard Kane might affect his daughter and other innocent people.

She hadn't considered how much she might grow to care for Ivy.

Or how hard it would be to look herself in the mirror every morning.

And she definitely hadn't considered the possibility that *true evil* might be afoot at the Flagstaff Kane Ranch—or that she might be aiding and abetting it.

But after Troy Laquay, the Yukon, and the dead man's Caro rental, there was no denying it—she'd become a pawn in a dark, dark game... and it seemed Becky had, too.

I have to find her before it's too late.

At this point, she no longer believed her mother killed Troy Laquay—either by design or by accident. Becky wouldn't have stuck around the ranch if she had. No, whoever rented that Yukon murdered Laquay.

And, somehow, Becky knew their identity.

Sandra had an unshakeable feeling her mother was trying to stop the killer from striking again. If there was one thing Sandra understood about Becky, it was that she considered it her job to fix other people's problems. And even though that made Sandra want to punch her fist through a wall, her anger at Becky would have to wait until *after* they found her safe and sound.

"Should we open the box? There might be a clue inside," Ivy said.

There could also be damning information about Sandra, but she no longer cared. "What are you waiting for?"

Ivy looked at her. "I'm going to open it. Of course I will. But I feel bad about invading Mrs. Winters' privacy."

And that was the difference between them. Sandra had no compunction about skirting the rules when it served her purpose. Maybe she'd take a page from Ivy's book in the future. But now was not the time to be constrained by the rules of etiquette. "I'll do the honors if you want."

"No. I don't mind taking responsibility. It might help us find her. We have a *duty* to look." Ivy opened the box.

From over Ivy's shoulder, Sandra could see a group of old photographs inside.

Ivy lifted the first one: Sandra as a baby, with a bow, almost bigger than her head.

Ivy flipped the photo over. On the back, someone had scribbled: *Sandra at nine months. Look at that bow!*

Wordlessly, Ivy examined the others, and then passed them on to Sandra. Some had inscriptions, some did not—but the milk was spilt now.

Here was Sandra in a frilly pink party dress blowing out six candles.

There was preteen Sandra sticking out her tongue.

Next came Sandra posing stiffly on the porch in front of their dilapidated house, her prom dress too tight around the belly—her beau staring into the camera like a dead man walking.

Beside her, she could hear Ivy's breathing growing more ragged by the minute.

Tears pricked Sandra's eyes but she would not let them fall.

All these years, her mother kept these. It was plain to see that she had once been the center of her mother's universe—and for the first time in forever, she felt like she still was.

Ivy's breathing seemed to stop.

Silence flooded the room, like water, threatening to drown them both. Sandra needed air, and there was only one way to get her head above her emotions. She had no choice but to tell the truth. There was far too much at stake. "Ask me whatever you want. I won't lie to you anymore."

"Why does Becky have all these pictures of you?" Ivy whispered.

"Mrs. Winters, Becky, is my mother." Her chest heaved, not with fear, but with pride. "What else?"

Ivy's hand went to her throat. "She's my *grandmother*?"

"No." Sandra spit out her answer before yet another lie could take root. "I'm sure she'd love that, but it isn't true. Becky, Richard and I have been lying to you this entire time."

SIXTY-EIGHT

SANDRA

"I-I don't understand," Ivy said.

The look on Ivy's face made Sandra want to curl up with a bottle of whiskey and forget she was the person responsible for causing her all this pain. If she hadn't shown up on Ivy's doorstep, none of this would've happened.

Not true.

She had to own her part in it, but Sandra wasn't responsible for Laquay's death.

His *killer* was.

And if Sandra had never darkened their door, Clayton would still be manipulating and controlling Ivy—keeping her world too small and her mind confused.

Richard would still be hiding the truth about her adoption from her.

No more lies.

Sandra was done with that. She owed Ivy the truth—she owed that to herself, too.

She didn't know everything, but she would tell Ivy all that she did. "Patsy and Richard adopted you. That much is true. But I'm not your biological mother."

Ivy was squinting at her, as if she didn't believe her. "In this photo, you look like you might be pregnant. I think I see a baby bump."

"You're right." Sandra swallowed back her tears. The truth was hard, but she was determined to tell it. "I did give birth as a teen. But I am *not* your mother, and that boy beside me is not your father. That's *Dalton's* father."

"Your ex-husband?" Ivy whispered the question.

"No. My ex, Jonathon Steele, married me three months before Dalton was born. I listed him as the father on Dalton's birth certificate. Legally, and in every other way, Jonathon Steele *is* my son's father. Even after we divorced, he was there for Dalton—until he couldn't be. The man you see in this picture, Dalton's *biological* father, is Jimmy Reeves." She paused. "Jimmy was the frigging love of my life. That story I told you about your bio dad, including the name, Michael Smith, was mostly made up. But I did base it *loosely* on Jimmy and me. The important thing to understand is that I have zero information about your family of origin. If I did, I'd hand it over."

"You lied to me!" Ivy rose on her haunches, her chin trembling. Then, she held up one palm and collapsed back into a sitting position. "And *Dad* lied to me. He knows you're not..."

"Richard knows Laquay hired me to impersonate your birth mother. But no one knew, not Laquay or anyone else, except Dalton and me, that Becky is my mother."

"But *why* did Laquay hire you? I can't believe Troy would do that on his own. This can't be true." Ivy began shaking her head, back and forth, back and forth—one long, continuous attempt to deny what she obviously didn't wish to believe.

"Laquay claimed *Patsy* put him up to it. I believed him, at first, but now I'm not so sure."

Ivy drew in a sharp, audible breath, then stared at her,

unblinking. She went so still, Sandra wondered if she'd heard what she'd said. Was she even breathing anymore?

"*That* is a lie," Ivy said, finally. Her voice had turned to hardened steel— its edge could cut glass. "If Laquay said Mom told him to hire you, or anyone else, to play the role of my birth mother, he was *lying*. She left me a letter. She *wanted* me to find my birth mother. And more importantly, she loved me. She would *never* do such a thing. Not my mother. Do you hear me?"

As uncomfortable as it was to have that combination of fire and ice in Ivy's eyes directed at her, Sandra was glad. Ivy *should* get angry, not only with Sandra, but with *everyone* who'd deceived her. "It doesn't make sense to me, either. I don't know who's telling the truth anymore. What I do know is that Becky recommended me to Laquay. She told him I was an actress, but like everything else, that was a complete lie. Like I told you at our lunch, I'm a teacher's aide at the school for the blind in Fort Worth, and at night, I wait tables. Dalton has a decent relationship with Becky, but for decades, she and I barely spoke. Let's just say my teenage pregnancy did not bring us closer together. For the past few years, since Jonathon got sick, Dalton's been in and out of trouble—he's particularly fond of picking fights with guys twice his size. I can't imagine what you must think of me, or of Becky, but I promise neither of us wanted to hurt you."

"Then why did you?" Ivy's chin was high, her spine straight.

Sandra had expected her to break down sobbing or possibly faint. But Ivy was tougher than she'd given her credit for. The more Sandra threw at her, the tougher she seemed to become.

If Sandra were Ivy's mother, she'd be damned proud. "Because I wasn't thinking about the consequences to you. I needed money. I want to send Dalton to the University of Texas. He's super smart and a fantastic photographer. He wants to study journalism, and he deserves a chance for a better life than the one I've given him. My ex, Jonathon, got sick with leukemia. He's in remission at the moment, but his medical bills bankrupted him. Jonathon doesn't have a dime left to help out with expenses. All my life, I've played by the rules. Until now, I earned my money the honest way. But it isn't enough. It never has been."

"So, even though it meant lying to me, Becky wanted you to get money for Dalton's school."

"She didn't seem to think she could stop what was happening. Somehow, she talked herself into believing it was for the best. That your parents only wanted to protect you."

"But you don't believe that."

"I do not." Sandra covered her mouth in shame. "I'm so sorry, Ivy. I wouldn't blame you for disbelieving every word I say, but I am telling you the truth now. Please don't hate me."

Ivy was calm. Too calm. Sandra wanted her to cry or yell or pummel her with her fist. But none of that happened.

"I don't hate you," Ivy said evenly. "You lied to me, but *yours* isn't the betrayal that stings the most. What you did was wrong, so wrong. But in a way, I'm in your debt."

Her composure was stunning. Was she in shock?

"If it hadn't been for you, I might never have known I have another family out there somewhere—and I *will* find them. I have a right to know who they are. And I wouldn't have known how treacherous my own husband can be. I would've gone on believing the sun rose and set with Dad, believed every word out of his mouth—and Becky's. She did what she thought was right for you and Dalton, I suppose. But she was like a second mother to me." Her hands were relaxed on her lap, her gaze unflinching, and proud. "I deserved better from *all* of you."

Ivy's phone buzzed.

With a rock-steady hand, she lifted it to her ear. "Yes, I'm okay. Did you find anything?"

Ivy nodded slowly, then dropped the phone.

Sandra had been waiting to see a crack in Ivy's new-found titanium veneer, and now, she did. Ivy's eyes were wide, her pupils dilated.

"What is it?" she asked.

"That was Detective Winthrop. Clayton has been released from jail."

"You expected he would be." So why was *this* the news that made Ivy's voice tremble? "What is it, Ivy? What's happened?"

"Kathleen told me to stay at the ranch and lock the doors and windows. She's sending a patrol car over. Clayton was released from jail *before* they completed the search of our house. Now, they want to bring him back in. They found..." She paused, drew in a long breath, clearly struggling with her next words.

"Take your time, go slow."

"They found a cell phone in Clayton's gym bag—it's Troy Laquay's. She thinks *Clayton* murdered Laquay. She thinks he might be on his way here. Looking for me."

Sandra catapulted to her feet.

"Where are you going? We're supposed to stay here and wait for the patrol car," Ivy said.

"Becky disappeared the same night Laquay was killed—she might've seen something. She must know something she shouldn't. We can't trust *anyone*, and we know Clayton is dangerous. He's free and she's in the wind—I've got to find my mother before something terrible happens."

She was already at the secret door with Ivy right behind her.

"It's not safe outside. Lock all the doors," Sandra said. "Wait for the police. And whatever you do, do not let Clayton in. Call Winthrop back and tell her everything I just told you."

"No. You need a driver—you don't even have a car," Ivy

said. "You can call Detective Winthrop after we get on the road. You'll tell her everything yourself."

Sandra didn't slow down. She didn't have time to stand still. "It's not safe. I can't let you come with me."

"You can't stop me." Ivy's breath was on the back of her neck. "I don't care what she's done. Becky is still family."

If only there were a way to outrun all the lies. To speed past the hurt, the betrayal from those she loved best, and start life over on her own terms. Ivy smashed her foot against the pedal, and her Mazda SUV surged forward. The speedometer read 50 mph, but she couldn't keep this up long. Ahead, steep downhills and sets of treacherous hairpin turns awaited.

But nothing was more treacherous than the killer targeting them.

Clayton?

Evidence was piling up against him, but what about Dalton and all those creepy photos he'd taken of her? Dalton had been in Flagstaff much longer than he'd claimed, and he'd been at the club the night someone tried to run her down.

Clayton was there, too.

Her jaw ached from clenching her teeth and she forced herself to relax it.

Keep cool.

You need to focus. Becky's life might depend on it.

Out of her peripheral vision, she noted that Sandra, who'd

just hung up with Detective Winthrop, had removed her seat-belt, apparently to search for her dropped phone. "Buckle up, please."

Sandra held up her mobile with one hand and yanked the shoulder strap with the other.

Ivy heard her seat belt click into place.

"I'm all for speed," Sandra said, "but let's figure out where we're going. I've got Dalton covering the downtown area. I say you and me head toward the San Francisco Peaks."

"Great minds. And I have a gut feeling about this. If Becky left the ranch, but she's still in the area, the first place I'd try is Lockett Meadow."

"Sorry to say, but you probably know my mother better than I do. I'm glad you came along. What's special about Lockett Meadow?"

"It was Mom's favorite hike, and we scattered her ashes there. I know Becky likes to go up to the meadow to think—she told me it makes her feel close to Mom." Ivy flicked her gaze to the rearview.

"Whoa. Take it easy," Sandra said.

Pulse revving, Ivy took a long breath, forcing her eyes back to the road in the nick of time to slow down for the first hairpin turn. "I think that's Clayton's Porsche."

"I think you're right—and dammit, he's gaining on us! How the hell did he get behind us?" Sandra asked.

"If he was headed for the ranch, he might've followed us from the turn-off. I need to keep my eyes on the road. This section is tricky as hell. Can you turn around for a better look? It's not like he has the only fire-engine red Cayenne in Flagstaff."

She'd seen at least one or two others around town. But she wouldn't bet their lives this was one of them.

"It's definitely him," Sandra said. "Now he's waving out the window for us to pull over."

"Oh, hell no. Call nine-one-one. No—call Kathleen again."

"Great plan, if only I had service." Sandra grabbed Ivy's cell from the console. "You got no bars either. What should we do?"

Ivy let up on the gas and put her hands at ten and two on the steering wheel. Clayton's Porsche SUV could both outrun and outmaneuver her Mazda—no question. She'd barely slept last night, and all day her eyelids had been threatening to close against her will—but the good news was, Sandra's revelations earlier, and the sight of Clayton's car in the rearview mirror, had gotten her adrenaline pumping. She was wide awake now, her heart turbocharged, her brain firing on all cylinders. The life and death stakes of their situation had sharpened her thoughts into a surgeon's scalpel. "Depends on him. If he plays nice, we play nice."

"And if he plays dirty?"

"Then we play dirty. He knows this road—but not like I do. And here's a fun fact about me. When I was sixteen, Dad hired a sheriff's deputy to teach me to drive. I have a few hypothetical tricks in my tank—but I've never actually attempted any of them."

"No offense, but I'm hoping he plays nice."

Raindrops!

"Dammit." Ivy slowed to thirty. The posted speed was fifteen. She chanced another look in the rearview. "He's too close. But I can't speed up until the road straightens out. Keep trying the cell phones."

"Yep. Nothing."

The drops of rain turned to sheets of water, pouring down her windshield and slicking the roads. Ivy switched on her headlights—it was mid-day, but the sudden storm had darkened the sky. Her knuckles ached from gripping the wheel. "We're about to hit a level stretch. You up for this?"

"Do I have a choice?" Sandra eked out a laugh that didn't sound real.

"You absolutely get a say. We're in this together. So, if you want to pull over and try to reason with Clayton, hear him out, we can do that."

"I don't like that option. What's behind door number two?"

"I can try to outdrive him."

"With the tricks you learned from the deputy sheriff *at age sixteen?* The ones you've never tried in real life?" Sandra turned her head. Sighed. Then reported back. "He's speeding up, like he wants to get beside us, maybe run us off the road. I'm up for dirty driving if you are."

And here came the widest, most protected part of the road-way. *Thank goodness.* But she couldn't accelerate too quickly, for fear of hydroplaning. Taking it nice and easy, she increased her speed.

Behind her Clayton took the bait.

Then, as he zoomed forward, she decelerated slowly.

There was no time to second-guess herself.

Any minute, the road would narrow and bend.

Time seemed to slow as she checked ahead and behind to be sure there were no other cars. It was one thing for Sandra and her to chance it, but she wouldn't risk another motorist becoming collateral damage.

Clayton's Cayenne pulled beside her.

He mouthed something at her.

She eased up on the gas.

The Mazda's nose rolled into position near the Cayenne's rear wheel—perfectly aligned for the special police maneuver she'd learned from the deputy.

Now!

She jerked the wheel, tapped his bumper, then hit the gas.

His Porsche spun out.

Over the roar of her pulse pounding in her ears, she heard the squeal of tires and then Sandra's victory scream. "You are such a badass!"

Her breath blasted out, as if from an air cannister.

Clayton's Porsche landed on the road's shoulder, facing the opposite direction. She whooped and pumped her fist, then watched the Cayenne getting smaller in her rearview mirror.

SEVENTY

SANDRA

If only Sandra could fast forward in time to the moment they found Becky, she'd tell her how much she loved her.

Please let her be safe.

At least they'd gotten Clayton off their tail. With any luck the cops had picked him up and were grilling him right this minute. But seeing as how Becky had been hiding out in a secret room, it was hard to feel good about her mother's judgment.

Sandra prayed she wasn't up to something dangerous.

They didn't know where Becky was—they'd been driving for hours based on a hunch. A good hunch, but still, it was only a guess. And although the cops liked Clayton for Laquay's murder, Sandra couldn't help thinking Richard was still in the mix—he'd lied to Ivy, and he had a solid motive for wanting to be rid of Laquay. No telling what skeletons a man like Richard had in his closet—and if anyone would know about them, it would be her mother, his longtime housekeeper.

Please, please don't do anything stupid, Becky.

She opened her window and breathed in the scent of pine and fresh mountain air, willing her mother to be picking flowers in Lockett Meadow, enjoying the kind of brilliantly beautiful day that follows a summer rain. But she kept imagining her with Richard, confronting him over some dark secret only the two of them knew. "Too much wind for you?"

"No," Ivy said. And that was about as lengthy a response as Sandra had gotten out of her for quite a while.

The drive from Sunset Crater up Forest Road 552 to the Lockett Meadow parking lot was maddening. Sandra had long since given up checking for a cell signal, and even though the storm had passed, the constraints of a tight-cornered single-lane road made it impossible to speed.

"You doing okay?" Ivy's silent treatment was killing her. She wanted them back on the same team.

"Mm."

"It's gotta be hard for you to hear that the cops think Clayton killed Laquay."

"Dammit." Ivy jerked the wheel to avoid an oncoming car on the narrow road.

Sandra had just about made peace with Ivy's reticence when she added, "It *is* tough. Even if Clayton is guilty, and we don't know for sure that he is, I can't believe I forced him off the road like that. What if he's badly hurt?"

"Sweetie, he was driving recklessly. He nearly forced *us* off the road, and the police warned us he was dangerous. You did the right thing. It's good that you feel badly about it, though. I'd be worried if you didn't."

"Thanks. I needed to hear that. It's not easy to figure out the right thing to do when it comes to people you love."

"*We* did what we had to do. We both agreed the best thing was to play dirty. Listen, Ivy. I know I hit you with a lot. But if we're going to find Becky, and figure all of this out, we need to trust each other."

Ivy let out a sigh. "Agreed. And I do trust you with my life. I'm just not sure I trust you to tell the truth."

"I don't know how to fix that, except to keep telling it. So here goes. There's something on my mind I haven't voiced, for fear of offending you. I worry you're in denial about Richard."

"How so?"

"If Clayton murdered Laquay, why do you think he did it? Those two had no beef that we know about. If Laquay was killed because he knew too much, who would benefit? I don't think the answer is Clayton."

"I see where you're going with this. You think Dad had a role in it. But you're wrong. My father isn't capable of such a thing."

"And yet Clayton is? All I'm saying is we need to be careful. I trust you. You trust me. That's it."

Ivy scoffed. "Like I said, I trust you with my life—only because you've already saved it once. But I'm still not sure you're telling the whole truth."

"I'll take it." *For now.*

Ivy slowed and veered into the parking lot. "We'll have to hike into the meadow from here. But I think our day is about to improve."

"I sure hope so. What's up?"

"That Jeep over there belongs to the ranch—Becky's the only one I know who has the keys. Her car is on its last legs, and Dad lets her use the Jeep for errands," Ivy said.

As they climbed out of the Mazda, Sandra's knees nearly gave way from the relief. They hadn't come all this way for nothing, and in a matter of minutes, she would be hugging Becky.

And there was more good news: Sandra had bars. She sent the message to Kathleen she'd typed out more than an hour ago and scanned the horizon.

Then, before she could slam the passenger side door, Ivy came around, reached in the glove compartment and pulled out a handful of scrunchies. She passed half of the colorful bands to Sandra.

"No thanks," she said.

"Take them." Ivy stuffed her half into her jeans pocket. "They're not for your hair. We'll attach them to branches along the way. When the cops get your message, they might come looking for us. Signal isn't reliable out here so I figure we better leave them a trail of bread crumbs."

"Smart," Sandra said, and then suddenly, her heart plummeted.

She'd spotted her mother's beat-up car parked in the very last row of the lot—Becky must've had it hidden near the ranch in case she needed to make her getaway.

Which meant she hadn't driven that Jeep up here to Lockett Meadow after all.

"Ivy, didn't you say no one else has the keys to the ranch's Jeep?"

"Yeah. Only Becky... and Dad, of course."

SEVENTY-ONE
KATHLEEN

Kathleen didn't love the bruise blooming on Clayton Pinnacle's left cheekbone. As she took her place across the table from him in the interview room, she frowned at it. Last thing she needed was to get a confession, only to have it disputed on the grounds he was confused due to his injuries. "You're sure he's been medically cleared?"

Officer Wadley shrugged. "Never even lost consciousness. But the uniform on the scene called the paramedics anyway. They transported him to Flagstaff Samaritan on a spine board as a precaution. Report I got says the trauma team cleared him, and then kicked him back to us in short order—lucky us."

Lucky indeed. It wasn't often she put out a BOLO and in such short order got her perp delivered up on a silver platter, or in this case on a spinal board. "You read him his rights?"

"Yeah," Wadley said.

"He's had an opportunity to confer with his attorney?" She turned to Odell Atkinson, one of Flagstaff's best criminal lawyers.

"He has." Odell Atkinson loosened his tie, then ran a finger between his neck and shirt collar.

"And, Mr. Atkinson, you're satisfied with Mr. Pinnacle's mental status?" She wanted that on the record.

"I am. Nice to see you, Kathleen. How are Danny and Dr. Sky?"

"Mom and Dad are well. Thanks. You stalling or buttering me up?"

"The latter. No stalling on our part. My client's eager to talk, but we want immunity."

She scoffed. "I bet. What murderer doesn't?"

"I didn't kill anyone." Clayton slumped in his chair. His dark, wavy hair, usually one of his finer features, was definitely the worse for wear—caked and clumped from sweat and dirt, bundles of it drooping over his eyes. "You can't pin this on me."

Odell put his hand on Clayton's shoulder. "Don't speak again until I say so."

"You've been informed your client is the prime suspect in Troy Laquay's murder?" Kathleen asked.

Clayton grunted. "I didn't do it."

"No?"

Odell smiled, unfazed by Clayton's disregard of his instruction. He was no doubt used to that from his clients. "If Mr. Pinnacle did not participate, in any material way, in the murder of Troy Laquay, and if he has information that leads you to the killer, then can we expect immunity in return for his truthful testimony?"

"That's a lot of *if*'s, but sure. I expect the D.A. would strongly consider that. We need to hear what he has to say first, and if he lies, there's no deal. And we're only talking for the Laquay case. Any other crimes your client may have committed are off the table."

"Understood." Odell squeezed Clayton's shoulder. "Okay, you can talk. Make sure you answer the detective's questions truthfully."

Kathleen glanced at the camera in the corner to be sure the

blue light was flashing, indicating it was recording. The captain was next door watching the feed. "Mr. Pinnacle, did you kill Troy Laquay?"

"No."

"What was his phone doing in your gym bag?"

"Someone planted it there. I think he's trying to frame me."

"Who?"

Clayton's gaze flicked about, glancing off the camera in the corner, before settling on his attorney.

Odell Atkinson nodded the okay.

Clayton put a hand on his neck and cranked his head to the side. "Richard Kane. That's who."

Kathleen pursed her lips. With effort, she kept her forehead from wrinkling. "Your father-in-law is trying to frame you for Laquay's murder."

"Since he's the one who killed him, that's my best guess. He told me that Laquay threatened him. Tried to blackmail him over some big bad secret he'd been keeping for years. He said they got into it one day, and he hit Laquay over the head with a lamp. He loaded the body up into one of the ranch's trucks and dumped him out by the trails, to make it look like a hiking accident. He never expected a bear to rip the body apart before it was found."

Clayton's deadpan delivery of Laquay's demise turned her stomach. A lot of things about this job turned her stomach, but it hadn't stopped her, yet, from doing it. "Did Richard tell you what this secret was? The one his lawyer was trying to blackmail him over."

"Richard told me that Sandra Steele is not Ivy's biological mother. He and Laquay hired her to play the birth mother. She's an actress, I guess. They tricked her, too, in a way. They told her it was Patsy that didn't want Ivy to know who her parents were. I get the feeling there's a lot more to the story. Why the hell would Richard work that hard to keep Ivy from finding her biological parents? What secret is worth that? And worth killing Laquay over? But that's all I know… except he paid Sandra one hundred grand to go away. Put her on a plane to Paris, but she never made it past New York. She turned up again the next day. It was the hundred grand that set Laquay off. Troy said he'd been keeping Richard's secret all these years, and he never got anything except his standard fee. When I remarked that the standard fee is what a lawyer is due, Richard said Laquay thought he deserved more because he'd 'sold his soul' for him. Then Richard told me he regretted what he had to do to Troy, but what he hated more was Sandra taking his money and then breaking her word. He said his word is his bond, and her word isn't worth a damn." Abruptly, he stopped, and looked down at his hands.

Kathleen noted blood under his nails. Probably from the accident, but they should test it. "Is that all? I need everything. Otherwise, there's no deal."

"I shot Richard with a crossbow."

Dammit. The dirtier Clayton's hands were, the harder it would be to convince a jury he was telling the truth. *If* he was telling the truth. If he'd tried to kill Richard, why would she believe he wasn't the one who killed Laquay?

"You're an experienced archery hunter, from what I understand. In a club and such. You missed pretty badly."

"I didn't miss. Richard convinced me to do it. I was supposed to graze him, and that's exactly what I did. He thought if someone tried to kill him, it could rule him out as a suspect in Laquay's murder—if it came to that. Only now I see it was a two-birds-with-one-stone kind of deal, because it makes me look guilty as hell."

"Is that it? When I say I need everything, I mean *everything*. Now or never. This deal's not coming around again."

His Adam's apple worked. "Richard almost killed Ivy. *He* was the one driving that Yukon."

"This story of yours is getting pretty far out. First, Richard hires a fake family. Then he tries to run over his own daughter, who, by all accounts, he adores," she said.

"It was a mistake. When he saw Ivy in the road, he mistook her for Sandra Steele. Can I get some water?"

The captain swung open the door and handed Clayton a water bottle. "You're aware it's a crime to lie to the police."

"Yes, sir."

The captain sent her a look that clearly communicated his opinion—Clayton Pinnacle was a lying sack of it. Then he strolled out of the room, leaving her to it.

She waited a few beats before asking Odell, "Is your client ready to continue?"

As Clayton sipped his water, some of it dribbled onto his shirt. Maybe the captain had unnerved him, or it could be from fatigue. He'd spent last night in jail, and likely hadn't slept much. Then he'd been in a minor accident, which she wanted to know more about—but that could wait.

"I'm ready. Let's get this over with," Clayton said. "I can't account for Richard's actions. I can only tell you what he told me. Richard said Sandra defrauded him by taking one hundred thousand dollars and then breaking her promise. He was worried, too, that she would figure out he killed Laquay. He tried to throw her off the scent. Tried to convince her he had nothing to do with Laquay's death by pretending he wanted to come clean to the cops with the truth about their scam. He said he was playing a game of 3D chess with her—but in the end, Richard didn't trust Sandra to keep her mouth shut."

"Can we back up a minute? Where and when did Richard Kane relay all of this to you?"

"Some of it the day Ivy and Sandra found Laquay's arm. And the rest at the Canyon Creek Club—just before he almost ran over Ivy by mistake. He said he'd set up a test for Sandra, and if she failed, he'd have to kill her."

"What kind of a test?"

"He left a planner with his schedule where she could find it —but only if she was spying on him. He notated a very important meeting at the Canyon Creek Club. He figured if Sandra showed up, skulking around, that would prove he couldn't trust her. If he couldn't trust her, he had to kill her. He explained how he rented a Yukon using Laquay's license. I don't know how he got into his phone, but he probably made the poor guy give him the code before he killed him. That night, when he met me at the bar, we both saw Sandra sneaking around outside. She was dressed all in black, with a hoodie pulled around her face. He told me he was going to run her down like a dog."

"I want to make sure I understand what you're saying. You claim Richard was trying to kill Sandra because of what she knew, and because she took advantage of him. But he mistook Ivy, who was, I will grant you, also dressed in all black, for Sandra. It was a case of mistaken identity."

"Right."

"It's one thing to be an accomplice *after the fact*, in Laquay's murder. But Richard Kane told you he was going to run down a woman on the street, and you did nothing to stop him."

"Only because I didn't believe he'd go through with it. I swear on my life. The way he told it, what happened with Laquay was more accident than murder. Richard's not a killer— I mean, that's what I thought at the time. I didn't want him to go to prison. He's Ivy's father—if she lost him, on top of losing Patsy, I worried she wouldn't recover from it."

"If you're so concerned about your wife, why dope her drink? You have to make me understand that, if you expect me to believe you care about her."

"I still had faith in Richard, and up until today, I was trying to help him. After the Yukon, Ivy was so scared someone was out to get her that she wasn't sleeping—but she wouldn't take any pills. And she wouldn't go to counseling. Richard and I both thought it would be easier on her if she believed she was misremembering how it went down. That she was confused because she had a concussion. And of course, it would be better for everyone if it seemed like a random accident. We talked about, you know, gaslighting her—just a little. Making her feel loopy and foggy-brained. That's the reason I opened up an allergy capsule and dumped it into her drink. I wish to hell I hadn't, but I did."

"And what about today? What were you doing out near the ranch?"

"I was trying to get to Ivy—to beg her forgiveness."

"Were you going to warn her about Richard?"

"No. Even this morning, I didn't believe he was capable of hurting Ivy."

"And what about now?"

"Now, he scares the devil out of me. After I heard you found Laquay's phone in my gym bag, I realized Richard was setting me up to take the blame for *everything*. Laquay, the crossbow incident, the Yukon. I love Ivy. And for her sake, I wanted to protect her father, despite everything he'd done. But he tried to frame me for murder, knowing how much that would hurt Ivy. I believe he *thinks* he loves her... but Richard Kane doesn't know what real love is."

"What proof do you have of any of this?" Her gut told her he was being truthful, but she didn't believe in going by her gut alone. She needed evidence.

"Ivy and Sandra sent off DNA swabs. When the results come back, they should prove what I said about Sandra being a phony. Once she knows the game's up, I think she'll confirm what I told you about Richard and Laquay hiring her."

In fact, on the phone earlier today, Sandra had already told Kathleen the story about the fake family.

But Kathleen needed more.

Clayton coughed, a rattly cough, and looked to his lawyer.

"My client is willing to take a polygraph," Odell said.

"We'll set it up." Kathleen nodded in Wadley's direction. "Put out a BOLO for Ivy Pinnacle and Sandra Steele. They phoned in earlier, but they're no longer answering my calls. If what Mr. Pinnacle says is true, then neither one of them is safe. Not as long as Richard Kane is on the loose."

SEVENTY-TWO

I see you, Becky.

It rained earlier, but now, the storm's blown over. At such high altitude, the air is thin, and the sun seems hotter. The sky seems bluer. In this windless hour, Lockett Meadow's placid pond is like a mirror. In it, I see the reflection of the San Francisco Peaks... and your troubled face. It's no surprise, Becky, that you chose this place, among the lupine, the penstemon, the yellow columbine.

Like my Patsy, you are predictable.

My footfalls, across damp grass, release the scent of crushed flowers, but they are too soft to be heard. It is only when I'm quite near that you spot my face reflected in the pond and turn.

"I think she's happy here, Richard."

As poetic as it would be, I can't do it here, where we scattered Patsy's ashes. The meadow is frequented by tourists and locals alike. But the spot I have in mind will be close enough for symmetry. "I know she is, Becky. Our Patsy loved this time of year best, early summer when the wildflowers bloom."

I don't ask where you've been. I'm looking forward to hearing what story you'll invent to explain your absence, though

I know very well you've been hiding in the room behind the secret door, all along.

You've taken so long to venture outdoors, away from the ranch, I was beginning to worry I'd have to kill you there. I don't mind being patient, though. I've been putting you off until the last possible minute. "You meant a lot to Patsy, and to me and to Ivy. You're part of our family, Becky."

"I guess you wondered where I'd gone. Why I took off like that."

"Your note explained you wanted to put yourself first for a change."

"Exactly. With Patsy gone, I thought it was time for me to make a new life. It hurt too much to say goodbye to you and Ivy—I'm sorry I wasn't brave enough. But I've really missed you both."

"And we've missed you. Finding your note on my windshield this morning was a wonderful surprise." You are bold to ask to meet me here—I'm impressed. "I hope this means you'll be coming back home, to the ranch. I promise to increase your salary. You can choose whatever furniture you like to go with your new accommodations in the Mountain Room. Extra vacation days are in order, I think. Even if you hardly use the ones you have." I play along. Let you think I don't know you've seen me for who I am.

I won't enjoy the kill—I'm not like that.

But I do love a good game of cat and mouse.

You walk toward the trees, in the opposite direction of the well-traveled Inner Basin Trail. This time of year, the aspens are getting their new leaves, green on top with pearly underbellies. They flutter in the sun, and in the wind, they chime like fine crystal.

This place is truly magical.

"Retirement isn't for me. I want my old life back, Richard. You don't have to bribe me."

"Not a bribe. You've earned a raise. I don't begrudge you."

I follow you deeper into the forest. "Where are we headed?"

"Patsy and I found a secret trail," you say with a coy smile.

Patsy never kept secrets *from me*. But I don't say so. I've come here often, over the years, with my wife. We'll have to thrash our way through tall grass and conifers. This is no trail, it's barely a foot path. Hidden and narrow. A mile or so in, we'll have to make our way single file, into a deep ravine. This spot will do very well.

Close enough for symmetry.

SEVENTY-THREE

Six Months Earlier, a cold autumn day

A mountain forest near Flagstaff, Arizona

My lovely Patsy. You and I face off in a grove of quaking aspen trees. Their lofty white trunks are crowned by a canopy of golden leaves. They hang over us like a shivering sun.

The trembling of the foliage is contagious.

I bend at the waist and place my hands on my knees, trying to still them. "Does Ivy know?" I ask.

Autumn leaves blow around us, drifting into thick, multicolored piles, intermingling with pale bark and trampled grasses. Light beams down between the trees, spotlighting you. The breeze wafting over my cheeks carries the crisp, pungent aroma of fall in the mountains.

"Ivy knows nothing," you say.

My pounding heart quiets, but only for an instant. The relief doesn't last. I've spent decades pretending the past never happened. But you won't let me hide any longer.

I understand what must be done, but I'm still resisting. Still playing mind games with myself, looking for an alternate ending. Trying to hold on to what's left of my humanity until the very last second.

There's a monster inside me, but I don't want to give in to it.

I hoped this day would never come, but deep down I knew it would. Secrets have a way of floating to the surface, like bloated corpses in a mossy pond. Now, my darkest secret has dragged itself out of the water and climbed up onto the bank.

Not a corpse at all.

My secret still lives, still breathes, still gasps air into its lungs.

Ivy can never know.

I flex my hands. Hands that have always protected you. Now, I imagine them closing around your neck. "Are you afraid, Patsy?"

"No, Richard. Are you?"

"I'm terrified. You and Ivy are my whole life. And now I have to choose between you. I can't stand the thought of losing either one of you."

"Then don't. There's another way, you know. You could tell the truth—that you paid Troy Laquay to hire a young woman, Sandra Steele, to play the part of Ivy's birth mother. I know she's a phony. You can't fool me and you won't fool Ivy."

"Why on earth would I do a thing like that?" It's too late now to make you believe me, but I have to try.

"Because you killed Ivy's father."

My breath stops. I can no longer feel my fingers.

As we circle each other, I make a feeble attempt to read your thoughts and fail. I'm glad I don't know what goes on in your brain, your heart. Faced with your essence, I could never do what must be done. "How did you find out? Was it Laquay who told you?"

"Don't blame him. In all these years, he never breathed a word to me about that poor young man. I found a note from you ordering Troy to stop me from searching for Ivy's birth parents. And that's when I remembered something. Ivy was only about two years old. A man, hardly more than a boy, showed up at the ranch. You argued with him and threw him out of the house. Then you stayed out late—I'm not sure you even came home that night. But the next morning, I found blood on your clothes. You told me you got into a fist fight with the same man at the Canyon Creek Club, and that you never wanted me to ask you about him again. I knew, in my heart, that boy was Ivy's father. They had the same eyes, Richard. I let it go, because I was afraid of losing you. And afraid of losing Ivy. I understood that boy could cost me my whole world. The honest-to-God truth is I was glad you got rid of him. But I didn't know you killed him. I realize now, I didn't want to know."

"So, this is all just a hypothesis, Patsy? You deduced it, but you have no proof. Well, you're wrong. That wasn't Ivy's father, and I didn't kill him. I never killed anyone."

Your sigh is deep. "Richard, I'm not a fool. Asking me how I found out is the same as a confession. And yes, Laquay admitted it when I told him I knew what you'd done."

"I swear that's not what happened. Please, believe me."

You shake your head. "I'll believe you when you tell me the truth. I know you well, Richard. If you lie, I'll hear it in your voice, read it in your eyes."

Perhaps there's still hope for me, for us, if I tell you everything.

No matter how small the chance, if you can hear the truth, and let us go on living our lives, I have to take it. "Ivy can never know. A young man showed up at the ranch, looking for Becky. While he was waiting for her, he saw Ivy, and then he lost it. He was shouting that Ivy was his daughter. That he never agreed to give her up. He said the mother told him she miscarried, but he could see that Ivy was his. I agreed to meet him at the Canyon Creek Club. I offered him money to go away, but he refused. I told him if we went to court, he'd never win. But he wouldn't see reason." My hands are ready but my heart has not let go of hope. I have to make you understand why I did it. What was at stake. "I invited him to spend the night in the bunk house, so we could talk more the next day. He came back to the ranch with me, and I shot him. Laquay helped me bury him and get rid of his truck."

Tears are streaming down your cheeks. You love me. I know you do.

"My God, Richard. You've lived with this all these years. That must've been terrible for you."

"Now you understand why you can never tell Ivy she's not our blood, why you *must* stop searching for her biological parents. All you have to do is drop the matter and our lives can go back to normal. I'll cancel the contract with Sandra Steele. No one will ever know."

"*We* will know. Richard, you have to go to the police. I promise, I'll stand by you. We'll get the best attorneys—you'd been drinking, and he threatened to take your child. You're coming forward on your own. You'll plead it out to the lowest possible charge, the least amount of prison time. You're a powerful man, you might even get off with probation."

"Patsy, it's not only about going to prison. I'm strong enough to withstand that. But our daughter will never forgive me for murdering her father. I'll lose Ivy forever—and that I cannot bear."

"You have to give her that chance, Richard. The lie must end, right here, right now."

I wish there were another way—not only for your sake, but for the benefit of my own soul.

Every muscle in my body tenses.

Here, today, in this astoundingly beautiful forest, I will bury my secret forever.

SEVENTY-FOUR

Lockett Meadow, near Flagstaff Arizona

The ravine is steep, and it would be easy to push you off the path, Becky. Watch you tumble to the rocks below. But if I get that close, you might do the same to me.

Is that your plan?

Are you waiting to take me by surprise?

Oh, Becky.

If you brought a weapon, as I suspect you did, I'll take it from you and use it against you. If you didn't, if you only want to talk, to make a deal of some sort, there are other ways.

I brought a knife with me, just in case.

But I doubt I'll have to use it.

At the bottom of the gorge, beside that rushing mountain stream, you won't have a chance against me. Patsy was athletic, and far younger than you, and even she was no match for me.

You're soft, small, old—it should be over quickly. If I can

avoid the knife, I won't have to hide a murder weapon—I don't want to use it, but if I must, I won't hesitate.

I could strangle you, like I did Patsy—although without Troy to help me cover up, that might not be advisable. Patsy's injuries, after we shoved her car off the cliff, obscured the signs of strangulation. But I can't do that now.

It might be best to simply hit *you* over the head with a rock. Another hiking accident. *Oh my, this terrain is dangerous.*

Regardless of how I do it, you will be out of the way.

I've gotten away with this before, and I will again.

In the real world, it only takes a trick or two to mislead the cops.

"It's beautiful." You look up at the sky with tears in your eyes. "Let's stop and rest."

We're on a precipice. "Can't you keep going? It's not much farther, and think how refreshing that stream will be when we get to the bottom. I can practically feel it splashing between my toes. We can take off our shoes and wade in, like Patsy loved to do."

You draw in a quick breath.

"I mean, anytime we came upon a mountain stream, she had her boots off in a flash."

"You've been here before, Richard. Why didn't you say so?"

No real reason to lie to you at this point. We have to stop playing the game sooner or later. When that moment comes is up to you. "I didn't want to spoil it for you since you thought it was your and Patsy's secret trail. But I confess the two of us came here a few times."

"What else do you want to confess?" Your tone takes a turn.

"Let's keep moving, shall we?"

"What else do you want to confess?" Now, you look at me with hard eyes. The hatred I read in them takes me by surprise.

"Are we going to do this here?" It's not my preference, but I can take you, precipice or no precipice. You're a fool if you believe otherwise. And you're a *damn* fool if you think I'll spill my guts so easily. Why should I? You can die curious.

You slip your hand inside your jacket and out comes a little lady-like Ruger. It's so small you could fit it in a purse. And it's pink.

Oh, Becky.

"I have nothing to confess. But it seems you do. You've been plotting my demise. You've been lying this entire time. You think I'm stupid. But, Becky, how could you possibly think I didn't know you were still at the ranch? Sneaking out at night to raid the kitchen. I built that ranch. There are no *secret* rooms— not from me. Now, be reasonable and put that gun away. Tell me what's gotten into you."

You shake your head. "*You* think *I'm* stupid. I only asked you to confess for the benefit of your own soul. Troy and I were friends. I already know everything."

I admit this is an unexpected development. You knew, and you didn't go to the cops? "How long?"

"I found out about the boy, Ivy's father, the day after you shot him. Troy was all torn up about it. He admitted he helped you bury him in the south pasture. And then you built that barn, way out there, for no good reason. Except you did have a reason, didn't you? You wanted to cement Ivy's father under the foundation."

"No comment. But if you believe that, you must be a terrible person. Becky, how could you keep quiet about a murder?"

You're crying big fat sloppy tears.

"I can't live with this anymore. Troy told me it was an acci-dent, and I believed him. He told me the boy wanted to take Ivy, and I believed him. He said you never meant to hurt him. So I kept quiet, because it wouldn't bring that poor kid back. But, after that day, I never let myself be happy. I gave up my sketches. All my pretty things."

I can't help myself. I let the sarcasm rip. "Your sketches. Those fashion drawings you used to do? I wondered why you started dressing like a nun. But you've punished yourself enough, dear. Just the same as if you'd done hard time."

"*I* didn't kill anyone." You wave the gun at me.

I consider lunging for it, but I don't think you have the guts to use it. I'm more likely to die from slipping when I go for it.

"I won't let you get away with it."

I've always liked you, Becky. You were good to Ivy. Good to Patsy. Good to me. But right now, I've lost all respect. You *did* let me get away with it. I'm not going to confess now. It's way too late to cleanse my soul. So there'd be nothing in it for me. "Put down the gun. Lay it at your feet, and then kick it over here."

Thunder cracks. Lightning flashes. Your hair lifts from the static electricity in the air.

You're a witch. A bitch.

"I'm going to kill you!" You scream like a banshee, which proves my point.

"That doesn't make sense, Becky. You'd kill me over an accident you *think* happened twenty-seven years ago? You need psychological help."

"It wasn't an accident. I didn't know that then, but I do now. I heard you arguing with Troy when I went to get my photo box from the secret room. I heard Troy say he wanted money. He said he deserved it for all he'd done for you. He said you shot that poor boy in the back of the head! And when Patsy found out"—she choked on a sob—"you strangled her. Troy helped you put *our Patsy* into the car. The two of you poured whiskey on her, and then you pushed the car off a cliff. I heard you tell Troy you were going to kill him. And I heard you tell him the reason —because he was the only person left alive who knew you killed Patsy... and that poor boy. Oh, my God. That poor boy. If only

I'd said something back then, you'd be in jail, and Patsy would still be alive."

"If you believe that, then you're the sinner. And it's too late to save your soul. I don't think you should put the gun down, after all. The best thing for everyone would be for you to put it to your temple and pull the trigger. Then this will all be over."

You raise your arm.

"Good girl."

You touch the gun to your temple.

A scream splits the sky.

I look up, and I see her, only a few yards behind, looking down on us.

Ivy!

A muzzle flash.

A deafening crack.

The stench of gun powder.

Ivy!

SEVENTY-FIVE
SANDRA

Sandra didn't remember racing down the treacherous path to the bottom of the ravine. It seemed a million years ago that she'd heard a thunderous crack, saw her mother's body fall, bounce, tumble down the side of the cliff.

Her ears still rang from the gunshot.

Her stomach roiled from the stench of smoke and blood.

"Mommy! Please, please don't die." She knelt beside her mother, then bent her face near her open mouth, felt the blessed breath of life on her cheek. She lifted her mother's wrist, and was rewarded with a faint but steady pulse. "Help! I need help over here!"

"Is he dead?" Becky tried to lift her head.

"Lie still. Your neck could be broken."

"Did I kill Richard? Tell Ivy I'm sorry. Promise you'll tell her."

Sandra's heart was pounding out of her chest, her hands were shaking, her mind racing. But this cut through the fog. Her mother had fallen from a cliff. She must be in excruciating pain, but she was worried about Ivy. "You're not going to die, because I won't let you. Now, lie still and shush."

"Don't shush me. The minute I pulled the trigger, I knew it was a mistake. I knew it would never change anything that's happened. Richard's death won't bring them back. Please forgive me. I love you so much. Where's Ivy? I need to tell her I love her. I need to confess my sins."

Her mother writhed on the rocks, agitated, confused.

If she wanted Ivy, then Sandra would get her for her—as it turned out, all she had to do was look up.

"How's she doing?" Ivy whispered.

"Ivy..." Becky tried, again, to raise her head.

"She's breathing. She keeps asking for you. And she wants to know about Richard." *Please don't let him be dead.* If her mother survived, Sandra didn't want her to have to deal with the guilt.

Ivy sat down and drew her knees to her chest. "I just left him to check on Becky. He's unconscious, but breathing. His pulse is steady. I saw it happen, Becky. I heard him taunting you. And I saw you shoot that gun straight up into the sky."

"I didn't shoot him? He's alive? Praise be." Becky raised her head again.

"You've got to keep still," Sandra said.

"If you let me talk, I will. But I will not die without telling you the truth."

"You're not going to die." This time it was Ivy who said so.

There they were. The three of them: Becky, bloody, broken, breathing fluttery breaths, flanked by Sandra on one side and Ivy on the other. Each of them grasping one of Becky's hands.

"I want to remember this. I never thought I would have such a beautiful moment. Give me a second to take it in," Becky said.

Sandra was too overcome to respond. She didn't recognize this sentimental woman.

"Take it in as long you want. We're not going anywhere," Ivy said.

"You might, after you hear what I've got to say. Richard did a lot of terrible things. I'm going to let the police tell you about most of them. But there's something you both need to hear from me. Richard killed your father, Ivy." Tears streaked down her cheeks, leaving dirty trails. "Jimmy. I'm sorry, Sandra, but Richard killed your Jimmy."

Her mother was badly injured. This had to be a delusion. "You don't know what you're saying, Mother. Richard never met Jimmy, and Jimmy is *not* Ivy's father."

"I know exactly what I'm saying. Your first baby didn't get placed with those professors in Austin, like I promised you she would. They wanted a boy, and they got one. The adoption counselor wasn't supposed to tell me. But she broke the rules. When I found out, I put the adoption agency onto the Kanes. This beautiful woman, Ivy, is your baby girl. Just like you are mine."

SEVENTY-SIX

IVY

Becky's words to Sandra echoed in Ivy's brain.

Richard killed your Jimmy.

Ivy is your baby girl.

A gossamer veil floated in front of Ivy's face, filtering the trees and sky into smudges of color, thick oily brush strokes of earthy greens and blue browns. The muffled sound of her heart beat in her ears, as if it, too, were swathed in delicate fabric.

"Ivy... where are you? Ivy..."

Richard.

She reached out to capture the floating veil, then opened her fist to find she was holding on to nothing but air.

It was an illusion.

Her whole life, up until this very moment, had been a mirage.

"Ivy... forgive me. I'm begging you. Ivy..." Richard's distant pleas pierced the air.

He was fighting for his life, only a few yards away.

In front of her, Becky lay on the ground, clinging to Sandra's hand, nodding her understanding. "Ivy, sweetheart. I'm okay. Go to him."

She shook her head.

She didn't want to go to him.

Didn't want to leave Becky.

"If you don't, you might regret it for the rest of your life," Becky whispered.

"I'm here," Ivy said.

The sight of Richard, lying supine, his face already beginning to swell, his lips cut and bruised, made her breath catch. One leg was twisted into an unnatural position, the bone sticking out like a broken tree branch.

"Ivy... you have to tell them what she did." When he spoke, it was as if his voice were being scraped across sandpaper. "Sandra pushed me off the edge. You saw her do it."

She cast her eyes up to the heavens and spotted two small figures at the top of the cliff. She couldn't be certain from this distance, but one looked like a woman, and the other a man, possibly dressed in uniform.

Another moan from Richard. His face was bloodless.

How long would it take for help to reach them?

No more than minutes.

Despite the steep, treacherous switchbacks, they were running it.

"Help will be here soon. I see someone on the trail—police, I think."

"Sandra has to pay for what she's done." Richard wasn't so hurt that he couldn't go after Sandra.

"You had a terrible fall. It's making you say crazy things. Becky told me everything, but I'm still here. No matter what you've done, I won't just sit back and watch you die."

"I'm not going to die." He let out a groan as his head dropped onto his chest. "You came back to me. You forgive me and that gives me a reason to go on. I'm going to fight like hell, now. But honey, you need to fight for me, too." He clawed at his throat.

"Don't try to talk. I can see you're in pain."

"Don't care. As long as you're with me, nothing else matters. But my throat is so dry. I could use some water."

A few feet to her right she recognized the small pack Richard carried with him on his hikes. A moment later she found a water bottle buried in the pack and wrapped her hand around it.

The world, the forest around her, came into sharp relief. Instead of smudges of color she suddenly saw towering tree trunks and crystalline blue sky.

No more illusions.

With water and pack in hand, she returned to Richard and knelt beside him.

Banishing the thought of what he'd done, she guided his hand, helping him, sip by sip, until he signaled he'd had enough to drink.

"I'm so grateful, Ivy. I knew, in my bones, you'd forgive me."

"I don't forgive you—I can't. But I do *understand* that you did... what you did to protect me."

"Call it understanding or forgiveness, you're too good hearted to hate me. You wouldn't be at my side, now, if you didn't love me."

"I don't know about that."

"Listen." He paused, lifting a hand to his forehead. "Sorry. Dizzy. Do you still see them? The police?"

She was sure of it now. That was Kathleen and Wadley. "They're halfway down."

"You'll back me up? About Sandra." Richard seemed to be getting his wind back, after only a few sips of water.

"You're confused. With a fall like that, you'll definitely have a concussion. That's why you keep insisting that someone pushed you off that cliff."

"I'm not confused. I *remember* Sandra pushing me. Ivy, that woman tried to *murder* me. I realize I have to answer for what I've done, but Sandra does, too. You can't cover up for her."

Ivy reached her hand into Richard's pack. "It'll be your word against ours. The cops will believe us, as they should, since we're telling the truth."

"No. You need to stay away from her. Sandra Steele is as much a killer as I am."

"But she didn't push you. That's your head injury talking. You know what doctors say about concussions. They mess with your brain, big time." She forced herself to smile.

His head wobbled, and his eyes jerked back and forth, like he was having trouble focusing on her face. "I see what you're doing. You're playing with me. Getting back for the gaslighting I dealt you. But you can't school the teacher. I know what I know. Sandra pushed me. You have to tell the truth."

She bent down to stroke his damp hair from his eyes. "You're sweating. And you look pale, but you're strong enough to keep up a conversation. I should go back to check on Becky now."

He reached out and gripped her wrist. "Please stay, just keep talking, at least until the police get here. You're doing me a world of good."

She knelt beside him and said a silent prayer for strength. "Would you like to hear a story?"

His eyelids fluttered, and he nodded.

"Sandra did not push you—" she started.

He rocked his head side to side in a "no". "I remember her hand on my back. And the hard push. I didn't fall. I didn't jump."

"All right then, maybe she did, but I'm trying to tell you a story. A secret I've never told anyone. You know the rules Mom taught me? Never talk to strangers. Always have a grown-up with you. I tried to be a good girl. But sometimes I wasn't. And one day, I went outside by myself, and I made a friend. He lifted me in the air, swung me around and hugged me. I thought he was the nicest man in the world. Except for you, of course. Then Mom caught me. She made me promise never to play with the man again. But I didn't listen. I broke my promise." Ivy's lungs felt far too tight, but she breathed through the discomfort and pushed on. "The very same night, a noise woke me. I went to my window, and, in the full moon, I saw him. I snuck out to play with him, even though I knew I shouldn't. I was about to run into his outstretched arms when I heard a loud pop. I fell down and covered my ears, and when I opened my eyes, he was on the ground—and *you* turned and ran away."

"You-you were there? I didn't see you."

"Stop interrupting, Richard. I ran to him. There was a lot of blood. It smelled strange—like that day someone shot you with an arrow. I *almost* remembered it when you and I were lying in the dirt. But I guess my mind wasn't ready to accept the truth."

Richard's face screwed up. He started coughing in fits and spurts.

The water bottle was close at hand but that wasn't what she reached for. She waited for Richard's spasms to subside before continuing. "I begged the man to get up. But he couldn't. He told me, *Go back inside, Ivy! Hurry!* I didn't want to leave him. Then he said he loved me, and I had to do as I was told so no one would hurt me. I went back to my bed, and I swore I'd never be bad again. I promised God to be a good girl and follow all the rules if he would keep the man safe. So, you see, all those nightmares I was having weren't dreams at all. They were *memories*, Richard. I saw you shoot my father. I saw you murder Jimmy."

"How long have you known?" he whispered, somehow managing to lift himself off his back and onto one elbow.

"While I was in the hospital, recovering from my concussion, I had one of my bad dreams. Not that same threadbare rug of a dream like I've had so many times before, but a vivid, fully woven tapestry. A dream that revealed *everything* to me."

She paused, giving him time to let it sink in, and herself time to gather her courage.

"But I forgot it all again. Or, I suppose, it would be more accurate to say I repressed it. And then, when I saw you with Becky on that cliff, and heard you yell that she should turn the gun on herself, my brain was still hiding the truth from me. And yet, somehow, my heart knew. I was glad when Sandra pushed you off that cliff."

"You don't mean that, Ivy. You'll forgive me. I know you will."

She pulled her hand from his pack, showing him the bright gleaming blade. Held it near her heart while he whimpered. "When I went to get you water, I found this in your pack. I realized you brought this hunting knife with you to kill Becky, and that is the exact moment I remembered *everything*. I see you, so clearly, now. My mind and my heart are singing the same truth. I want you to know how sorry I am."

"But you said you understood. I did it for you, Ivy. For our family."

"I understand what drove you to it more than you know. But I'm not finished with my story. You see, I promised to follow the rules if God would keep *him* safe. That was the bargain I made. But the man died anyway. I've been following the rules, all this time, for no reason. When I say I'm sorry, I truly mean it. I'm sorry that when she pushed you off the cliff you didn't die. But maybe it's for the best, because now I have the chance to get justice for Mom and Jimmy and all the other people whose lives you've ruined. A chance to save Sandra."

"Put the knife down, Ivy. My little girl doesn't want revenge."

"Not revenge—justice."

"You'll never get away with it. Police... are ... coming." He had to know it was over, but he kept talking, kept pressing.

He'd meant it when he said he'd keep fighting.

She leaned over his body, positioning the knife between his chest and hers. "Get away with what? Don't you remember? When you jumped off the cliff you fell on your knife."

He moaned, then whispered, "Ivy, it's not too late. You won't be able to live with yourself if you go through with this. Trust me when I tell you a secret like that will ruin you. You'll spend the rest of your life afraid of someone finding out the truth."

"I can live with that." She checked to be sure the sharp end of the blade rested directly over his heart and the butt of the handle against her breast bone.

She embraced him.

Hugged him tightly, pressing against him with all her might until he stopped struggling.

Until his warm blood soaked through her thin shirt, drenching her chilled skin.

Until, finally, his hand dropped to his side.

And, still, she held him.

The world went silent save for his shallow, agonizing breaths—then those, too, ceased.

She continued to rock his body, eventually coming back into herself. Back to a new world—a world filled not with the lies of her father, but with terrible, secret truths of her own.

Racing footsteps grew louder.

The police were almost upon them, but it was too late. Richard's face was blue.

When she pressed her cheek to his, she felt as if she'd swallowed a block of ice. First, her arms began to shake, and then the tears began to fall—for her mother, for Jimmy, for *all* of Richard's victims, both living and dead.

Kathleen was shouting at her. "Hang on! I'm almost there! Rescue 'copter is on its way!"

"Help! Help! He needs help!" Ivy yelled back.

Then she curled his lifeless body closer and whispered in his ear, "You really are my father, Richard—see how well you've taught me. I'll do *anything* for family."

EPILOGUE
IVY

Ivy hoped the kid-friendly set-up at the Flagstaff Family Services Center wouldn't be off-putting to Jimmy's mother, Diana Reeves. A mural of Winnie the Pooh, frolicking among fluffy clouds, decorated the back wall. A yellow plastic slide cascaded into a pit of multi-colored balls, and a muted Disney movie scrolled across the screen of a television mounted in the corner.

Hardly an ideal venue for meeting her paternal grandmother, but at least it was neutral ground.

Ivy and Clayton had formally separated. Because of his cooperation with the police, he wasn't prosecuted as an accessory in Laquay's murder, or for the crossbow incident. But by his own account, on many occasions, he'd administered tranquilizers and antihistamines to Ivy without her knowledge. For that, he was charged with, and had pled guilty to, multiple counts of assault and reckless endangerment. He was presently occupying the marital home while awaiting sentencing.

Ivy had moved back to the ranch so that she could oversee

its operations while arranging its sale—it would've been unthinkable to invite Jimmy's mother to the site of his murder.

After the authorities released Richard's body, Ivy had returned, alone, to Lockett Meadow, and scattered his ashes in the same location they'd scattered Mom's. She hadn't forgiven him—but she'd honored his final instructions because that was what Mom would want her to do.

She didn't know if she deserved forgiveness or punishment for her actions, but she'd resolved to live in the present, and to do her best to be a good daughter and a good sister because that, too, was what Mom would want.

Some days, it was impossible to believe the man she'd called *Dad* had murdered Mom and Jimmy, too—and Laquay. Or to acknowledge the pain he'd caused Becky... After her fall from that cliff she'd required a double hip replacement and surgery for a fractured femur.

Some days it was impossible for Ivy to believe *she* had ended Richard's life. She'd pretend, instead, that it had been some traumatized facsimile of herself who could not be held accountable. *Out-of-her-mind Ivy* hallucinating floating veils, or *Little-girl Ivy* sleepwalking in a bloody nightgown. Given her history of confusion and nightmares, and the picture Clayton and Richard had tried to paint of her to everyone who'd listen, she'd have a decent shot at an insanity defense.

But it turned out there was no need for an insanity defense, or any defense at all.

No one questioned the women's version of events—Becky fired a gun into the air and fell. A terrified Richard jumped off the cliff when he heard the gunshot. When Ivy got to him, he was lying prone, after falling on his own knife. She flipped him over and held him in her arms, tried to comfort him, but he was already gone.

Most days, though, Ivy didn't make excuses—not for herself or for Richard.

Most days, she preferred the pain of the truth over the comfort of lies.

And today, like every day, she carried that secret burden with her.

Now, Ivy took a seat in one of the folding chairs arranged in a circle in the center of the room.

Sandra, Dalton and Becky were already seated.

Also present was Sherry Grissom, a counselor provided by the center—her services came with the rented space.

"We're still waiting on Diana, I believe. In the meantime, please fill me in, with as much detail as you'd like to share, about your family's special circumstances." Sherry Grissom spoke in a soft, non-judgmental tone, casting a bemused glance around the circle, before her gaze settled back onto her clasped hands.

Ivy pegged her as well-intentioned. She didn't mind her presence, as long as she didn't try to fit their family into some preconceived notion of what families should be.

After a few seconds of silence, Becky offered a polite, but wholly inadequate, response. "We're a blended family."

"That's an understatement," Dalton scoffed, stretching his legs and placing his hands behind his head. "Don't get me wrong. I like the way this tribe is coming together. But I don't think 'blended' paints the picture. Sounds so... homogenous. So normal. We're more of a hash."

"Interesting." Sherry nodded. "You're all meeting Diana Reeves, for the first time?"

Sandra fidgeted with the hem of her blouse. "Everyone except me. I knew her when I was a teenager. I think it's fair to say she didn't like me. But not many moms would approve of a teenage son's pregnant girlfriend."

"Not true." An older woman stood in the doorway, shoulders back, head held high.

When Jimmy's bones were excavated from the south pasture of the Flagstaff Kane Ranch, the story had made national news. Ivy recognized her paternal grandmother from the media—her graying hair, cut short and blunt, the way the bridge of her nose curved. But those images hadn't conveyed Diana Reeves' powerful presence. The impact of canny brown eyes, daring you to look away, her sorrowfulness worn proudly like a crown.

Ivy could well imagine how intimidating she must have seemed to Sandra when she was younger.

Diana crossed the room and took her place in the family circle, occupying the last empty chair. "I didn't dislike you, personally, Sandra. I wanted what was best for my son."

"And that wasn't me," Sandra whispered.

"No," Diana said. Her voice held a certain raspy depth that sometimes comes with age. "It was not."

Sandra didn't protest—and given the intimate nature of matters between her and Diana, Ivy didn't feel it was her place to do so, either. She suspected those two were going to need both time and privacy to work through a difficult past.

The counselor remained silent—not interfering, but not facilitating either. Ivy stole a glance at her phone: 11 a.m. It would be time to leave soon.

She'd hoped to clear the air before Jimmy's service. "Diana, I'm Ivy. I'm so sorry for your loss. I don't want to pressure anyone, but we're here, together, in a safe space, so if anyone needs to say something, this is a good opportunity."

Diana tugged at her wispy bangs. "I'm sorry for your loss, too, Ivy. And Sandra... what I want to know is did you love my Jimmy?"

"Like I've never loved anyone." Sandra's eyes filled with moisture as she lifted her gaze to meet Diana's.

"Then why did you give up his baby? And in all these years, why didn't you tell me about Dalton? I had no idea. You can't blame me for being hurt."

"This is my fault, more than Sandra's." Becky jumped to her daughter's defense.

"Okay, then. Here's your chance to explain how I wound up with two grandchildren I've never met, and a son buried beneath a barn with a bullet in his head."

"It's important not to assign blame," the counselor piped up, remembering her role at the worst possible moment.

"I'll assign blame where I see fit. Who are you?" Diana asked sharply.

"The volunteer counselor. Not to be uncivil, but Sherry, stay out of this," Becky said. Then a look of agreement passed between her and Diana. "As I was saying, I have to shoulder much of the blame. Sandra and Jimmy were kids. Fifteen and sixteen when Ivy was conceived. Sandra, I'm sorry I wasn't around enough, that you didn't feel supported enough to care for a child. Jimmy got scared and ran—some of that's on you, Diana. And if you understand why your son made the decision that was best for him, you should give my daughter the same grace. Sandra, do you want to explain about Dalton?"

"You should explain it in front of everyone," Dalton said. "But I want to say something first. I questioned all along why Becky dragged us into this scheme unless Ivy actually was my half-sister. That's why I stalked you, Ivy. Becky let so many things slip to me that I think, on a subconscious level, she *wanted* the truth to come out. That's why she got Laquay to recruit us to be Ivy's 'fake' family."

"Is that why you took all those photos of me?" Ivy asked Dalton.

"Yeah. I was trying to work out if there was a family resemblance, at first, and then I guess I got carried away with the idea of learning everything I could about you. I never thought you'd turn out to be my full-blooded sister. And I never meant to scare you. That's what I wanted to get off my chest. Okay, Mom, go ahead. Tell Diana what you've already told the rest of us."

Sandra gripped the edge of her seat. "As we all know by now, I put Ivy up for adoption. I was sixteen when she was born, and I didn't think I could care for her as a single mom. I didn't know where she'd wind up, but I made a specific request that her parents be educated. Becky handled a lot of the details, and became friends with the adoption counselor. They got very close... *too close*, and the counselor told Becky information she shouldn't have—that the couple who were originally set to adopt Ivy opted for a baby boy at the last minute instead. Becky then steered the agency toward the Kane family. For the record, I had no idea about that. I thought Ivy had been placed with two professors. I moved to Fort Worth to get away from my memories—and from my mother. Becky and I weren't getting along."

Counselor Sherry was on the edge of her seat, as enthralled as the public had been when the story broke.

"About two years after I put Ivy up for adoption," Sandra continued, "Jimmy showed up at the café in Fort Worth where I worked at the time. He'd grown up a lot. By then, I was eighteen. He was nineteen. He said he regretted running off, and he wanted to be a standup guy and do the right thing by me and the baby. I felt so ashamed for putting her up for adoption that I lied, at first, and told him I'd miscarried. One thing led to another, and Jimmy and I spent a beautiful week together. When he asked me to marry him, I couldn't keep up the lie. I told him the truth. That it was a closed adoption and I didn't know where our baby girl was. He didn't believe me, though, and I now know he went to the Kane ranch to get more information out of Becky. After that, I never heard any more from him. I thought he ran off again because he couldn't forgive me. Then I met Jonathon Steele, and he married me, knowing I was carrying another man's child."

Diana rose and hurried to Sandra, threw her arms around her. "You wanted a family for Dalton, and you gave him one. It's not your fault the professors wouldn't take Ivy."

Ivy lifted one shoulder. "Because I wasn't a boy. But I *am* a professor. So there's that. If it's any comfort."

"And I'm going to UT next year on Richard Kane's dime," Dalton said. "I've been lucky to have Sandra as my mother, and Jonathon Steele as my father. I wish I could've known Jimmy. But Diana, you and I and Ivy and Sandra and Becky—we still have the chance Jimmy never got. We can still be a family—even if we're a crazy, messy, hash of one."

"I think Jimmy would want that," Diana said, her eyes brimming with tears. "I've been alone a long time, and I'd love to be part of the mix. There's a lot of obstacles ahead, overcoming the barriers that time and distance have built. But I want to be there for my grandchildren—for you, Dalton. And for you, Ivy—I know Clayton's upcoming sentencing hearing is going to be hard on you. But if you'll let me, I'll hold my head up and stand next to you in the courtroom. And I want to say how grateful I am. I want to thank you, Ivy and Dalton, for seeing to it my son finally gets a proper burial. The service starts soon, doesn't it?"

"I'd be honored to have you by my side in court or anywhere else you like. And yes, we need to leave soon, or we'll miss Jimmy's remembrance. I think we can all fit into one car." Ivy climbed to her feet and, for the first time, embraced her grandmother, astounded at how holding a complete stranger felt like coming home.

Dear Reader,

I'm honored that you have taken time from your life to read my work and have invited my characters into your world. Creating stories and then sharing them with you so that you can shine your own light on them, reading through a lens shaped by your own perceptions and imagination, is such a joy. I hope you enjoyed the journey!

If you'd like to be the first to know about my next book, please sign up via the following link. Your email address will never be shared and you can unsubscribe at any time.

www.bookouture.com/carey-baldwin

If you loved this story, I would be very grateful if you could leave a short review. Reviews are one of the best ways to help other readers discover my books. They don't need to be long or clever. You can make a big difference simply by leaving a line or two. Building a relationship with readers is one of the best things about being a writer. I love hearing from you, so please stay in touch by connecting with me on my website or social media. Thank you very much for reading!

Love,

Carey

KEEP IN TOUCH WITH CAREY

www.careybaldwin.com

instagram.com/authorcareybaldwin
bookbub.com/authors/carey-baldwin

ACKNOWLEDGEMENTS

Thank you to my readers! You are the reason I write.

Thank you to my fantastic editor, Natalie Edwards, who gave me brilliant insights into making the story better and who has shown such care and thoughtfulness in all our work together. Thank you to my eagle-eyed copyeditor, Donna Hillyer, and my proofreader, Jennifer Davies. Thank you, thank you, thank you, to Kim Nash, author community director, and publicists extraordinaire Sarah Hardy, Noelle Holten, and Jess Readett. Thank you to Ellen Gleeson, publishing director, and Alba Proko, head of audio publishing. Thank you to Peta Nightingale, contracts, rights, and translation director, Mandy Kullar, desk editor, and Hannah Snetsinger, editorial manager. Thank you to *all* the directors and publishers as well as all the individuals in marketing, art, and the entire team at Bookouture who champion every book by every author they publish.

Huge thanks and a million hugs to my dear friends and brainstorming, critiquing, beta-reading geniuses: Suzanne Baldree and Paula Burgess. And a very special thank you to John Baumann, who, when he heard I was writing this book, generously shared his own personal and inspiring story with me.

To my family: Bill, Shannon, Erik, Kayla, Lumi, Sarah, Junior, Olivia, Marlene and little Scout—I love you truly, dears!

Turning a manuscript into a book requires the efforts of many people. The publishing team at Bookouture would like to acknowledge everyone who contributed to this publication.

Audio
Alba Proko
Sinead O'Connor
Melissa Tran

Commercial
Lauren Morrissette
Hannah Richmond
Imogen Allport

Cover design
Toby Clarke

Data and analysis
Mark Alder
Mohamed Bussuri

Editorial
Natalie Edwards
Charlotte Hegley

Copyeditor
Donna Hillyer

Proofreader
Jennifer Davies

Marketing
Alex Crow
Melanie Price
Occy Carr
Ciara Rosney
Martyna Młynarska

Operations and distribution
Marina Valles
Stephanie Straub
Joe Morris

Production
Hannah Snetsinger
Mandy Kullar
Ria Clare
Nadia Michael

Publicity
Kim Nash
Noelle Holten
Jess Readett
Sarah Hardy

Rights and contracts
Peta Nightingale
Richard King
Saidah Graham

Dear Reader,

We'd love your attention for one more page to tell you about the crisis in children's reading, and what we can all do.

Studies have shown that reading for fun is the **single biggest predictor of a child's future success** – more than family circumstance, parents' educational background or income. It improves academic results, mental health, wealth, communication skills, and ambition.

The number of children reading for fun is in rapid decline. Young people have a lot of competition for their time, and a worryingly high number do not have a single book at home.

Our business works extensively with schools, libraries and literacy charities, but here are some ways we can all raise more readers:

- Reading to children for just 10 minutes a day makes a difference
- Don't give up if children aren't regular readers – there will be books for them!

- Visit bookshops and libraries to get recommendations
- Encourage them to listen to audiobooks
- Support school libraries
- Give books as gifts

Thank you for reading: there's a lot more information about how to encourage children to read on our website.

www.JoinRaisingReaders.com